'You must take this letter to the Queen.'

The Abbesse sat down and drew a sheet of paper towards her. 'I am telling her that you have formed an attachment with her god-daughter and wish to marry her. You will, in due course, be requesting the King's permission to be married as soon as the royal assent is given. As a special favour, I am also asking her if she will find a place for Teresa at Court. Perhaps as a lady-in-waiting.'

Crossing the floor in two swift strides, Guy placed a firm hand over the sheet of paper. 'You cannot do this! You must not! It is too much to bear! I cannot, *will* not, be forced to marry a frivolous, empty-headed child from the convent. You must know that in the matter of my marriage I had other hopes, other plans.'

For the first time throughout this strange nightmarish interview he looked directly at Teresa. There was no liking in that look. His expression was one of loathing, as though the sight of her was abhorrent to him. Clearly, the thought of marriage with her filled him with detestation. His words confirmed this. 'My God!' he exploded. 'I think I would rather the Bastille!'

After graduating from Bristol University in 1973, Una Power travelled and lived on the Continent, enjoyed reporting and interviewing for BBC Radio Bristol, and lectured in Social Sciences in England and Southern Ireland. Her art student son Robert encouraged her to write which she now does all the time in her Irish country home. For recreation she abandons her garden and typewriter and samples Dublin theatre.

Previous Title

THE BRIDE SALE

INTRIGUE AT VERSAILLES

or

THE WICKED DUC

Una Power

MILLS & BOON LIMITED
ETON HOUSE   18-24 PARADISE ROAD
RICHMOND   SURREY   TW9 1SR

First published in Great Britain 1989
by Mills & Boon Limited

© Una Power 1989

Australian copyright 1989
Philippine copyright 1989
This edition 1989

ISBN 0 263 76571 7

Set in Times Roman 10 on 10¼ pt.
04-8910-91109 C

Made and printed in Great Britain

CHAPTER ONE

'SISTER CLOTHILDE, who is that very handsome man who calls upon our Abbesse?' Teresa looked quizzically at the flushed face of the nun who helped her tend her plot of garden in the convent grounds.

'Worldly affairs need not concern you, Teresa. You are to take the veil, remember.' Sister Clothilde looked disapprovingly at her young charge.

'Aha! I suspect a mystery.' Teresa's eyes sparkled with mischief, for she loved to tease Sister Clothilde. 'Is he, perhaps, a lover from her wicked past?'

'Mademoiselle Rochefoucourt!' Poor Sister Clothilde was outraged, her emotions overcoming her natural timidity. 'That young man is her nephew, he is at the court of King Louis the Fourteenth at Versailles. Out of kindness and family duty he pays his respects to his aunt——'

Teresa interrupted her. 'Ooh! I do not think I like the sound of someone who pays respects and feels dutiful.' She pulled down the corners of her pretty mouth in comic dismay.

'I see that you are determined to misunderstand everything I say. Nevertheless, I shall continue. Our Abbesse deferred her entry to the convent when her sister and brother-in-law died, in order to bring up her niece and infant nephew, for there were two children. That you should imply that our dearest and most revered Abbesse should be guilty of any impropriety as to have...' As words failed her, she stabbed agitatedly at the ground with the small trowel with which she had been weeding the garden.

Genuinely contrite, Teresa bit her lip, attempting to suppress her smiles. 'Is it so very wicked, then, to have a lover?'

Red with embarrassment, the nun looked flustered, her face a study of indecision. 'I hope you are not aware of the grave import of your words. It was a mistake to allow you to spend so much time with Mademoiselle Marie Besneval—she is frivolous and silly, and not a fit companion for a girl destined to enter the noviciate. The next time some young lady is obliged to leave the court for a time and stay here in the convent, I shall request that she be housed at some distance from you.'

Teresa was dismayed, for the young girls who boarded temporarily at the Convent of the Sacred Heart in Villepreux had been a constant source of amusement and entertainment for her. She had particularly liked Marie Besneval, for she was elegant, fashionable, and loved to gossip about court affairs.

Upon being informed that under no circumstances would the Abbesse permit her to wear powder or lip salve in the convent, Marie had shrugged disdainfully, but looked with wicked drollery at Teresa.

'Tcha! I do not care, for who is there to flirt with here? Now, if I were at Court at this hour, I would be dressing to go to...' And she had proceeded to relate to an enthralled Teresa stories of the parties, balls and masques which she frequently attended.

'Do you not long to be there still?' Teresa had wondered. Marie had made her see the gay and glittering world that the Sun King had created.

'Of course. But I was a little indiscreet, so the Queen thought I should benefit from a retreat from Court life. She is very religious, is our dear Queen.' An expression of impish amusement had accompanied these words, and Teresa could not help laughing in response.

'How I should love to go to Court,' she had admitted to Marie. 'But it was my mama's wish that I take the veil, and she made my godmother, Queen Maria Teresa, after whom I am named, promise that I would be brought up here in the convent and become a nun.'

It was gratifying that her new friend had instantly understood how sorely this prospect tried her. 'It is a great shame, for you are very pretty, and if you were at Court you would become the rage in no time at all.'

The rage of Versailles! What a glorious vision those words had conjured.

'The King much admires your sort of looks, for he loves pink and white skin and fair hair. You might even become his mistress.'

These words had shocked Teresa, but she had attempted not to show her feelings—and failed.

Laughing, Marie had exclaimed, 'I have dismayed you, little puritan! Perhaps it is as well that you are to remain in the convent, for you would be a great figure of fun at Court if you were to blush like that every time someone spoke of these matters. Little else is talked of at Versailles. It is a terrible punishment to have to stay here for the rest of your life.' Marie had looked around the tranquil cloister in which they had been sitting, and then at Teresa with real pity.

Feeling conscience-stricken, for the seven years she had spent with the nuns had been happy and content, she had reassured Marie. 'Indeed, I cannot think of it like that. When my parents and brother, Armand, died of fever, I was very glad to come here. The nuns have been very affectionate.'

Abandoning her light-hearted manner, Marie had directed a shrewd look at Teresa. 'You are well dowered, are you not? That always makes a difference to the good nuns. Their bounty increases with the size of a person's fortune. Your father was a very wealthy man, and your mother was as rich as she was beautiful, I have heard.'

Teresa had recalled that she had been a very bewildered and unhappy ten-year-old child when she had come to the convent. The nuns had petted and indulged her and showered affection on her. No, she could not believe that they were kind just because she was rich.

'I have been very happy here, Marie. It is my home.' Honesty had compelled her to admit this.

'Well, my friend, do not underestimate the power of money. It has the loudest tongue in France.' Casting her eyes heavenwards, she had sighed deeply. 'You can have no idea of how very expensive it is to live at Court. I have to employ all sorts of schemes and strategies to survive. This gown,' she had fingered the billowing primrose silk, 'cost a great deal of money. But it is an investment.'

Teresa's expressive blue eyes had shown her lack of comprehension.

'An investment for what?' she had asked.

Impatiently Marie had replied, 'To catch myself a rich husband, of course. How can you be so simple, Teresa? If I am fashionably dressed, and present a good appearance, then I might even snare the Wicked Duc himself.'

'Do you love him?'

A little shriek, half amusement, half vexation had greeted this question. 'My poor Teresa! What has love to do with marriage? The Wicked Duc is the handsomest man in France, if you admire very dark looks, which I do not. They say that every woman at Court is in love with him. In the past he even killed the husband of one of his lovers. All these things make him very attractive to women. But he has the one attraction which I find irresistible—he is very, very rich.' She had breathed these last words with such a reverential air that Teresa had burst out laughing. 'Ah, it pleases you to laugh at that. But let me tell you that the world is not kind to those who are poor.'

'I hope that I never like a person better because they are rich, or despise them because they are poor.' Teresa had spoken with some heat. Greatly in awe of Marie, and seeking to emulate her manner, she would have been glad to have used her as a model of behaviour if she ever got to Versailles, but she could not agree with her views on the subject of money, and had felt compelled to speak.

'Then it is as well that you are to remain in the convent, *chérie*.' She had spoken drily, and Teresa had been uncomfortably aware that Marie thought her views foolish.

When Marie had returned to court, Teresa missed her society greatly. While she could not share Marie's more cynical opinions, she did love her wit and conversation about the Court, and the people—beautiful and scandalous—who lived there.

Looking about the herb garden, breathing in the sweetly aromatic air, listening to Sister Clothilde's gently complaining voice, Teresa was seized with a vast restlessness. It was true, she did love the convent and the nuns, but she did not wish to spend the rest of her life with them.

'What happens to me if I do not choose to take the veil?' she asked Sister Clothilde.

'Not take the veil?' The nun regarded her blankly. 'But, what sort of question is this? You *must* take the veil.'

Teresa's mouth rounded in dismay. 'But I wish to go to Court,' she blurted out.

Taking Teresa's slim hand in hers, the nun looked at her with real compassion. 'My dear child, life at Court is not a good life. There is much corruption beneath the surface. I know that Marie Besneval has been filling your head with all sorts of tales, and you believe that you would like such a life. But, believe me, you would soon come to hate it. Your dear mother was lady-in-waiting to the Queen——'

'I know! She came with Queen Maria Teresa from Spain and left the Court to marry my father.'

'Whatever she saw at Court did not please her, despite her love for the Queen. And as the Queen is your godmother, we must assume that they were very close. So earnestly did she desire to protect your future that she made the Queen promise that you would be placed in a convent and, in due course, take the veil. When you are older, and have been here longer, you will see that it is the most wonderfully fulfilling life in the service of God and humanity.'

I do not want a wonderfully fulfilling life, Teresa cried out silently. All her being rebelled at the thought. I want music, jewels, gorgeous gowns, masques. I want to go to a ball at Court and be admired by the Wicked Duc.

'Do you think that I might be allowed to go to Court for a few months? I would so like to see Marie Besneval once more.'

The nun shook her head regretfully. 'I know how you must miss the society of a girl of your own age, Teresa, but it is impossible for you to go to Court. You would have to wait to be invited by the King or Queen. In your circumstances, it is unlikely that the Queen would invite you. You must pray for the grace to accept your destiny, and decide to be happy and content here.'

Rising gracefully, Teresa brushed a few bits of brown earth from her plain grey gown. 'Perhaps in time that will happen, Sister. I had better hurry and wash, or I will be late for prayers. Would you put my gardening tools away for me?'

Without waiting for the nun to reply, Teresa hurried away, anxious that she should not see the tears in her eyes. Entering the back door of the convent, she hurried up the stairs to her room, and, closing the door behind her, allowed tears of vexed disappointment to fall. Lately she had begun to indulge the hope that she might write to Marie, begging her to invite her to come to Court. Now it seemed that such an invitation must come from the Queen. If she were to write, could she be sure that the Abbesse would send the letter? Her conscience might tell her to ignore such a request. Marie's words returned to cause her further discomfort. Perhaps it was true— perhaps the Abbesse really did want her dowry. Teresa knew that, at her dying mother's request, her lands had been sold and that either the Queen or the Abbesse held her money.

Going to the window, she stared out at the long, straight road that led from Villepreux to Versailles. It was only a few miles away, but it may as well be in the sky, for it was unattainable. Suddenly, her small room seemed like a prison from which she longed to escape.

A stir in the courtyard below arrested her attention. A groom had mounted the box of a light travelling coach and was moving to the front door of the convent. Sighing deeply, she looked with envy at the vehicle. If only she could simply walk out, step into the coach and command the groom to take her to her godmother! He would not obey her, naturally. The coach probably belonged to the nephew of the Abbesse. How fortunate he was, for in a few minutes he would be leaving the convent and returning to Versailles.

An idea began to form in her mind. Perhaps she could write a note and beg him to convey it to the Queen. If she told him of her desperate plight and begged him to keep the affair secret, he could scarcely refuse her.

Opening a drawer, she took out her writing materials and spread them on a table. With an enormous effort of concentration she attempted to write the note, and regretted most sincerely her frequent inattention in reading and writing classes, for she found the simple task of composition a great labour. If she did not make haste she would be too late. Already she thought she heard the vehicle moving, and, going to the window once more, she saw that the groom had climbed down from the box and was walking the horses to the gate. Evidently, his master was delayed. If only she could contrive to talk to him privately, she was sure that she could convince him to speak to the Queen on her behalf. Whenever she had used her most coaxing ways on any of the nuns, she had always been successful. Sister Clothilde had referred to him as a young man; he was not young, he must be at least thirty, but he had a kind face and she did not doubt her ability to persuade him. But how and where to speak to him privately? The only place she could do that was in his own coach. No sooner had that idea entered her head than she sped from the room with all the impetuosity deplored by the Abbesse, and a few moments later found herself in the luxurious, though stuffy, interior of the coach.

Clasping her hands in her lap, she silently rehearsed a fluent speech which should make him pity her dreadful plight. Some slight noise outside caused her to shrink against the silk lining of the coach, afraid that she might be discovered by one of the nuns before she had had a chance to talk to the nephew of the Abbesse. Feeling the vehicle move, she was surprised, but assumed that the groom was returning to the front door of the convent. Any moment now he would open the door, enter the coach, and she would make her speech; in a few minutes she would be back in her room, her mission completed.

The coach began to rock and sway; it was moving at great speed! Pulling aside the small curtain at the window, she looked out to discover that the coach was bowling along the road to Versailles, and already they had left the convent behind. For one moment she was tempted to remain where she was and allow fate to take its course. But she could not leave the nuns in this callous fashion—it would be improper and show a lack of gratitude. Obviously the nephew had decided to make the return journey on the box of the vehicle—that he might do so had not occurred to her. She had better attract some attention and make them return to the convent immediately. Calling out was useless, for they could not hear her above the sound of the horses hoofs. The glass windows seemed fixed into position, and it was quite impossible to open them. If only she could find some object with which to bang the roof of the vehicle! But in vain did she rummage in the pockets and under the seats—there was nothing there.

Sitting back on her seat, she began to feel apprehensive. It was one thing to have crept into the coach in the hope that she might have a few minutes' conversation with its owner. But her common sense told her that to be travelling along the road to Versailles, alone in his company, was quite another matter. The nuns would be justifiably furious. Often she had pondered on the nature of the indiscretions that caused young girls to be banished from the delights of Versailles to the convent. Was this the sort of act they had committed? she wondered. Hideous visions of social ostracism began to assail her. Whenever she had thought of Versailles, she had imagined herself there, a great success, the rage of the Court—the object of the attentions of the Wicked Duc. There would be fun and gaiety and triumphs. But she had learned that, whatever one did, a scandal must never be created or advertised. With only the vaguest notion of what an indiscretion was, she was acutely aware that discovery was infinitely worse than the crime. If she were discovered in such circumstances, her glorious career would be ignominiously ended before it had even begun.

Their progress had slowed and, from the sounds she could hear, it was clear that they had entered the town of Versailles. Curiosity overcame caution, and she peeped from behind the curtain. So many buildings! So many people! There were labourers, clerks, bakers, finely dressed men and women, all going about their business; Teresa stared at them, open-mouthed and fascinated. The men walked with a suggestion of swagger in their gait, the women, hips swaying, looked with coquettish invitation at the men. Teresa felt a small wave of distaste sweep over her, and hoped that while she might become fashionable—the rage of Versailles even—she would never appear to be so vulgar as some of these women.

That the owner of the coach, the nephew of the Abbesse, was a popular and well-known man was evident from the number of times the vehicle stopped while greetings were exchanged. Eventually, however, they turned into a quiet avenue situated parallel with the main street. A jumble of modern buildings, many of them quite ugly, characterised the main streets of the new town; but here, in this avenue, the houses were large, elegant and of beautiful proportions. Many reminded her of the convent, for they were built from mellow stone with slated roofs, and boasted long windows which afforded glimpses of luxurious gold and white interiors.

They stopped before one such house, and Teresa leaned forward to look with interest at the loveliest house she felt she would ever see in her life. Tubs of bright red flowers flanked the shallow steps which led to the front door; pillars supported a fine porch. The owner jumped to the ground and stood beside the coach. She saw a tall, well-made man with broad shoulders and military bearing. Eyes as dark as his hair were set beneath thick brows that gave a curious effect of frowning. How had she formed the impression that he was kind? Reserve and pride were stamped across his handsome regular features. He might have very good looks, she thought, but they were marred by the forbidding coldness of his expression.

When he spoke, Teresa felt an unexpected shock, for his voice was quite unlike the feminine tones that she had been used to hearing; it was crisp and deep.

'Take the carriage to the stables, I shall not need it again today—I intend walking to the palace. You may have a holiday until tomorrow.'

Teresa's prepared speech died, unuttered. Her confidence deserted her, leaving in its place the greatest reluctance to talk to this intimidating stranger. Feeling a slight lurch as the groom gave a quiet word to the horses, she decided that she had better speak quickly. Tapping the window, and attempting to smile, she sought to attract his attention.

If he was startled at the sight of a young girl sitting in his coach, he concealed it admirably. With a snort of impatience he signalled the groom to stop and wrenched open the door.

'What is the meaning of this? Who are you? Are you trying to rob me?' A moment ago his voice had been cool and authoritative; now it held an unmistakable note of menace. Arrogant dark eyes surveyed her from the top of her flaxen, braided head to the tips of her toes. There was no warming of his expression, and she felt that he must despise her plain convent gown and unfashionable person. Speech was impossible.

'I am waiting, *mademoiselle*, for an answer. As you are doubtless aware, I am an extremely busy man. If you have some idea of robbing my coach, you may search in the pockets and assure yourself that they are empty.'

Teresa had felt uncomfortably aware that she did not present a good appearance, and had felt intimidated, but this last remark kindled her indignation.

'Of course I am not trying to rob your coach! How foolish you must be to entertain such a notion. Would

I have tapped on the window to attract your attention if that had been my purpose?'

Instantly, she regretted her words, uttered impetuously. Rucfully, she thought that they were very far from those planned in her optimistic imagination.

'I want you to take me back to the convent at Villepreux,' she blurted out.

Looking thunderstruck, his forbidding brow darkening further, he snapped, 'Do you mean to tell me that you have been in the coach since it left the convent? I had thought that you had this moment entered.'

'I crept in while it was in the courtyard. I wished to have some speech with you. But you travelled on the box, and I could not make you hear me when I called out.' Rather breathless, her heart-shaped face very flushed, she ended her little speech, perfectly sure that he had not understood a single word she had spoken.

'If you wished to speak to me, why did you not do so at the convent?'

For some reason, she was quite unable to answer this direct question. Certainly, any story of persecution or a desperate plight would sound very foolish—even to her own ears.

'You had better come into the house and explain yourself. It is most inconvenient,' he added impatiently, 'for I am extremely busy. So, I warn you, *mademoiselle*, that your explanation had better be a good one.'

Without waiting for an answer, he nodded dismissal to the groom and walked to the door of the house. Feeling that it was useless to argue with him, Teresa followed, hoping to convince him of the necessity of returning her to the convent without delay.

A deeply bowing servant dressed in plum-coloured livery opened the door, while another hovered solicitously, waiting to relieve his master of his hat and coat. Teresa looked around her with unconcealed admiration, much to the disgust of the two servants.

It occurred to Teresa that the older and more stately of the servants seemed far grander than the master, for his plum-coloured livery was much embellished with gold braid, while his master wore a plain, dark jerkin over a white lawn shirt. His dark hair was unpowdered and he affected no jewellery or adorning ribbons. Even his leather boots were not as glossy as the servants' buckled shoes. Yet, for all that, he had an air of easy command and an unconscious assumption of authority over all with whom he dealt.

'Shall I bring the young person to the kitchen?' The stately servant's eyes had flickered over Teresa. Plainly, he thought her a fellow servant, and once again she was mortified by her drab appearance.

She had been about to blurt out a denial of his assumption when it occurred to her that she was in an awkward position. If it became known that she, Teresa Rochefoucourt, godchild of Queen Maria Teresa, had visited a single man alone, a scandal would be created. Perhaps he was married, but, somehow, she felt that he was a single man. As though reading her thoughts, her host directed a look at her that contained only the merest hint of warning. They were in silent but mutual accord.

'Not at all, Pierre. I shall interview her myself.' He spoke easily, but with dismissive finality. Bowing, Pierre threw open the nearest door and withdrew.

Teresa could not help but contrast this lovely house with the austerity of the convent. Gilded chairs, small, polished tables, fine paintings and gleaming mirrors bore evidence of the wealth and refinement of the owner.

'How very beautiful your house is!' she blurted out. 'How very much I should like to live here.'

'You are not the first female with such a design,' he responded with irony. 'But, as such an event is extremely unlikely, we need not consider it.'

This reply, designed to snub, Teresa had no doubt, depressed her unaccountably. Without inviting her to sit, he folded his arms across his chest and waited for her to speak.

Feeling at a distinct disadvantage, for she was of diminutive proportions and had not realised how very tall he was until he towered over her, she began. 'The Abbesse, your aunt—at least I think it is the Abbesse's plan, for that is what Sister Clothilde told me—wishes me to enter the convent. It is not precisely her own plan, for my mother planned it with the Queen, who is my god-mother——'

'You are the Queen's godchild?' he interrupted her without ceremony. 'Holy Trinity! Now here is a pretty coil.'

It was a very small satisfaction to her that he no longer looked impatient and forbidding; now he looked at her with hard, wary eyes. 'Continue!' he commanded curtly.

'I live at the convent; I have since I was ten years old. But I do not wish to stay there. I want you to help me leave the convent and go to Court and become all the rage——'

'You wish what?' So thunderously angry was he that she recoiled. 'You wish to leave the convent in a clan-destine manner, deceive my aunt, and become the *rage* of Versailles, and you wish me to aid and abet you? You must be quite mad! What in the name of heaven gave you the idea that *I* could or would help you?'

Feeling more muddled than ever, for he seemed genu-inely angry and outraged, she hardly knew how to con-tinue. But she had but one chance to get to Court, and it was represented in the shape of this man. She *must* try to make him understand.

'I hoped that you would speak to the Queen and per-suade her to ask me to stay at Versailles. I do so much wish to go.'

'Why did you not go to my aunt and tell her this? No one would have forced you to enter the convent against your will. This is 1678, not the Dark Age.'

Why had she not simply gone to the Abbesse and told her? It seemed so simple and reasonable.

'I acted impulsively,' she mumbled. 'Sister Clothilde always says that I act without thinking, and indeed I do. I am a very stupid person at times, but when I saw your carriage waiting in the courtyard I thought that if I ran out and spoke to you, then you would speak to the Queen on my behalf. You could remind her about me—she may have forgotten, for I have no relatives to speak for me.'

There was an unconscious pathos about her words, and his expression softened very slightly. 'Oh, please do not refuse me, for I have heard such wonderful stories from Mademoiselle Marie Besneval of Versailles. I long so much to go to balls and banquets, to go out in a gondola, to meet the Wicked Duc——'

'The Wicked Duc?' he snapped, his frown pronounced, an ugly glitter in his eyes. 'What are you talking about?'

'Oh, have you not heard of him? Marie and all the other girls from Court talked about him all the time. He is quite the most exciting man in the whole world. Of all the men at Court, he is the only one who does not fear the King. All the gamblers are quite terrified to play cards with him, for he always wins. And if anyone said even the smallest wrong word to him, he would draw his sword and cut them to ribbons. They say that he is the finest swordsman in France, and all fear him.'

By now her eyes were shining rapturously, and he looked at her with contempt.

'Would you make a hero out of a bully who would draw a sword on a man for the sole reason that he had spoken an ill word?'

Flushing, she eyed him wrathfully. 'I see what it is. You are jealous! The Wicked Duc is the boldest man at Court, and, because all the women have fallen in love with him, the other men are all wild with jealousy. Do you know that once he fell desperately in love with a young lady, and when she chose another in place of him he challenged the poor man to a duel and killed him,' she paused dramatically, 'and then spurned his faithless love.'

Teresa saw with apprehension that, far from inspiring her host with a love of the Wicked Duc, she had further angered him, for there was a whiteness around his firm mouth and a grim set to his lean jaw.

'Is that indeed what they say about the man? Such words are uttered with too much ease at Court. If you are to go to Court, *mademoiselle*, then you would do well to cultivate a discreet tongue in your pretty head.'

It was as though he had been about to say a great deal more, but had decided against this. The ingenuousness of her expression convinced him that she had had no malicious intent behind her foolish prattling. Certainly, he thought her very pretty: large, vivid blue eyes, brilliant and lustrous, were set in a heart-shaped face which was framed by very fair hair. With her clear, unblemished skin, perfectly shaped mouth and naïve exuberance, the Court would describe her as adorable, taking, popular, pretty, a Court ornament—but never the rage. To become the rage of Versailles she would need brains and wit, like that of the King's official mistress, the opulently lovely Marquise de Montespan. Versailles abounded with just this pretty child's sort of frivolous, empty-headed femininity; she would find herself very much at home. This was exactly the sort of girl he most despised—life at Court was boring enough for someone of his restless, masculine nature, but girls like this made it tedious beyond bearing. Hers was the fresh, rosy fairness that most appealed to the sensuous Bourbon King; yes, she would enjoy life at Court. He felt some sympathy with her desire to escape convent life, for he had longed for years to escape from Versailles and return to his Provençal estates; but for that he needed the King's permission. That permission was always denied him.

'I would like to help you, *mademoiselle*, but I cannot think that any application from me would aid your cause. Indeed, I almost laugh to think of the comment it would occasion if *I* were to ask the Queen to invite you to Versailles. It would immediately be assumed that I had an ulterior motive.' He smiled thinly.

'But you are so old!' Again she had spoken heedlessly, and once again regretted the impulsive tongue with which she had been born. When the servant had offered to take her to the kitchen, both she and her host had allowed him to continue in the belief that she was a servant seeking employment as an easy way of dealing with any embarrassment attendant on the situation. But, to her relief, instead of being offended he threw back

his head and laughed, and immediately looked far less
forbidding.

'I like your style of dalliance, *mademoiselle*, for it is
calculated to appeal to masculine vanity.'

'I am sorry, please, say you forgive me,' she coaxed
prettily, imps of mischief dancing in her eyes, a smile
curving her mouth. 'That was not well said of me. I
assure you that I mean to become very expert in the art
of dalliance.'

'A very commendable ambition; I wish you success.
Now,' the moment of brief accord was past—he looked,
once more, forbidding, 'I must take you back at once
to the convent. The sisters will be at prayer, and it is
possible that your absence will not yet be remarked on.
I suggest that you go straight to your room and write a
letter to the Queen, which my aunt will have conveyed
to her. If the Queen is disposed to think kindly of your
mother——'

'She did! My mother was one of the Queen's closest
friends. I have heard the Abbesse tell Sister Clothilde
that when my mother left Court after her marriage, the
Queen said that she had lost her only friend.'

'Then you need have no doubt that she would be
pleased to welcome the daughter of so valued a friend,
for she is the soul of kindness.'

Pulling on the bell-rope which was situated beside the
marble fireplace, he seemed satisfied that his business
with her was concluded. This was confirmed when the
servant entered the room.

'Have the carriage brought round, and inform any
callers that I expect to be back in Versailles within the
hour.'

These plans were not at all to Teresa's liking—she
thought that once she was dispatched back to the convent
this man would forget all about her. Even if she were to
write to the Queen, as he suggested, she was sure that
the Queen must receive many such requests for a place
at Court. Despite her youth and inexperience, Teresa was
an intelligent girl, and felt that her chances of winning
the Queen's favour in this matter were very slim. Also,

in honour, the Queen might feel herself obliged to obey the request of her friend and former lady-in-waiting, and insist that the daughter should remain in the convent.

This man was clearly someone of importance; the style of his house and domestic arrangements spoke of wealth and authority. Teresa was sure that if he spoke people listened with respect. How could she persuade him to speak on her behalf? She must attempt to detain him a little while longer.

'Is it not proper to offer visitors some form of refreshment?' she demanded.

'Most improper,' he responded crushingly. 'Since my staff believe you to be a maid in search of work, I am anxious that they should continue in that belief.'

Flushing with embarrassment, she very much wished that she had the social grace with which to reply with aplomb to his statement—and, moreover, to make such a reply that would leave him feeling crushed and humiliated.

Once more he appeared to guess her thoughts, and he spoke, not unkindly, for a smile lurked in his dark brown eyes. 'I know, I know. And if they all but only knew it, you are all set to become the rage of Versailles. I have done you a service, you foolish child. If it became known that you were here, in my home, alone with me, your reputation would be destroyed for ever—despite my advanced years.'

Inwardly raging, for he had laughed at her ambition and made her unguarded pronouncement about his age seem foolish, she was learning her first lesson about the adult world. Concealing her feelings, and schooling her features into a pretty smile, she spoke archly. 'Are you quite sure that the servants do not suspect that you are trifling with me?'

Far from discomfiting him, these words amused him hugely. Eyes glinting with enjoyment, he smiled and showed a row of strong white teeth.

'Ah, but my servants know that when I make love I do so with the utmost seriousness; I never trifle. And,' he smiled at her blushes, 'my taste is for ladies older, and more beautiful than yourself.' There was a teasing note in his voice, and Teresa blushed yet again. 'This habit of blushing is quite charming, my dear, but at Versailles it would be considered gauche. Come, let me take you back to your convent. Stay there for another year, then think about coming to Versailles. Believe me that my conscience would not allow me to assist you in any way with your absurd ambitions.'

CHAPTER TWO

THE journey back to the convent was not a happy one for Teresa. The silent man sitting, apparently deep in thought, opposite her had made it quite clear that he would not assist her in any way. If restless impulse had driven her to creep into his carriage, then it had only been heightened by her recent, if brief, experience beyond the convent walls. It seemed to her as though she had subtly changed; conversation with this man had been challenging and somehow exciting. Recalling the stories and descriptions of flirtations and dalliances that Marie had regaled her eager ears with, she could not possibly accuse this man of flirting with her, or even of paying her flowery, extravagant compliments. Yet he stirred her senses indefinably. Perhaps it was his air of worldly wisdom. Fervently she hoped that the young men of Versailles were not all like *him*, or how dull and correct they must be! Doubtless his attitudes and behaviour sprang from his pious aunt's guardianship of him.

Despite her feeling that he did not wish for conversation, she found it quite impossible to sit opposite someone in the close confines of the carriage and remain silent.

'I believe that everyone at Versailles gambles all the time. It must be most exciting to gamble,' she breathed ecstatically.

'No,' he replied shortly.

Stung by the snub, she could not resist saying, 'I believe the Wicked Duc, when he is not wooing ladies and fighting duels, is a very great gambler and frequently wins and loses thousands of *livres*. Is that not *very* adventurous?'

He had been looking out of the window, but now directed a curiously hard stare at her.

23

'I am not sure which you think the most *adventurous*—the gambling or the duels.'

'Why, both, naturally. What a silly question to ask. Do you know the Wicked Duc? You did not tell me, when we talked of him earlier.'

'When *you* talked of him,' he corrected her. Sounding weary and bored, he spoke again, softly. 'Yes, I know him. I would hardly describe him in the terms you have used, and I am sad to think that people would make a hero from so contemptible a rogue.'

'You *are* jealous!' she retorted.

'And, *you mademoiselle*, are a bore. Did your guide and mentor, Mademoiselle Besneval, not advise you that, whatever you do at Versailles, you must not be a bore. It is accounted a worse sin than all the others put together.'

The very absence of the intention to insult in the studied observation made Teresa acutely uncomfortable, for he spoke as though he truly believed in his own words. How dared he? Yet innate honesty compelled her to admit that it was, at the very least, bad manners to speak continually of the Wicked Duc to one who was not his admirer.

As though wishing to temper his words, he spoke more kindly, 'I had not realised until you spoke that Versailles was such a very foolish place.'

'And doubtless you think that I should be very much at home there,' she retorted with spirit.

'Bravo!' He looked at her with something like approval. 'I must confess that such a thought had entered my head. But if you will accept my advice, you will do as I bid you earlier. Stay in the convent for another year.'

'Because you think that I am not clever enough for Versailles?' she demanded.

'Because I think you too good for Versailles,' he responded gravely.

His unexpected words caused her to fall silent. Too good? Did he mean that she had conveyed the impression that she was as pious as the good nuns?

'I have already explained that I have no turn for convent life. I admire those who do good works,' she spoke tactfully, anxious not to let him think that she was criticising the Abbcsse or the other nuns, 'but I do not want to devote myself to a life of prayer and contemplation.'

As though bored by her, he looked away, and there was no further conversation between them until they approached the Convent of the Sacred Heart.

Looking up at the mellow edifice before her, Teresa felt profoundly depressed. In a few minutes she would be back in her own room, her mission a failure. Her ambitions had been laughed at, she had been advised to stay in the convent for another year, she had failed to impress one who must surely be a notable, if somewhat unfashionable, member of Louis's court.

Her intention of slipping away unseen to her own room was not to be fulfilled, for the courtyard was full of nuns. As Teresa and her escort alighted, the nuns dispersed either separately or in clusters, averting their eyes from the pair and blessing themselves. Teresa wondered what it could mean, while the Abbesse's nephew looked grimly about him before striding to the front door and going into the convent.

Had her unfortunate flight been discovered? She must instantly explain to the Abbesse that it had all been a most regrettable accident. Aware that she would also have to explain that she preferred to tell a complete stranger that she would rather go to Court than enter the convent, Teresa foresaw that her coming interview with the nun was not likely to be very happy. Sister Clothilde edged towards her as she was crossing the threshold of the convent.

'Oh, Teresa! Whatever made you do it? If I said anything that caused you to run away with that wicked man, please forgive me. Indeed, I shall do a month's penance.' Pausing to wipe her perspiring brow with a corner of her snowy wimple, she gazed at Teresa with anxiously pleading eyes.

Giving her a brief hug, her conscience smarting, Teresa hurriedly reassured her. 'Dear Sister Clothilde, nothing you said caused me to run away, as I shall tell the Abbesse.'

Sister Clothilde's distress made Teresa feel very guilty, and a deepening sense of her own folly made her even more apprehensive about her coming interview with the Abbesse. But a spark of rebellion made her feel irritated that so much should be made of an absence of so short a time. The nuns, her friends and family for seven years, had looked on her as though she had been plagued. It was not as though she had been away from the convent in the company of a stranger. The man was the nephew of the Abbesse—as old as he was correct!

Prepared to defend herself, Teresa faced the Abbesse across the large, shining table that separated them. The simply furnished room contained a few small chairs for the comfort of visitors, but the Abbesse did not invite either of her guests to sit.

'How could you, Guy?' She addressed her nephew with solemn reproach. 'How could you abduct an innocent young girl from my care and protection? Have you no sense of shame? Is there never to be an end to your villainy and folly? Always in the past I have been your greatest defender. I brought you up; you are as a son to me. When I felt my task was complete, I left Provence and entered this convent. There has never been a day when I have not prayed for you and wished that you could find the contentment that I feel you crave. When I hear stories about you—and, yes, even here we hear about you—I have always believed that at heart you are a good and kind man. You have grieved me this day, and disappointed me unbearably.'

There was as much sorrow as reproach in the nun's voice and manner, and Teresa was astounded. Abduction? Folly? Villainy? This staid and sober man? Impossible! For a moment she felt like laughing aloud at the absurdity of it. However impatient she might feel at the nun's reaction to her little escapade, she could not allow this man to take the blame for her silly actions.

'You mistake, Abbesse. Your nephew did not know I was in the coach until it reached Versailles. We went into his house for a little while, and then he brought me straight back here. We had planned that I should go to my room, and not tell anyone where I had been. It is a great pity that you found out.'

If Teresa had hoped that her words would provide some explanation which would appease the nun, she was very wrong. For the first time she detected a family likeness between the two. There was anger and hostility in the brown eyes and a hard set to the mouth.

'You *planned* that I should not know anything about your escapade? You planned to deceive me? I have given you licence, Teresa Rochefoucourt, and much affection, but you have betrayed me this day. For seven years we thought that you had been happy among us, yet you chose to repay that by creeping away. I cannot believe that you entered the coach by anything other than design. You were seen, but by the time I was informed the coach had left.'

'It was an accident, truly,' Teresa said, close to tears. 'I wanted to talk to your nephew, to ask him if he would speak to the Queen on my behalf so that I could go to Versailles. I do not want to take the veil,' she ended on a note of desperation.

'Then why did you not tell *me* so?' the Abbesse demanded reasonably, surprised out of her anger. 'It is *I* who could have helped you with that decision, not my nephew. I cannot pretend that your inheritance would not have been most welcome, but there would never have been any question of compelling you to remain with us.'

Teresa recalled, uncomfortably, that her actions had been guided, if somewhat obscurely, by the words that Marie Besneval had spoken to her. Now, she believed that the Abbesse was not the sort of woman who would have forced her to take the veil.

Throughout this exchange, the man had remained silent. Only his white face and erect bearing showed any sign of the anger that he had thus far suppressed.

'You will have to marry her, Guy. There is no other solution to this business.'

If her words had astounded Teresa previously, she was now wholly transfixed. Marry this man?

'For the Lord's sake, Eugénie,' he burst out, 'no one, save ourselves, knows of this, I give you my word. Directly I discovered her, I brought her back. It is an incident which is now closed.'

The Abbesse rapped the table sharply with a lightly clenched hand, her face strangely worldly-wise. 'Every sister here knows of your joint departure. If you think the religious habit protection against a gabbing tongue, then you know little of women, despite your reputation. You took Teresa into your house—that was stupid, for your servants must all know it. If you think that this affair can be a secret, I am amazed.'

Through clenched teeth, he spoke furiously. 'There *is* no affair!'

'Mistakenly, I took you for a villain this day, Guy. But I never thought to take you for a fool. Do you think that I am so far from the world that I do not know that they call you, with some past justification, the Wicked Duc? Every one of your actions is of immense interest to those who watch you and gossip about you.'

Regarding his aunt coldly, he spoke with anger barely controlled. 'It is many years since I earned that most obnoxious title. I behaved so out of boredom. Ever since a certain incident which involved the death of a close friend, my actions have been those of a sensible man. I have never dishonoured anyone...'

He went on speaking, but Teresa was unable to concentrate on anything he said. She felt as though she were participating in a nightmare. So, this was the Wicked Duc! That aunt and nephew discussed matters of grave import, she could not doubt. There was very much more to their conversation than acrimony over the events of this afternoon. They seemed oblivious of her presence, engaged in a battle of wills; it was beyond her comprehension. The realisation that she had made a dream-hero of this very ordinary and quite old man tugged at her

heart sickeningly. It was her first taste of disillusionment. Was this the sort of man that women in Versailles
fell in love with? Did he really represent the ideal of
romantic masculinity? No wonder the men did not care
much for him—she inclined to their view.

'Do not argue with me, Guy, for I see, as I have always
seen, that you are as rebellious as your father. Think
carefully what his fate was before you reject my plan. I
have always used what influence I have to protect you,
but there would be little I could do in this case.'

'I am still a virtual prisoner at Versailles!' He spoke
with such anguished bitterness that Teresa was startled
out of her reverie of self-pity. 'I want more than anything to return to my estates, but that is denied me.'

'If you had behaved with more circumspection, I could
have continued to urge the Queen to use her influence
with the King on your behalf, and allow you to return
to your home. But what do you do? Take this foolish
girl into your home! It will look to the world like abduction—you will convince no one that matters were
otherwise. Are you aware that her mother was a dearly
loved lady-in-waiting to the Queen?'

'Yes.' He was tight-lipped.

Not once had he looked at Teresa throughout this
painful interview, and she could guess what he must be
thinking of her. That she was the cause of his predicament made her long to beg his forgiveness.

'Then you must know that you would not be forgiven.
If you alienate the Queen, you will never return to your
estates, for she is your only ally at Court. Those who
pretend to be your friends are simply waiting to see you
in the Bastille, and, after gaining the King's favour,
would wait to have your lands conferred on them.'

'Must I always suffer because my father was a
Frondeur? It was he who rebelled, not me! I was only
a child then.' Once more the anguished bitterness in his
voice moved Teresa.

'You have never troubled to conceal the fact that you
dislike being at Court. You would have done better to
dissemble more.'

'You did not bring me up to dissemble, Eugénie.'

'Even so, you would have done better to have kept your views to yourself——'

'They are all so stupid, vain and pompous at Court. You can never know how it galls me to have nothing to do all day but bow and scrape to the King. To make idle conversation about nothing at all is the most tedious of pursuits. Paying Court to painted, perfumed women, who are more like simpering dolls than real people—faugh!' He made an expressive gesture of repugnance with one well-shaped hand. 'Behind their smiles there is viciousness and intrigue. They are not people I could ever love, and their way of life has no appeal for me.'

So savage was his tone, so strong were his words, that a glimpse of the ugliness beneath the façade was revealed to Teresa. She shied away from the picture he presented. It could not be true! Because he disliked Court, and was old and embittered, his vision was darkened by his own thoughts and emotions. He could not be talking of the Versailles of her dreams!

'It is of no moment whether I share your views, Guy. But you, above all people, must know that the King considers any criticism an act of disloyalty. To sneer at Versailles is to sneer at the King. There are people in the Bastille who have committed less heinous crimes—be warned! I believe that the King has affection for you—that is one reason he keeps you so close. You are of an old and illustrious family; he likes to have such people around him. When you choose to exert yourself, you are a witty and charming companion. If asked, I have heard, about affairs of state, you give the King good advice. You should put yourself forward more, in this serious way.'

Teresa saw that the Abbesse was almost pleading with her nephew, but the taut lines of his face did not soften.

'If I allow the King to depend on me that much I shall never be able to leave Versailles.'

Teresa watched them both, the family likeness now very pronounced, face each other across the large writing-table. The nun sat down and drew a sheet of paper towards her. Dipping her pen into the ink-well, she began to write with a steady hand. Without looking up, she addressed her nephew, still writing.

'You must take this letter to the Queen. I am telling her that you have formed an attachment with her god-daughter and wish to marry her. You will, in due course, be requesting the King's permission to be married as soon as the royal assent is given. As a special favour, I am also asking her if she will find a place for Teresa at Court. Perhaps as a lady-in-waiting.'

Crossing the floor in two swift strides, he placed a firm hand over the sheet of paper. 'You cannot do this! You must not! It is too much to bear! I cannot, *will* not, be forced to marry a frivolous, empty-headed child from the convent. You must know that in the matter of my marriage I had other hopes, other plans.'

For the first time throughout this strange nightmarish interview he looked directly at Teresa. There was no liking in that look. His expression was one of loathing, as though the sight of her was abhorrent to him. Clearly, the thought of marriage with her filled him with detestation. His words confirmed this. 'My God!' he exploded. 'I think I would rather the Bastille!'

The merry brightness that had always filled Teresa's world exploded into dust as she experienced her second disillusionment of the day. No one had ever hated her; on the contrary, she had been loved, petted and indulged—first by her family, and then by the nuns. She expected to fall in love with a handsome, romantic young man who would write poetry about her, sing songs in her praise, walk in the gardens of Versailles, all the time declaring his unending love for her. But she was not to have this; instead, she was to be married to a man who regarded the Bastille, that dark place without hope, as a fate preferable to marriage with her. At his side she must learn to see Versailles through his disillusioned eyes—as a place not bright and beautiful, but filled with intrigue and mystery.

Occasionally in the past, in order to win her own way, she had forced tears to her eyes; now they spilled, unbidden, down her damask cheeks.

'I do not wish to marry this man! He is too old and not at all romantic.' How foolish her words sounded. How little they represented the welter of emotions which she was experiencing, but could barely understand.

For the first time in that interview a lightness wafted into the air. The Abbesse put up a hand to her mouth to hide a tiny smile.

'If you think that, Teresa, you must be the only woman in France of that mind.'

It was several days before news arrived from Versailles that they were to expect a visit from Queen Maria Teresa. The nuns, under the Abbesse's direction, were harried into intense activity as the convent was cleaned until it sparkled. Flowers were placed everywhere and the chapel resembled a floral bower more than a place of worship. The gardens received extra attention, for the nuns were expert gardeners and farmers and they were always proud to show the results of their labours to their royal patron. Only rarely did the Queen dine with the community when she visited them, but when she did she insisted that, like the nuns, she ate in the refectory. The long tables were polished with beeswax until they shone; the benches were given equally loving attention. There was an air of holiday, joyful and glad, over the entire community, for the grave, sweet Queen was dearly loved.

Sister Clothilde explained to Teresa that the Abbesse had not deemed her worthy of her attention.

'Naturally *I* believe that you acted without thought, Teresa, that is ever your way. But how many others would believe that? The Queen would not be able to receive you at Court if your reputation were destroyed. Your *dot* is very large, so you need not fear that you would not receive a marriage offer. But it might not be one that you would like.'

'I do not like *this* one!' Teresa spoke passionately, for she was deeply upset. 'He dislikes me very much. Can you imagine my feelings when he told me that he would rather go to the Bastille than marry me? His aunt tried to persuade him, but he became very angry. It was a long time before she could convince him that it was the only thing to do.'

She and Sister Clothilde were dusting books in the library; now she pushed some books aside and began to pace up and down the room in an agitated manner. The nun looked with lively alarm at the ill-treatment of the precious books.

'He does not even wish to live at Versailles, he wants to bury himself away on his estates. It will be terrible! I think I would prefer to remain here; at least you all love me,' she ended with a slight catch in her voice.

Quietly restoring the books to their shelves, Sister Clothilde searched in her mind for some words that would bring comfort to the unhappy girl. The community would never accept an unwilling novice, and she had shown herself to be that. Guy Denis, Duc d'Abbeville, was a proud man, a man of courage and resourcefulness; his estates were vast and his wealth reputed to be unlimited. But his father had been a Frondeur—one of those who had rebelled against the monarchy. Louis was an unforgiving King and a demanding man. If he chose, he could have the Duc cast into the Bastille; he chose, instead, to command Guy to live, under his surveillance, at Versailles. The Duc had experience of the world and people that was beyond the comprehension of a girl of seventeen. Forced unwillingly into a marriage with such a girl, he could make her life very difficult. Sister Clothilde's whole life had been spent within the walls of the Convent of the Sacred Heart at Villepreux—happy, contented years—yet she knew that Teresa lacked the wiles and the experience to make the Duc fall in love with her. That they should both appear to be entering into the marriage with feelings of mutual loathing, filled her gentle soul with misgiving. Having no comfort to offer, she tried to turn the conversation into more cheerful channels.

'You will certainly enjoy being at Court; there will be so much for you to see and do. Can you not think about that instead?'

Suppressing a sob, Teresa picked up her duster and began to clean some empty shelves. It was pointless, she felt, to attempt to explain anything to an elderly nun. There was a quality about the Duc that frightened her. There was something strong and unassailable; she felt that he had the power to crush her and cause her deep unhappiness. The coming of the Queen, on her account, filled her with dread; a few days ago it would have filled her with ecstasy.

Henri Deschamps, as angelically fair as his companion was satanically dark, attempted for the third time to extract the cause of the Duc's savage humour from him.

'I wish you would not question me, Henri, for I am loath to tell you the cause of my present unhappiness. Ah, you need not look with that expression. For once, I am the victim and not the author of my difficulties.'

Henri was perplexed. Many times he had seconded his friend in a duel, ridden into battle with him, diced and fenced with him, but he had only once before seen him in such a bitter and despairing mood. Henri liked the aimless, sociable life of the courtier—it suited his own charming indolence—but he knew that his friend did not like the Court. It surprised everyone that two men so very different should be such firm friends.

'Do you hunt today? The weather is fine, and we might have some sport. It might help to lift your spirits, for you labour under some terrible load. As to your being a victim,' he raised an eyebrow and grinned quizzically at his friend, 'I cannot believe that the noble, but very wicked Duc d'Abbeville is a *victim*.'

'Do not call me by that foolish title!' snapped Guy, his eyes darkening. 'You may believe me, Henri, for I speak the truth—every single action I committed, every act of folly which earned me that despised title, was carried out through boredom or frustration. I would far rather have been looking after my estates.'

Henri's youthful face clouded with quick sympathy. 'I know that, Guy. But I believe that your very unwillingness to gamble makes players seek you out. Your lack of interest in the married state makes women desire you more——'

'And my loathing of killing forces every young fool with a rapier to challenge me to a duel!' The Duc spoke with weary contempt.

Henri watched his friend's darkly brooding face. 'I have wanted to change places with you so often. The lovely Marie adores you——'

Without ceremony, Guy interrupted his friend. 'You would be welcome to change places with me, Henri. Lovely as Marie is, and I do like her very much, my destiny lies with another.'

The two men had been throwing dice in the chamber given over to the courtiers for their own leisure. As there were several other courtiers in the room, all engaged in dicing, gossiping and drinking wine, they had been talking quietly. Now Henri, casting aside the dice and abandoning his lounging position, sat up quickly.

'What is this? You are promised to another and you made love to Marie?' Henri was angry.

A wry smile twisted the Duc's mouth. 'Easy, my friend. Do not vent your anger on me. I know well how enamoured you are of the lovely Marie. *She* would have me make love to her. As I said already, I like her well enough, but I have not been so cruel as to trifle with her or make her believe that I have feelings other than those of purest friendship for her.'

Rebuked, Henri flushed, his flash of anger subsiding. 'Oh, I know that she has no smiles for me while you are here in Versailles.' Sighing deeply, he knew that Guy spoke only the truth. But how he longed for Marie to bestow on him the dazzling smiles and pretty, coquettish ways that she lavished on the handsome Duc. Marie, with her capricious whims and dusky curls, had captured his heart from the very first moment she had made her début at Versailles.

'You have not answered my question, Guy.' Henri was frowning. 'You hint that you have a marriage planned.'

'*I* have not planned it. Oh, curse it! I may as well tell you the wretched story, but I beg that you will not repeat its substance to anyone.' Receiving a nod of assurance from an interested Henri, he looked down at the dice he held in his long fingers, his face a study of unhappy abstraction, before he began to speak.

'My future bride is not, as most people supposed, Marie Besneval, but a girl of seventeen who resides, as she has done for the past seven years, at the Convent of the Sacred Heart at Villepreux. She is silly, ignorant and with no thought in her head beyond dressing up and showing herself off prettily to every fool in the palace. She had the grossest of all the female stupidities, for she decided to make a hero out of "the Wicked Duc".' Derisively he looked across at the astounded Henri. 'Is that not a fitting reward for me? If she has any notion of the conduct expected of a Duchesse, then I have yet to see it.'

Henri was now as appalled as he had previously been astounded. 'How comes this, Guy? What ever made you contract such an unsuitable alliance?'

Briefly Guy d'Abbeville related the circumstances of his forthcoming marriage. 'And this is the girl with whom I must spend the rest of my life! My God! Henri, you can have no idea of the bitterness I feel. Even in the matter of my marriage I am powerless to choose for myself. This boring, aimless existence I live has been made bearable by the thought that one day I could return to Provence with a bride of my choice, and together, as companions, we could watch our children grow. Now I must look forward to life with a girl who cannot hold a rational conversation, and, moreover, dislikes me every bit as much as I dislike her.'

'On my oath, Guy,' Henri was distressed, 'I never heard a sorrier tale.' Sucking in his cheeks and turning down his lower lip, Henri considered the matter for a moment. 'However, I cannot see that you have any alternative but to marry the girl. When it became known, as surely it would, that you carried off the Queen's virginal godchild, then it would be the Bastille for you. Make the best of it. You have never had any difficulty in making girls fall in love with you. Woo her, win her heart, then mould her to your ways.'

'Love! I am not interested in her love; that emotion can never exist between us. But I shall certainly mould her. It was her stupidity that caused this damnable coil, and that is something that she will never be allowed to forget.' Speaking savagely, with an angry glitter in his eyes, he did not notice that Henri shuddered and looked away. 'In the meantime,' he ground out, 'unless I am to be a laughing stock throughout France, I must pretend that I am all delight and happiness at the prospect of marriage with a badly dressed girl who has rarely been beyond the walls of her convent for several years!'

Rising from a deep curtsy, Teresa looked with interest at the serenely lovely face of the Queen of France. Years of childbearing had devastated her figure; the constant humiliation of witnessing her husband's ill-concealed and frequent infidelities had saddened her. But there was beauty in her large, dark eyes and sweetness in her grave smile.

'How very like your mother you are, Teresa. It is not at all surprising that the Duc should have fallen in love with you.'

Teresa blushed, for there was a quality of truthfulness and piety in the Queen and she hated the thought that she must deceive her. They were in the room set aside for the reception of visitors of the highest rank; it was furnished with velevet-covered chairs and a few small tables which held bowls of roses.

'The Abbesse speaks very well of you—she tells me that you are a good girl and will make a suitable wife for the Duc. You must know that I have a very special affection for him, and have longed for him to marry and enjoy the comfort and security of family life. It is arranged that you will return to Versailles with me, where you will become a lady-in-waiting.' Smiling with real affection, the Queen continued, 'It will remind me of the many happy times I spent with your mother when I came to France as a young bride.'

If the Abbesse had not been watching her, Teresa would have blurted out the truth, but she stood beside the Queen's chair throughout the short interview.

'You will share a room in the palace with another lady-in-waiting, Mademoiselle Marie Besneval——' She broke off, a faint smile curving her mouth, for Teresa had exclaimed joyfully. 'I hope that you will be able to exercise a beneficial influence over that young lady, for she is a little wild on occasion. But she is a very sweet girl, and she will be able to show you all your duties besides being your friend and companion. The Princesse d'Elbeuf will instruct you in matters of dress and court etiquette, for you must know that at Versailles etiquette and appearances are very important.'

'You are very kind, *majesté*. I shall do my very best to serve you well.' Impulsively, she burst out, 'You cannot know how happy it makes me to be going with you to Versailles.'

Smiling with warmth, the Queen looked at her with twinkling eyes. 'I believe that you are thinking of your Duc. But I must tell you that you must not speak of your forthcoming marriage to *anyone* until the King's permission has been granted. At Versailles we are subject to the King's word. If you were to speak of your marriage, you would incur his displeasure. Now, do not look so solemn, for I am but giving you a little hint. Go and find Mademoiselle Besneval—she is in the garden with one of the sisters.'

Dismissed, Teresa curtsied and withdrew from the room. Hurrying to the gardens, she was torn with joy at being reunited with her friend, and a greater joy at being told that she must not mention her coming marriage to anyone. Never had a piece of news been so welcome. Perhaps the King would refuse his consent! It was only a tiny spark of hope, but enough for her to cling to. In the meantime she would put all thoughts of her marriage, and the Duc, who was more disagreeable than wicked, right from her mind and prepare to enjoy life at Versailles.

Marie, a pretty hat tied over her dusky curls to protect her fine complexion, was stooping gracefully over a rose bush. Teresa looked with unfeigned admiration at her billowing silk skirts and longed for the moment when she might dress so elegantly. Glancing up, she saw Teresa and, abandoning her contemplation of the convent gardens, ran to her friend, hands outstretched in a charming gesture of welcome.

'How good it is to see you once more, Teresa.' Her eyes danced with mischievous mirth. 'We are to be friends together and serve the Queen. Had you come to Versailles a little while ago, we could have made many follies together. But now I am on my best behaviour, for I am to be married.'

Leading her to a bench, which was situated at the end of one of the many gravelled walkways in the garden, Teresa turned to stare at Marie with pleased astonishment.

'But this is wonderful, Marie. I knew nothing of this! You should have written to tell me, for you are frequently in my mind.'

'Am I?' Marie raised delicately arched brows. Then, with a little laugh, she said, 'I can assure you that when you are at Court you will have little time or inclination to think of all this.' Wrinkling her nose with distaste, she swept a slender hand around the garden in a disdainful gesture.

'I have been very happy here,' murmured Teresa, for she felt uneasy that Marie should make fun of the place in which she had been very happy for the past few years.

'My love!' Marie gave an affected little shriek. 'Never let anyone at Court hear you utter such words! You would be laughed at, and I would not be able to support our friendship if you became an object of fun.' Despite Marie's laughter, Teresa felt that her friend spoke with a degree of seriousness, and it disturbed her. That Versailles glittered she had expected, that the ladies and courtiers should have such shallow values disquieted her.

Perhaps Marie only displayed an unusual sense of humour, Teresa thought.

'Come and sit beside me on this stone bench; it is quite clean and will not spoil your lovely gown,' invited Teresa. 'And tell me all about your forthcoming marriage.'

Twitching complacently at her low neckline—could I *ever* wear such an immodest confection? wondered Teresa—Marie allowed a smile of pure triumph to spread over her face.

'I am to be married to the wealthiest and most handsome man in France. When it is known that we are to be married, I shall be the most envied girl in the land. Already there are hints of the marriage, and other unmarried girls—of which there are a *great* number in Court—and their mamas all look at me with hatred. Ah!' she sighed ecstatically. 'It is truly *wonderful*.'

'Do you love him?' Teresa could only suppose that Marie had not mentioned this because she might consider the subject indelicate.

'Love?' Marie's velvety brown eyes widened in real astonishment. 'When a rich noble proposes, one does not enquire if one is *loved*. Or care, for that matter,' she added. 'One merely thanks providence for the opportunity——' She broke off, seeing that her friend was regarding her with dismay. 'Oh, tra-la! I will lose patience with you, Teresa! Marriage—at least, marriage for our class—is about making a suitable business arrangement. If the couple like and esteem each other, so much the better. Love will follow later. It is better to occupy an unloved but secure position than to be *loved* by a nobody.'

Teresa was stung by the admonition. 'I can recall that you expressed yourself very differently that last time you were here. You were deeply enamoured of the Wicked Duc——'

'Rest easy!' Marie gave a shrill little cry of amusement. 'If that is your worry, then cease! For that is the name of my betrothed.'

Teresa directed a look of blank astonishment at Marie. 'The Wicked Duc?' she repeated.

Eyes dancing with glee, Marie made her mouth firm. '*Not* the Wicked Duc any more, for he will reform when we are married. Guy Denis d'Abbeville.'

CHAPTER THREE

TERESA stared unseeingly at the massed flower-beds and green, scythed lawns. What had the Duc said about having 'other hopes, other plans'? Was he referring to his marriage with Marie? Inevitably Marie would have to be told that the Duc was marrying another. It was obvious to Teresa that for some reason he had not divulged his new plans to her. The Queen had said that she must make no announcement until the King's permission had been granted. But it was not fair that such important news and, moreover, news that affected her so directly, be concealed from Marie Besneval. Teresa was in a wretched state of indecision. Concealment was alien to one of Teresa's open, sunny disposition.

'I shall have some sharp words for Guy tonight,' Marie said blithely. 'There is a rumour that he has seduced some servant girl! He was seen taking a young girl—a very plain young girl, by all accounts—into his house on the Avenue du Vieux Versailles. How I shall tease him! When I am Duchesse d'Abbeville I shall ensure that my husband behaves with more discretion. If he must take little servant girls into his house for several hours, then it *must not* be in daylight for everybody to observe him.'

Putting trembling hands to flushed cheeks, Teresa implored Marie.

'Enough! I beg you not to continue——'

Marie gave a laugh that was half-way between vexation and amusement. 'Really, Teresa! You must not act in this silly way if you hope to make something of yourself at Court. You are very beautiful, and you have the sort of looks much admired by the King—you could easily become the rage.' She nodded with the worldy-wise air that had formerly entranced Teresa. 'But at

42

Court you must behave like a lady and not like a convent-girl.'

In the few days between the arrangement of her marriage and the arrival of the Queen, Teresa had only thought of the wretchedness of her own position: her distaste for the marriage; her fear of her future husband; her possible removal from Court before she had had a chance to taste its delights. Now she perceived that her impulsive action would bring unhappiness to Marie also, and was genuinely grieved. Dared she confess to Marie? If she did, then she would lose her only friend at Court, for she hardly thought of Guy d'Abbeville as a friend. The Queen had imposed silence on her, but her conscience troubled her badly. The consequences of her actions were borne upon her, and left her with little desire to go to Versailles.

'The Marquise de Montespan was telling me the other day that the King is in hourly expectation of receiving an application for my hand from the Duc.'

'The Marquise?' Teresa barely knew how to reply to Marie, so confused and unhappy were her thoughts.

'Really, Teresa! Did you never attend to a thing I told you about Court? The Marquise is the King's mistress. The most beautiful and influential woman at Court, she is a great friend of mine. As the King will very much favour your looks, I do not think that she will like *you* very much. But I am your good friend, so do not let that trouble you.'

'But what of the Queen?' Teresa demanded, glad to talk of something other than Marie's forlorn hopes for her marriage.

Shrugging and giving a pitying laugh, Marie glanced sideways at Teresa. 'At Court, or, at least,' she amended, 'the part of the Court that *counts*, the Queen is reckoned a nobody.'

Until now Teresa had been in affectionate awe of Marie, on whom she unconsciously patterned her behaviour. But she could not allow such a callous statement to pass without challenge.

'I could never think of the Queen as a nobody, or be happy among people who could so describe her, Marie. It grieves me that you should number among them.' There was unexpected dignity as well as reproof in her voice and manner.

Reddening, Marie looked with annoyance at her acolyte. 'I merely told you how matters stand at Court. It is as well to be realistic about these things. I am sure that I fervently admire the Queen's piety. But those who hold power are those who hold the King's attention, and, even if I do not put the matter into words, it is true that the King has had a number of mistresses. De Montespan is his official mistress and, as such, wields great power. If you wish to succeed at Court, then you must be noticed by her.'

Acknowledging the truth of her words, and feeling that she had been unduly censorious of her friend, Teresa was still left with the uncomfortable feeling that life at Court was not as beautiful as she had painted it in her fertile imagination.

A number of soldiers and guards in blue and silver uniform stood stiffly to attention as the Queen's coach drew up at an entrance on the south wing of the palace. Liveried servants hurried forwards to let down the steps of the coach and assist their royal mistress into her private apartments.

Teresa had a confused view of sumptuous rooms with painted ceilings, bas-relief here, an enormous blue-grey marble fireplace there, and sea-green wall-hangings.

'I have my suite of rooms here.' The Queen indicated a series of rooms interspersed by galleries and corridors. 'I live here and perform my official duties from my own quarters. You will find it all very strange at first, but soon you will think it all very cosy.'

Teresa repressed a merry smile—she could not think of a less appropriate description for these vast rooms than cosy.

'The *Salons des Nobles*,' murmured the Queen. 'I do so love this room.' On she swept, apparently oblivious of bowing flunkeys and clusters of gaily clad men and women.

Everywhere the women were all dressed alike, and all wore the same style of hair—cut in layers and bunched on either side of the face. In young women, like Marie Besneval, it was charming and attractive; in older women it was faintly ridiculous. The gowns were broad over the hips and gave the waist—even the Queen's—a tiny appearance; a profusion of petticoats, knots of ribbons and great quantities of delicate lace entranced Teresa. She was still not sure if she would feel quite comfortable in such low-cut necklines, but she would dearly have loved to exchange her plain gown for one of the bright silks or gorgeously coloured brocades.

It was one of the duties of the Princesse d'Elbeuf to arrange a roster of ladies-in-waiting. 'Your duties will not be too arduous, Mademoiselle Rochefoucourt—you will stay with Mademoiselle Besneval at first. The Queen desires you to become acquainted with the Court and acquire some clothes before you are presented in public.' The kindly Princesse smiled at her vaguely, her eyes already straying to the list of cardinals and duchesses that she was obliged to check before the Queen received them at six o'clock. Then her attention was claimed by the Duc, who had that moment entered the great reception room.

'Ah, Guy, allow me to present to you Mademoiselle Teresa Rochefoucourt.'

Nodding, he replied laconically, '*Mademoiselle* and I have already met. The Queen commands me to escort you to the chapel,' he addressed Teresa.

If the Princesse was surprised that so notable a personage as the Duc d'Abbeville should claim the notice of an insignificant and newly arrived lady-in-waiting, she did not betray this. Waving them away with a vague gesture, she returned to a perusal of her list, merely advising Teresa to present herself to the Queen on the following morning after mass.

In silence, the Duc accompanied his future Duchesse through the state apartments and into the chapel. It was as ornate as the rest of the palace, and smelt of flowers and incense.

'My aunt, the Abbesse, wrote to me charging me with the office of attending to your spiritual welfare. I promised her that I would bring you to the chapel and ensure, thereafter, that you attended your devotions. Courtiers and ladies here tend to be lax in that respect.'

His tone told her nothing of what his feelings must be, but she suspected that he found the duty onerous and distasteful.

'There is no need for you to be concerned for me, Duc. I am quite capable of looking after my own spiritual affairs.'

Taking her hand, he turned her to face him. 'I dare say you are, Teresa. But, henceforth, you will be guided by me. If you need to know anything, ask me. When you are in need of guidance, I shall direct you.'

Teresa's heart sank; he sounded so much like an elderly tutor and unlike her vision of a lover that she felt a profound depression threatening.

'Let us go outside,' she said quickly. 'There are things that I would like to ask you about, and I cannot feel easy here.'

'By all means,' he assented. 'It is a fine afternoon, we could walk in the park. The King, as you will soon discover, is proud of his gardens.'

Teresa felt more at ease as they walked in the warm sunshine. A solemn, oppressed atmosphere had attended their visit to the chapel, and she had felt uncomfortable. More than ever, she was conscious that Marie Besneval expected to marry him, and that he was bound to her by ties of duty and circumstance that were repulsive to him. That the Wicked Duc should be responsible for her spiritual welfare would, under other circumstances, have delighted her ready sense of humour. She could not resist pointing this out to him.

'As my future wife, there is a code of conduct which I expect you to adhere to. In your ignorance you cannot be expected to know what it is, so I must instruct you. As to my being a *fitting* person, you may well be right in your assumption that I am unfit. At least, I was in the past. There were circumstances...' he hesitated as though trying to decide whether or not to speak '...which compelled me to change my way of life, and I assure you that I have little deserved that silly title for a long while.'

There was a curiously pained expression in his fine dark eyes, and she was touched and curious. 'May I ask what the circumstances were?' she asked timidly.

She had the feeling that he hesitated again before speaking. 'The Queen promised to be my ally at Court, and speak to the King on my behalf to help me return to my estates. For that reason I altered my way of life, and attempted to reconcile myself to life at Court.'

Without quite knowing why, Teresa felt very strongly that there was some other cause of the Duc's change from wild young man apparently embroiled in every devilry the Court had to offer to the weary cynic who chafed at the bonds which held him at Versailles.

They were approaching a bench which overlooked a fine display of formal flower-beds. Pausing by the bench, she asked if it were in order to sit.

'Versailles is not so rigid that rules govern the procedure of sitting in the park.' The Duc grinned, and looked less forbidding and more approachable.

Taking advantage of this, she sat on the bench, patting her skirts into order. 'There was another reason, I think?' she enquired gently.

Instantly his mood of lightness disappeared. 'Mademoiselle Marie Besneval has been gossiping. You would do well, Teresa, to choose your companions carefully at Versailles. I shall tell you who it is wise to consort with, and those you should avoid.'

For a long moment, Teresa looked full into his eyes and saw that he was startled as well as angry. How hypocritical the man was! Her instinct had been right—there *was* another reason for his change of behaviour, and he had talked to Marie of it. A man with the reputation that he had earned was scarcely in a position to tell her with whom she could associate.

'Do you say that Marie is not a fit companion?' she
enquired, deceptively meek.

Stirring restlessly, he looked away from her. Then,
taking a seat beside her, he spoke. 'That is not precisely
what I meant, as I think you know. I would not have
you gossip unwisely, nor be seen in the company of the
foolish and frivolous.'

'That cannot be a fair description of Marie, surely?'
Teresa demanded. 'At one time you were going to marry
her. Indeed,' wrath was flaring through her, making her
speech impulsive, 'I cannot credit that you would choose
one who was frivolous and foolish.'

Leaping to his feet, he dragged her up and glared down
at her irefully. 'That is a lie, Teresa. I insist on an
apology.'

'Do not attempt to bully me, Guy. I refuse to apologise. Marie herself told me that she was to be married
to you. Did she speak without foundation?' Teresa marvelled at the cool way in which she managed to control
her outward emotions and ask that question.

This direct attack seemed to take him aback and he
wavered. 'I can promise you that I have never asked
Marie Besneval to be my wife,' he replied eventually.

'Yet she felt so confident of your affections and in-
tentions that she believes, even now, that you and she
are to be married.' Despite her size and youth, Teresa
combined dignity and reproach. 'It would seem that your
reputation is still deserved, Guy,' she ended quietly.

Taking her hand, he held it for a moment, returning
her serious look. 'Whatever may be the shortcomings of
my character and personality, I promise you that I shall
be ever faithful in our marriage.'

Raising her hand to his lips, he kissed it lightly, as
though sealing some contract between them more solemn
and binding than the unwilling marriage they were about
to enter into. It was Teresa's turn to be taken aback; she
had not meant to wring such a promise from him. Her
motive in challenging him about his affairs with Marie
had been prompted by his high-handed attitude to
herself. Now he believed that she had some jealousy

towards him, and this irked her. Yet his solemn promise had reassured her—of what, she was not quite sure.

In a mood of uneasy accord they returned to the palace without further conversation.

Marie was delighted with her few days' holiday—she loved nothing better than visiting her dressmaker. 'She is very good and very cheap. You can have no notion of how very expensive it is to dress at Versailles. Look,' Marie pulled a bolt of figured green silk from the shelf in the corner of the room she shared with Teresa. 'This material alone costs twenty or thirty *livres*, then add to that the cost of making it up.'

Losing interest in Marie's silk, Teresa gave herself up to the sheer pleasure of looking about the room, which was situated up a stairway above the Queen's apartments. It was cluttered with clothes, fans, jewels and mirrors; the dressing table was littered with enamelled boxes, combs, pots of powder and oils, and the air was redolent of the light, sweet perfume that Marie favoured. Sure that she was going to be blissfully happy here, Teresa examined in minute detail every object of that fascinating room, exclaiming over and over again as she discovered treasure after treasure, until even Marie, worldly and sophisticated, was obliged to smile at her enthusiasm.

'First we must arrange to have your hair cut—you cannot be seen in public looking like a milkmaid. In the meantime, you can wear this.' She pulled a lovely silk gown of azure blue from the rack. 'It does not become me, I cannot think why I allowed Celeste to persuade me to buy it. You can wear these slippers with it.' She tossed a pair of little blue satin slippers with jewel-encrusted heels on to Teresa's bed.

'They are lovely, truly beautiful. But are they suitable for a walk into the town? I understood that the dressmaker lived in the town.'

'Walk? Merciful heavens! We do not *walk*. We will ask Guy or his friend Henri Deschamps to provide us with a coach.' Smiling archly, Marie observed that Teresa blushed every time the Duc's name was mentioned. 'You need not blush like a little ninny, Teresa. I do not anticipate that your morals are in any danger of being corrupted by my Duc. You are not at all to his taste.'

It was the moment for disclosure, but Teresa remained silent, mindful of the Queen's request of her. Her earlier slight misgivings about life at Court had disappeared, and she was determined that she would enjoy her brief sojourn there. With the optimism of youth, she felt that something would happen to save her.

Celeste was very young. Somehow Teresa had expected that she would be much older. In her mind she had compared her with the convent seamstress, a lady of great skill and maturity. Celeste was about Marie's age, twenty-one or twenty-two. Despite her youth, Teresa immediately recognised that she had unusual talent as she entered enthusiastically into all the plans for transforming the dowdy girl from the convent into the rage of Versailles.

'But, *mademoiselle*, you have excellent taste!' she exclaimed. 'That ivory silk will make you look *ravissante*—so fragile, so feminine. Do you not agree, Mademoiselle Besneval, that your friend has natural *flair* for choosing just what becomes her?'

Thus appealed to, Marie was forced to agree that the little friend she had considered provincial had displayed quite remarkable good taste. A riding habit of rose-pink velvet might not appeal to Marie's more practical nature, but on Teresa it was sensational.

Throughout the fitting, ordering and discussion of many gowns, petticoats and coats that were to be made up, or altered and sent on to the palace, money was not once mentioned. No fool, despite her lack of knowledge about the world beyond the convent, Teresa knew that the clothes would cost a great deal of money.

'How much do I owe you, Celeste? And when must I pay—?' she asked with the innocent charm that had already begun to bewitch the few people she had thus far met at Court.

Marie, eyeing her with impatience, broke in. 'We shall not discuss that now, Celeste. *Mademoiselle* is not yet in the way of things at Versailles.'

Outside in the street on which the dressmaker's establishment was situated, Teresa demanded an explanation.

'It is not the done thing to talk about money—it is considered extremely vulgar, Teresa.' Marie spoke with asperity.

Dismayed but undaunted, Teresa persisted. 'I still do not understand, Marie. How am I to pay if I do not know how much the bill is likely to be? I am not sure how I go about obtaining my money, but I do not want to overspend whatever allowance the Queen will make to me.'

Pulling a dust cloak over her broad hooped skirts, and pulling up the hood to protect her exquisitely coiffured head from the clouds of dust thrown up by the many carriages and wagons on the busy street, Marie did not at first answer. They were going along the street to meet Henri and some of his friends at Gaston's Inn, where a repast awaited them.

'I hope that you are not going to continue in this tiresome manner,' she thus addressed a surprised Teresa. 'One never pays one's bills at Versailles.'

'I could not possibly take clothes from Celeste and not pay for them.' She was quite shocked at the idea. If necessary, she had decided she would abandon her scruples and try to behave like other ladies at Court—but that could never extend to refusing to pay a little dressmaker who must rely on her trade as her sole means of support.

'Do not look so censoriously at me! It is a great honour for Celeste to be noticed by anyone at Court. Think how her business will increase when she is able to boast that she has dressed two of the most beautiful young ladies at Versailles.'

Teresa refused to be coaxed or diverted by Marie's cajoling tone, but, as they were stepping over the threshold of Gaston's and being welcomed by him, she could not tell Marie of her feelings.

Henri Deschamps had accompanied them into the town and, while his fair charges were with their dress-maker, he had attended to some trifling matters of business on his own account. Rising, and smiling good-naturedly, he kissed the hand of first Teresa and then, more lingeringly, of Marie.

'Are you pleased with me? I have obtained Gaston's finest private parlour.' Henri spoke gaily, but he watched Marie's face with a slight air of anxiety.

Shrugging, Marie looked briefly around. 'I expected no less,' she responded.

As he fussed around the room, Gaston watched the party with an expert eye. He knew and liked the frank Henri Deschamps. The little Mademoiselle Besneval, like her friend, was one of the many youthful and innocuous members of the Court. There was one other gentleman expected, and he had not arrived yet. Gaston was puzzled by the presence of the older lady who sat at the head of the luncheon table. The sharp face of Madame de Thiange, the intimate of the Marquise de Montespan, wore an expression of amused malice as she watched the flaxen-haired young lady with the shining blue eyes. Frowning as he deftly laid the table with heavy silver and arranged a dish of small cakes more appetisingly, Gaston tried to recall when he had seen her at his es-tablishment before. Many men and women hired rooms in utmost secrecy at his inn—perhaps to deal with a Paris jeweller; to speak privately to an apothecary whom they could not consult openly; maybe for the purposes of witchcraft, for black magic was practised at Versailles. Discreet and imperturbable, Gaston had impressed upon his wife and staff the need to look bland and incurious, to hear nothing, to know nothing. But Madame de Thiange did not belong in her present company, and Gaston was curious and alert.

It was impossible to remain out of humour when Henri had gone to such lengths to please his party. The table was loaded with every delicacy, and when Teresa refused wine Henri promptly ordered a little pot of chocolate. She rewarded him with a dazzling smile. With a little gurgle of infectious laughter she pointed to the array of dishes.

'You had better tell me what they are, Henri. For I am used to very simple convent fare, and have not the least idea what you offer.' This was accompanied by another smile, and Henri, who was rarely appealed to for help or information on any subject, was delighted.

'Trout pâté, trifles of every description, chicken tartlets——'

'Henri! I swear that I shall not eat a mouthful if I am obliged to hear you talk about the food as though you were a cook in a pastry shop. I beg you! Spare my feelings. I am sure that your young friend will learn all she needs about food from the tasting of it. That is the best way to learn about life—to taste it first.' A smile curved her thin painted lips, and there was mockery in the eyes of Madame de Thiange.

Marie laughed and dug Henri slyly in the ribs with the fan she carried. 'I do believe that Madame de Thiange has put you to the blush, Henri. You are as bad as poor little Teresa Rochefoucourt, who for once is *not* blushing. You two would make a very good match of it.'

This did make Teresa blush, even though Madame de Thiange's sally was incomprehensible. The door opened to admit the last of their party, and Teresa was grateful that attention had been diverted from her rosy countenance. She had expected that Henri's friend might be another young courtier, for he was popular and had many friends at Court, and was wholly unprepared for the entrance of the Duc d'Abbeville.

What a contrast he formed to Henri! A moment ago she had thought Henri quite the handsomest and most magnificently attired man she had ever seen—his pale blue coat adorned with silver trimmings was of the very height of fashion. The Duc wore a plain, dark coat that his groom would have despised, a fall of lace at his throat did nothing to distinguish his appearance, yet she had the conviction that he was more masculine than Henri.

Quickly dismissing such disloyal thoughts about her generous host, she turned her attention to the pastries in the dish at her elbow, for she felt a blush stealing over her cheeks again as his dark eyes lighted on her face.

'We have been teasing this young lady, Duc—she is blushing at the thought of marriage with Henri Deschamps. She is learning how to flirt in the most enchanting manner.' Madame de Thiange's voice had altered subtly as she addressed the Duc—it had become more throaty and her eyes gleamed softly.

'I was not *flirting*,' Teresa avowed, blushing again and causing the two ladies to trill with pleasure.

'May I introduce the most charming and decorative acquisition that we have had at Versailles for many a long time, Duc?' Henri spoke gallantly, his amused glance resting for a long moment on Teresa's flower-like face.

Marie observed these signs of favour with some annoyance, for she was accustomed to Henri's devotion to her own person.

Bowing slightly, his face inscrutable, the Duc spoke with some reserve. '*Mademoiselle* and I are already acquainted, Henri.' Taking a seat, he affected not to notice the effect his words produced. Henri lifted an eyebrow and directed a look of surprised comprehension at Teresa, Madame de Thiange's eyes narrowed thoughtfully, but Marie Besneval's look of annoyance turned to outrage.

'How comes this, Teresa? You did not tell me that you knew Guy d'Abbeville!' Her voice was sharp with suspicious surprise.

'I did not know when we met who he was, Marie...' How very stupid her words sounded! Was it with such skilful repartee that she had hoped to make an impression on the Court of Versailles?

'You were not introduced?' demanded Madame de Thiange swiftly, her avid stare taking in the discomfited face of Teresa and the polite mask of the Duc.

'You must recall that my aunt is the Abbesse of the Convent of the Sacred Heart, where *Mademoiselle* had been until recently a boarder. As I visit my aunt regularly, it was inevitable that sooner or later I would have the pleasure of meeting *mademoiselle*. Henri, I really hate to quibble with so very good and amiable a host, but I feel that this wine is not good. And nothing,' he smiled charmingly at Marie and Madame de Thiange, 'is more injurious to the complexion than wine that is not good.'

Leaping to his feet, Henri immediately summoned Gaston to complain of the wine, while the ladies exclaimed with dismay that the Duc was perfectly right.

Teresa, aware that he had deliberately diverted attention away from her, smiled with shy gratitude at him, but already he was selecting some food with care, and seemed wholly absorbed in this task.

When Gaston had insisted on bringing a fresh supply of his best Orléans wine to the table, with profuse apologies, and had personally filled each wine-cup, it seemed as though the incident had been forgotten.

Madame de Thiange exerted herself to be gracious to Teresa, who, under her skilled questioning and sympathetic looks, told her all about the expedition to the dressmaker and her disgust at the prevailing habit of not paying one's bills. With a trill of laughter, Madame de Thiange recounted this to the Duc a few moments later, and Teresa had the mortification of seeing that the company appeared vastly entertained.

The Duc had already spoken of her ignorance and stupidity, and she thought now that she detected a look of censure from him. Shrugging in the manner of Marie, she directed a look at him, as full of unconcern as she could muster.

'I am aware that it is not considered fashionable to pay one's bills at Versailles, but *I* am going to pay mine. That young woman is obviously from a poor background, for her establishment is hardly a wealthy one. She might have to support her whole family from her earnings——'

'My dear, there is no need to speak with such heat!'
Madame de Thiange admonished her, and Teresa thought
that she winked at Marie. 'In Versailles, we do not even
think of menials, let alone talk of them.' Smiling at the
Duc, she addressed herself to him. 'Your aunt has trained
her badly in the ways of the world, Duc.'

'I do not think so,' he replied laconically.

His indifferent manner began to annoy Teresa. How
in the name of all that was wonderful had he acquired
the name of the Wicked Duc? Although only a few years
older than the light-hearted Henri, he *seemed* much
older, and so very staid and sober. How could the vivacious Marie bear the thought of marriage with him?
With a pang, Teresa realised that she must put an end
to all Marie's hopes and dreams of becoming a Duchesse.
Would she ever forgive her? Life in the Bastille would
be preferable to marriage with Teresa Rochefoucourt,
he had said, and nothing could have occurred to make
him alter his mind.

Henri, sensing that his little luncheon party was beset
by uncomfortable undercurrents, attempted to create a
lighter atmosphere. 'Are there any little bits of gossip
or scandal circulating that might interest me?' he demanded gaily, looking around the table.

'Only the usual nonsense,' replied the Duc, his eyes
mocking the company. 'Gossip is a bore.'

'Really! Does nothing interest you? Are you bored
with everything?' Teresa blurted this out before she could
stop herself.

Raising her thin black eyebrows in surprise, Madame
de Thiange looked at Teresa, a speculative look in her
eyes. 'You seem on uncommonly intimate terms with
Guy d'Abbeville for one who could only have met him
in a convent.' Seeing that her words had made Teresa
uncomfortable, she persisted with a laugh. 'Only those
on the most intimate terms may be angry with each other,
Teresa. Witness the constant friction between long-
married couples. I assure you it is true.' Directing a
mockingly flirtatious glance at the Duc, she continued
in the throaty tone she appeared to reserve for him alone.

'There was a little bit of gossip, Guy, concerning yourself.'

Pausing in the act of lifting his wine-cup to his lips, he looked at her steadily over its rim. 'There is always gossip about me, *madame*. I am accustomed to it by now.' He spoke unencouragingly.

Leaning her chin on one slim hand, she achieved a saucy smile. 'Ah, but this is a little different, and of very recent date. It is said that you were seen entering your house in the Avenue du Vieux Versailles with a very young lady.' She looked at Teresa with a malicious glint in her eyes, and her gaze wandered deliberately over the girl's elegantly dressed flaxen hair. 'A lady with flaxen hair. Is that not strange?'

'Since I do not recall the incident, I assume that it was of no importance to me,' responded the Duc with indifference.

A tension seemed to have descended on the party: Marie's face was once more suspicious; Madame de Thiange was chagrined that her shaft had not found a mark, and the bloom had faded from Teresa's cheek.

Feeling that Madame de Thiange was baiting the Duc, and mindful that she had placed him in this position, Teresa tried to mend the situation.

'Perhaps you were interviewing a servant, Duc?' she asked a trifle breathlessly.

With a brittle laugh, Marie interpolated. 'The great Duc d'Abbeville, interviewing a servant? Nonsense! I confess I did hear something of this rumour myself, and meant to tax you with it, Guy.'

'If it was a *servant*, then she was dealt with with uncommon courtesy, for it is rumoured that the Duc then escorted her off in his own coach,' remarked Madame de Thiange.

Henri stirred restively; the conversation was not at all to his liking. A young man of easy and indolent temperament, he liked his friends to share his moods. Lighthearted gossip was both stimulating and entertaining; this deep interest in the Duc's private affairs was, in his presence, bordering on the impertinent.

'Well, that was very civil of him, I am sure. Although what concern it can be of ours——'

Madame de Thiange cut Henri short with another trill of the laughter that Teresa was beginning to find increasingly irritating. 'But it is of interest, for perhaps Mademoiselle Teresa might know of the young person.'

Opening her eyes wide, and attempting to keep an expression of incredulity on her face to mask her dismay, she stammered, 'I? How could I know, *madame*?'

'Because the coach travelled in the direction of Villepreux. Is that not where your convent is situated?' Smiling broadly, Madame de Thiange saw that if she had failed to rouse any embarrassment in the Duc, she had succeeded admirably with Teresa.

'Good heavens!' Henri laughed easily. 'How on earth can a young lady recently arrived at Court be expected to know what the Duc does?'

Henri's laughter, so spontaneous and natural, did much to banish the tension which had gathered in the past few minutes.

'You all assume that this ridiculous rumour is correct. If I ask you not to repeat it,' the Duc's voice was smooth and held only a hint of barely concealed laughter, 'you will instantly repeat it to ten or twelve of your closest friends. Indeed, you almost convince me that there *is* something in what you say, and fill me with an urgent desire to meet this young lady. If she *is* a young lady.'

They all laughed at this, and the rest of the meal passed with the Duc chatting with the utmost amiability with Marie Besneval, who flirted with him outrageously, and Madame de Thiange, who was successful in capturing his attention for much of the conversation. Teresa was surprised when he laughed, for he was attractive as well as handsome, and she could at last see why Marie wished to marry him. Henri entertained her with courteous ease, seemed delighted to tell her about the balls, routs, card parties and picnics that she could anticipate at Versailles, was flattered by her request that he teach her to ride, and disappointed when the Duc frustrated the task which would have enchanted him.

'I am going to teach Teresa to ride.' He spoke as though the thought afforded him little pleasure.

'Oh, I would much rather Henri taught me,' she said. Again she had spoken without thinking, and was furious with herself. In the few minutes she had been speaking with Henri, she had been aware that he had been regarding her with warm admiration in his blue eyes, and the sensation had been delightful. Now, the Duc was spoiling everything! Would that always be so at Versailles? she wondered miserably.

'Nevertheless, I gave my aunt a promise that I would instruct you in all the necessary accomplishments at Court, and I must honour that promise.' He spoke evenly, but there was a hint of steel in his eyes, and his voice was no longer the flirtatious one in which he addressed the other two women.

'The aunt at Villepreux,' murmured Madame de Thiange. 'Naturally.'

Their repast finished, they rose to depart. Marie had gone to talk quietly to the Duc who lounged at his ease near the window. Madame de Thiange was occupied with finding her gloves, and Henri was assisting her. Teresa felt that the room had become oppressively hot—the day was fine and warm, and she longed to walk in the fresh air. If she mentioned that she would like to walk back to the palace, no doubt the Duc would frustrate this desire, as he was probably going to frustrate anything that might give her pleasure in the future. Miserably, she was conscious that, while he was present, she would have very little fun and no flirtations. How to become the rage, she fumed, if she was obliged to do everything he told her? Nothing could be worse, she thought, than a reformed Wicked Duc!

Thanking Henri for finding her gloves, Madame de Thiange bestowed a practised smile on him and then raised a coquettish eyebrow at the Duc.

'Do you invite us to go to your house, Duc? Or is that a treat reserved for very special people?' This was spoken with the archness that she had used earlier, and with a faintly malicious glance in Teresa's direction.

'You do me too much honour, *madame*. I would never subject very special people to the rigours of my poor house here in Versailles, especially when my servants are from home. I would rather do as Henri does, and entertain in an inn.'

'Are your servants *never* home, Duc, when you entertain your friends?' Despite the smile which remained fixed on Madame de Thiange's cleverly painted face, the malice was now quite pronounced.

Her animosity temporarily forgotten, Teresa had an irrational desire to defend the Duc—prompted, she believed, by her growing dislike of the clever woman with the silver tongue who insisted on baiting him.

'Good heavens! *Madame*, is this another lesson I am learning? Do tell me, for you have been at Versailles for such a *very* long time, and must be quite the oldest person I have met yet. At least,' she amended sunnily, 'you are years and years older than I. Is it fashionable to talk continually of servants? I mean, does one question one's friends and acquaintances continually about servants? Do tell me, *madame*, for I am convinced that if there is one subject upon which you are expert, it is that of the servant class.'

Madame de Thiange's lips thinned, and she drew in her breath in a sudden spurt of unconcealed anger. The assembled company, lips twitching, suddenly busied themselves with departure and looked anywhere but at Madame's angry face, or Teresa's enchantingly ingenuous one.

They were all in their turn surprised, however, when the Duc, holding the door open for Teresa, bestowed an amused glance down at her and whispered, 'I can fight my own battles, you absurd baggage.'

And she, quite unabashed, responded with a mischievously twinkling smile.

CHAPTER FOUR

'You never come to my bed any more, Louis. Do you not know how that grieves me?' The King's mistress hissed passionately.

'I am sorry, Athénaïs, but affairs of state demand much of my time and attention. Since I prefer to conduct my business alone, there has been little time for leisure.'

The gentle irony of his words was not lost upon her, for Athénaïs de Rouchechouart-Mortmart, Marquise de Montespan, was as astute as she was opulently lovely.

'If I have interfered in affairs of state too much——'

'I should never use so vulgar a phrase,' rebuked the Bourbon King, who had perfected the etiquette of the Court to a fine art.

'—it was because I cared so much for you and our children.' She appealed to him, her face softer, her temper gentler. 'They are the most handsome and the most intelligent children in the realm. Are they not, Madame de Maintenon?' This she flung over her shoulder to a woman who sat quietly stitching in the corner.

Just lately, Madame de Maintenon had irritated her prodigiously. Everything irritated her—slight blemishes on her snow-white skin, the King's increasing lack of interest, the feeling that she was no longer the hub of Court life.

'All the King's children are handsome and intelligent.' Madame de Maintenon spoke in her usual colourless tone.

'You are as good as you are diplomatic, *madame*.' The King accompanied these words with a look of warm gratitude tinged with admiration.

A tiny doubt flared through the Marquise, to be quickly dismissed. It was not conceivable that rumour could be true, and the King could be interested in the dull, pious woman who so reminded her of Queen Maria Teresa. But where the Queen was transparently good, the governess had shadows of guile and secrecy in her sombre eyes. Madame de Maintenon, an able governess, maintained her privacy, appeared to consort little with others at Court, sought no favours, yet knew everything that went on. Dark rumours attached to her name, and the whispers grew louder with each day that passed.

One rumour in particular had caused the Marquise exquisite mirth, and she had laughed it to scorn, it was really too stupid! It was said that she used the black arts in her efforts to capture the King as a husband! Athénaïs tried, and failed, to imagine that stout, ponderous form dancing naked before a satanic altar. Aware that she herself had been instrumental in the past in spreading many rumours, she determined that this one should be quelled with all speed. If she could only discover the source of the rumour. For there, she was certain, were her enemies. Many were jealous of her power over the King, and wished her reign to end.

It was with a pang of regret that she recalled that day, a mere four years ago, in 1674, when she had been crowned the King's official mistress. She had been magnificent in a gown of gold, embroidered with gold, and the King had been besotted by her. Now he was withdrawing from her. Surely he could not prefer that holy turnip in the corner? She was more intent upon her stitchery than satisfying a man.

Another vision rose to torment her: a great quantity of ringlets framing a heart-shaped face, rosy with youth and beauty. Large, sparkling blue eyes that had fascinated the King with the ingenuous enjoyment they mirrored. Tantalised and jealous, she spoke more sharply than she had intended.

'That new lady-in-waiting to the Queen—she came mightily mysteriously to Court, did she not? Who appointed her?'

'The Queen is responsible for her own appointments.' He spoke with pronounced hauteur and she flushed. Did Madame de Maintenon smile in that sly, secretive way of hers? No, she was becoming fanciful. Better to concentrate her energies into coaxing her King back to her bed. She would use whatever means she had to hand.

The King walked slowly to the chamber where he received his Queen every morning, his thoughts absorbing him. It was a mistake to have allowed his mistress so much licence in state affairs—he must concede that. Those who had delicately attempted to inform him of this, he had dismissed brusquely, and under her guidance had not dealt kindly with them. It had been part of his plan to bring every member of the aristocracy under his complete subjugation. He would never forgive them for the way they had treated him when he was a boy. No! His next mistress would be kept in the background, he determined. There would be no part for her to play in the running of his government, neither should she be allowed to push her favourites into positions of prominence, nor situations of power.

'A thousand pardons, sire, but you requested my presence this morning.' The Duc d'Abbeville bowed before the King, and, straightening up to his full height, gave his sovereign the open smile which so much endeared him to Louis.

'Yes, Duc, please attend me directly I have returned from the Queen's reception. I have some matters of importance to put to you.' His gesture of dismissal was also a salute of friendship. He admired the young man who had distinguished himself in battle, and adorned the Court so gracefully.

Queen Maria Teresa curtsied before her royal husband and smiled at him with uncritical affection. Bowing ceremoniously over her hand, he then led her to the high, fringed chair beside his own. Her women, who attended her, retired to a discreet distance, and waited in attitudes of deference while the royal pair held their daily consultation. As always upon these occasions, the Queen was attired in full Court dress—the overskirt looped back by knots of ribbons to reveal an elaborately embroidered underskirt. The many petticoats made even her thickening waist seem small and dainty. Her kindly face was devoid of any of the make-up favoured by the ladies of the Court, he was pleased to note, for he loved his sweet-natured Queen. Maria Teresa never embarrassed him with scenes or tantrums, she always conducted herself with regal composure—a perfect Queen of France.

They chatted for some while upon a number of topics. In previous years, the King had been a trifle bored by his Queen's liking for religious life. Naturally, he attended mass each morning, but he did not expect to make religion his sole point of reference. However, of latter years he had become aware of the fine balance between good and evil, and of the necessity of acting with wisdom and piety. The full weight of decision-making must always fall upon his shoulders, but he was glad to feel that his actions were guided by a power infinitely greater and more worthy than himself. He had never felt so close to Maria Teresa as now. The fire of their early passion had burnt itself out—no one woman could permanently satisfy the sensuality of a Bourbon—but it had been replaced by a tender companionship that satisfied him. She had become his close friend.

Occasionally his gaze strayed to the lovely countenance of Teresa Rochefoucourt. The azure gown became her admirably, lending depth and brilliance to her blue eyes; a smile seemed to hover perpetually around her perfectly shaped mouth. There was a sweet merriment about her that he liked and wished to explore, for he had wearied of demanding women. Versailles abounded in men and women who constantly craved his attention, and went to extraordinary and foolish lengths to capture it. His ego was such that it never occurred to him that he lay at fault. It was at his own insistence that all life revolved around Louis, the Sun King. Nobles were expected to loiter aimlessly all day about the corridors and draughty reception rooms of the great palace, for a glimpse of their King. Every action was performed in public and according to a solemn and unvarying ritual. That any could be bored by life in the palace was beyond the King's comprehension.

'Your new lady-in-waiting has grace and dignity that enhances our humble Court, Maria Teresa.' He loved to refer to Versailles in that fashion with his Queen—it was one of a number of shared jokes.

'Indeed she does, sire.' The Queen had observed without jealousy Louis's scrutiny of the girl. 'You must recall her mother—I brought her with me on the occasion of our marriage. She was a very lovely girl, the daughter of our ambassador.'

'Yes, I do recall. She married. I recollect that I was most disappointed, for I considered that with her looks she could have done a great deal better for herself, although he had fortune.'

'They were very much in love, and brought each other great happiness, sire. As much happiness as we have brought each other.'

The King patted her hand, and smiled tenderly at her. 'Talking of ambassadors puts me in mind of a little matter I would seek your advice upon.'

Much gratified, the Queen nodded her acquiescence—she would never have dreamed of interfering in affairs of state, and never proffered her advice uninvited, but she loved it when the King asked her advice, for it recaptured bygone days of intimacy.

'I had thought to make the Duc d'Abbeville an ambassador. What say you to that idea?'

'I had thought,' she selected her words with care, 'that he wished to return to his southern estates.'

'He does, but it is not my will.'

'Is that wise of you, sire? You who are so wise in all things.'

'I wish to have my nobles here in Versailles, under my eye and thumb. Else they can be sent abroad upon my business. There shall never be another Fronde. Never again will a King of France be humiliated. There shall be many nobles, but there is only one King.'

He spoke with unaccustomed bitterness which moved his wife to cover his bejewelled hand with her own. 'Ah, my dear heart, can you not forget that? It is all in the past. Those who caused a little boy to hide in his own palace are long since punished. You were not your own master, you had no control over the nobles who caused the rebellion.'

'I am in control now. I shall bring them all grovelling to me.'

'Are you not being a little unfair to d'Abbeville?' she persisted. 'Is it really necessary to punish the son for the sins of the father?'

'I do not punish him!' The King was distressed, for he considered himself scrupulous on all points of justice.

'But he has served France well. Recall that you showed me the reports of his bravery and courage in battle,' she coaxed him. 'Indeed, I hoped you would send him back to his estates, for he is a man who needs much occupation. He is like a restless animal prowling about the palace—until he departs there is not a female heart safe from him.'

'That is the problem.' He waved an impatient hand. 'Not the silly women! But sending him back would be fraught with danger.'

Frowning, Maria Teresa looked at her King. 'Danger? Whatever can you mean?'

'He is ambitious and energetic. Can you not visualise what it would be like if I returned him to his estates? He is liked and respected among men—a seasoned soldier, an owner of vast estates which take a veritable army of men to work. If he were to combine with one or two others of like mind, he could raise a force which would threaten the monarchy and the future of France. No! I will not risk being threatened with a rebellion. He must remain at Versailles.' He looked obstinate. 'If he defies me, he will go to the Bastille.'

'You would not give him cause to love you, sire.' The Queen was gravely disturbed, but continued to urge the Duc's cause with quiet good sense.

'I do not need his love of me, I need his loyalty to majesty.' But he had shifted uneasily upon the plush seat, and drummed his fingers upon the arm of the chair.

'I think that if he had a wife and children, and much to occupy him, then he would be busy and content and wish nothing to threaten that existence.'

Much struck by this point of view, the King turned gratefully to his Queen, and, clasping her hand, raised it to his lips. 'What an excellent woman you are, Maria Teresa! How I value your counsel.'

Blushing like a girl, she allowed him to raise her from her chair with his inimitable courtesy and escort her from the chamber.

Teresa was reading to the Queen in a clear, if somewhat hesitant voice; it was a pity, thought the Queen, that her learning had been neglected. Evidently she had not inherited her parents' innate love of learning—perhaps she could encourage that. It was very pleasant to have as a companion one who was young, charming and, as yet, unspoilt by Court life. Despite her apparent preoccupation with learning, the Queen was well aware that beneath the glitter of Court life there lurked undercurrents of evil. The many ladies who attended her so assiduously and courteously could, and probably would, shift their allegiance overnight if they thought that it would advantage them. Sighing, she thought again of those days when Teresa's mother had been her dear and trusted companion. Now that there was no one in whom she could confide, she had learned to hide her feelings behind a tranquil mask.

She was glad that this pretty child, whose prettiness was about to blossom into real beauty, was to become betrothed, for it would grieve her deeply to watch her become corrupted by the Court. It was strange that she seemed so reluctant to discuss the Duc—perhaps she was shy. No, she was not shy, there was a confidence about her manner and bearing. That some degree of intimacy and understanding must exist between them was taken for granted—they wished to be married. When one of her ladies, unaware of this, had attempted to hint that

Teresa and the Duc were upon terms of deeper intimacy, she had gently quelled her. She would have failed badly if scandal attached to the godchild who bore her name, and the perpetrator should discover that she could be a wrathful as well as gentle Queen.

'I should like you to read to me every day, Teresa, if you should not object.'

'Oh, Your Majesty, how kind you are. How could I object to anything that would give me so much pleasure? Besides,' she grinned, 'I shall be able to show you my new gowns. They are very lovely, and so many of them!' She hesitated, unsure of how to continue, for she wished to broach the subject of money. 'I should very much like to be able to pay Celeste—that is, the dressmaker—as soon as the gowns are made and delivered. Only...'

'But you do not have any money. It is a simple matter to arrange. Most of your money will transfer to the Duc on the date of your marriage; my own attorneys will arrange all that for you. In the meantime, you are to have an allowance in order to present a creditable appearance. However much in love with you he is, I am sure the Duc approves of your appearance so much more now than when he saw you in the convent. Your new hair-style and clothes become you. There is also the matter of your mother's jewellery. Assuming that you would enter the convent and have no use for it, she bequeathed it all to me. Now I feel that it would be fitting for me to give it to you. It is a beautiful collection. I shall have it ready for you when you attend me tomorrow afternoon. Perhaps you would care to bring the Duc with you.'

Curtsying out of the royal presence, Teresa hoped that her dismay did not show on her face. It had been a great honour to sit with the Queen, and she stored up everything to tell Marie, for young ladies-in-waiting did not usually have the opportunity to have a talk with the Queen. If she had to bring the Duc it would spoil everything! Also, it would be soon obvious that there was a lack of affection between them. The more she became acquainted with the Queen, the less she liked deceiving her.

'Did the Queen ask you to her reception this evening?' Marie demanded, her attention on her own face as she sat before the dressing-table.

'No. She did not mention it. But she did ask me to bring the Duc with me tomorrow.'

'Pass me that clip, I wish to try it in my hair. Bring the Duc where tomorrow?' Covertly Marie watched Teresa's troubled face, reflected in the mirror.

'To see her. She wished me to read to her again. And I am to have some of my money. There are also some jewels that belonged to my mother.'

Marie frowned uneasily and thought again of the scene in the inn yesterday, when some disturbing quality of intimacy appeared to exist between Teresa and the Duc. Could the girl be unaware of the significance of the Queen's summons? Certainly she had not questioned the summons; equally certainly she disliked it. Could it be that the Queen had thought of arranging a marriage between her god-daughter and the noble Duc? With mounting anger, Marie was convinced that this must be the case. Teresa must have been the girl seen entering his house in Versailles, and that could only mean that the pair were secretly betrothed.

'Well, then, you will have to summon him, will you not?' she said brightly. 'Or perhaps I could tell him for you, for he escorts me to the firework display this evening, then we go on to the Queen's reception. It will be such fun—you cannot imagine how splendid the firework displays are. Do you know that on one occasion a rocket landed on the roof of the indoor riding arena—that large, circular building near the main courtyard—and it was hours before the fire was put out. I thought it vastly diverting.' Her laughter rang out at the recollection.

Shocked that such an event was considered amusing, Teresa asked, 'Was anyone hurt?'

Shrugging slim white shoulders, Marie attached the bright clip among her dusky curls. 'One or two of the guards, I believe.'

Rising, Teresa removed her light slippers and put on a pair of shoes. 'I think I shall go for a walk in the park; it is such a beautiful afternoon, and I have nothing else to do,' she said with a sigh.

'Do not sigh and frown so,' Marie relented a little. 'Your new gowns will be here in a day or two, then you will be able to go everywhere. To play cards with the Queen even—that I like best of all.'

'Does the Queen play cards?' Teresa was astonished, and could not imagine the Queen indulging in what seemed a somewhat sinful pastime.

'Do not act the simpleton all the time, Teresa.' Marie was tart. 'Of course she plays cards, and very glad we are to play with her. For when she loses,' Marie rubbed her middle finger against her thumb, right under Teresa's nose, 'she pays up immediately. Her losses have been very much our gains, I can tell you. You will soon find out for yourself.'

Louis the Fourteenth, at forty, was, in his own opinion, more refined and good-looking than ever. Alternating between a vengeful brooding on the past and a contemplation of present glories, he occupied his time at Versailles in commanding the minutest details of Court life. It was a source of exquisite pleasure to walk about the gardens of Versailles and, in observing the formal arrangements, the fountains, the flower-beds, the canals, to know that he had as much control over the natural environment as he had over the lives of his courtiers. The abject desire of his subjects to please him gratified him.

Strolling languidly along the path which bordered the gardens, with the Duc d'Abbeville, he reflected again that, no matter how deferential the man was, there was some part of his nature which always eluded the King. Beneath his courtesy and respect there was a hardness of purpose; while his loyalty might be given to his King, there would never be affection. That irked Louis—he liked to think of himself as the centre of the universe, the one being to whom all eyes turned with complete adoration.

There had been occasions when the Marquise de Montespan had complained that the Duc disliked her, and that had irritated him, although he had never seen evidence of this supposed dislike. Upon reflection, it was probably that the Duc had not been enslaved by the lovely Athénaïs—at one time that would have mattered very much, for the King liked all to concur with his taste, but now it was a matter of indifference.

Now, the Duc talked of marriage. This was a strange start—very little occurred at Court of which the King was not cognisant. And the Duc wished to marry that charming little lady-in-waiting, a protégée of his Queen. Pity, he had an eye for her himself. Curious, too, that Maria Teresa was only just saying that he should find a wife and settle down to married life. Was there some plot afoot? How he hated and feared these Court subterfuges. Yet, Maria Teresa would lend herself to no plot against him.

'I should be most grateful for a favourable answer, sire.' The Duc bent his head gravely.

'It would be churlish for me to refuse, d'Abbeville. Then I suppose you will wish to be returning to your estates, to install your bride?'

'I should hope that you would allow this, sire. It is my dearest wish to go home.' The King's indecision elated the Duc, and he had raised the subject of his own accord! Perhaps this marriage would be no very bad thing, after all.

'We shall see, we shall see. I do not like to be hurried into making rash promises.' The King chose to be querulous.

Damn, thought the Duc to himself. Hurried! Be damned to him! I have been kicking my heels in this infernal puppet show for a long time and I have had enough. But he knew that to show irritation or impatience was to court disaster, and he must tread warily.

Ahead of them, admiring the fountains, was a slight figure in a hooped, frilled gown of azure blue. The Duc would willingly have turned his steps in another direction had he been master of this situation, but he was not master. The thought of coming face to face with Teresa filled him with distaste—she was the cause of his misfortune, he could not contemplate her without loathing. It was true that she had shown a certain quick wit and aplomb in her handling of the malicious Madame de Thiange, which in anyone else he would have applauded, but it was probably only her desire to demonstrate her new Court manners.

'I believe that your intended bride is just ahead of us, d'Abbeville. How very fortunate. Or has she been lurking about in the hope of waylaying you, in order to discover whether I choose to give you a favourable reply? I like such ardour, I like it.' Pulling in his stomach, and with a new brightness of eye, the King bore down on Teresa.

Until that moment, the Duc had imagined that he would greet with a certain relief the King's refusal to his proposed marriage; its only redeeming feature, apart from averting possible disaster, was that it would enable him to return to Provence. In Teresa as a person he could not have believed that he would ever have a great deal of interest. He supposed that after their marriage she would bear him heirs, attend to her domestic concerns, occasionally appear at Court with him and generally fill the role of a wife of convenience. It was very far from his original hopes and dreams—he had longed for a companion, a friend, a confidante. Yet now, observing her blushes, sparkling eyes, and heart-shaped face framed with thick flaxen curls raised to the King like a flower to the sun, he wished that she would turn to him with such joyful radiance. Chiding himself for his own irrational and inconsistent feelings, he introduced her to the King, and watched with mounting ire as the King raised her up, gallantly kissing her fingertips and calling her the newest jewel of Versailles. Jewel of Versailles! Poppycock!

The only glance she gave him was so full of anxious enquiry that the King laughed delightedly and pinched her chin. 'Ah! Duc, see how she looks at you. I can see that she is mad for your nuptials. It would be unkind of me to return no answer. Come, I give you both my blessing to your betrothal! Does that not fill your pretty soul with delight, *mademoiselle*? I can see that it does, only you are too shy and maidenly to show it. Walk with us, my child. We would like your company. Tell me what you think of my gardens. Are they not the most splendid sight you have ever seen?'

Falling into step beside them, Teresa hoped that her agitation and disappointment did not show too clearly. 'I think that they are the most magnificent I have ever seen, Your Majesty.' She did not add that she could only compare them with the convent gardens—such an observation would have been superfluous.

'And how do you like being at Court?'

'I love it, Your Majesty. It has been my dearest wish for ages, and now that I am here I am so very, very happy.' The unfeigned enthusiasm and the wide smile delighted the King.

'That is what I like to hear! I am going to insist on a long betrothal, Duc. I cannot allow you to spirit such a charming addition to Versailles away until I have had a chance to show her all our entertainments. There is to be a small reception, just for a few of my close intimates, on Friday. You must both attend, and we can announce the date of your betrothal. It shall take place in the royal chapel; there shall be music by Lully. Afterwards we can have a really splendid ball.'

Louis was happy in arranging entertainments. France might be in the direst peril, from hostile foreign powers, a poor economy, or any of a number of causes, but Louis was content to plan new and more stupendous entertainments.

'I hunt this afternoon, Duc. Do you care to join me? No, no I shall not insist, I can see that you wish to be with your delightful *mademoiselle*.' He pinched her cheek. 'I shall look forward to your presence on Friday; it shall enhance my evening.'

The King, observing the departing couple, thought how very handsome they were. Perhaps Maria Teresa was right—she often was. If he were married to that charming girl, the Duc would have little time to think of rebellion. She would occupy and delight him; he would never wish to threaten the King's position.

Meanwhile, the happy couple were arguing hotly in suppressed whispers.

'How could you have behaved so stupidly, waiting about in the gardens?' the Duc demanded angrily.

'I was not waiting about! How could I know that you would be walking with the King? I know nothing about you, nothing of your habits, only that your manners are atrocious.'

'And yours, *mademoiselle*, are simpering and affected. It made me sick to see you using Court tricks on the King. By heaven, it did not take you long to learn to flirt.'

She stopped and faced him. 'I was *not* flirting.'

'For goodness' sake, do not stand still, or the whole world will know that we are quarrelling. Keep walking, and stop that scowling, it does not become you.'

Feeling that his admonitions were grossly unfair, but unsure of their cause, she was wise enough to keep silent. The King liked her! And while he liked her, he wished her to remain at Versailles. If only she could! While she had the King's favour, he would wish her to remain, and the date of this evil marriage would be deferred. What a glorious piece of news.

'The Queen has requested that I bring you to see her tomorrow afternoon, Duc. Are you able to accompany me? If you are not, I dare say that I can make your excuses.'

Not at all mollified by her pacifying tone, he responded instantly. 'I do not need a Mademoiselle Rochefoucourt to make my excuses to my Queen. Naturally, I shall be there.' He had in fact been going to refuse. 'You may meet me in the long gallery, near the

Queen's apartments, at two o'clock. I must regretfully leave you now, as I have an engagement with a friend.' With a curt nod he was gone, striding along the pathway that led to the extreme end of the palace.

Great diamonds blazed and flashed timeless fire. Entranced, Teresa hung over them, lifting first one and then another, holding them out for the Duc to admire. Smiling mechanically, he nodded, admired and made civil replies to the Queen's polite enquiries.

'Indeed, Duc, you must not marry Teresa too quickly, for she is already quite a favourite with me. I should very much dislike the thought of losing her.'

The tiaras, bracelets, necklaces, rings and brooches were spread out on a piece of black velvet on a low table in the corner of the Queen's small sitting-room. Here Teresa was kneeling, examining her mother's jewellery. As she held up a tiara, her eyes were devouring its beauty when the Duc replied, 'Teresa once told me that she wished to become the rage of Versailles. I must congratulate her on achieving her object in so short a time.'

Looking directly at him, her attitude one of supplication, her eyes flashed blue fire that was not a reflection of the gems she held. How very long ago it seemed that she had uttered those words. How young and innocent she had been! He must know that she had associated those words and those dreams with other dreams—dreams which could never be fulfilled now that she was to be his wife.

The curious contradiction in attitude and expression intrigued him. The look she had directed at him was wholly adult, full of bitter comprehension and sadness. Shocked, he considered her position anew. Although she had cried out against the proposed match that he was too old and not romantic, he had never doubted his ability, should he choose, to make her fall in love with him. An empty-headed, frivolous girl would make an easy conquest. Subconsciously, he had thought that she would probably fall desperately in love with him and become even more tedious and boring in the process— it had happened before. Now he was not at all sure.

CHAPTER FIVE

GASTON surveyed the distinguished company who graced the dining-tables of his inn. To have so many aristocrats sit down to one of his excellent dinners was good for business; personally, he did not care who they were, so long as they paid. Running an experienced eye over the elegantly dressed courtiers, he looked again at the five men who occupied the corner table near the open hearth. He did not like them. Those who constantly forgot to pay an overdue bill were sure to receive the slowest service and the poorest of the fine wines from Gaston's cellar. The men in the corner, listening intently to the handsome, arrogant Charles Villiers, were the sort of courtiers who disdained to pay a bill. Yet he did not press them. There was something he feared as well as disliked about Charles Villiers. What was it? he wondered. Watching the man pour bumpers of red Orléans wine for his companions, a smile tilting his mouth, Gaston shuddered, convinced that the man was evil and the subject of his conversation undesirable. Summoning a waiter to clear the table next to which he was standing, he took the tray and new bottle of wine that the man had been carrying.

'Gentlemen, allow me to present you with a bottle of wine, as a compliment.' He had hoped to overhear something of their conversation, for Villiers and his chief crony, Richard Beauchamp, older than their friends, were courtiers of the highest rank.

'We do not accept compliments from inferiors.' Villiers spoke to Gaston insolently.

Bowing and retiring from the table, Gaston flushed.

'However, you may leave the wine,' Villiers mocked him, 'as a tribute.'

His companions laughed at the retreating patron, but Beauchamp queried his friend uneasily. 'You have not the habit of winning the love of the common people, my friend.'

'Faugh!' Villiers looked disdainful. 'I care not a snap of my fingers for the common people. I value my hounds more highly.'

'And yet, Charles, if we are to succeed with our rebellion, we need someone to lead us who brings the people as well as the nobility with them.'

'As always, you are right, Richard. I believe that I know just the man to lead us.' He spoke softly, unwilling that he should be overheard. 'Guy d'Abbeville.'

'd'Abbeville?' Richard Beauchamp was incredulous. So were the others, who stared blankly into the handsome, smiling face of Charles Villiers. 'Impossible! Guy is a friend of the King, known for his frequent protestations of loyalty. He would never lend himself to our plans.'

Refilling his glass, Villiers stared into its ruby depths, an unpleasant smile playing about his mouth. Unlike his friends, he wished to plot rebellion against the King for the power that success would bring him. Crippled by the cost of living in Versailles, forced to watch revenues from their estates dwindle in their enforced absence, the others had become obsessed with wealth. Charles Villiers played for higher stakes. For years he had watched and waited until an opportunity such as now presented itself. 'I believe that we could give him cause to hate the King. When a man like Guy d'Abbeville hates, he seeks revenge.'

Impressed by his manner, though still unsure, Beauchamp regarded his companion, aware for the first time that motives beyond mere financial gain might lie behind his willingness to plot rebellion. 'What cause could we give him?'

'Marie Besneval has told me that she believes d'Abbeville is to become betrothed to the Rochefoucourt girl, very soon. If we could persuade the child that it would be a great thing to become the mistress of our foolish King, then we have our weapon. D'Abbeville is too proud to become a cuckolded husband. Unlike many of our complacent husbands, he is too aware of his worth, his name.'

'What if the King does not take her to his bed?' Richard needed more assurance.

'Have you no eyes in your head?' Villiers looked about the table, gratified that the company shared his view. 'Of course he will take her, she is just the sort to appeal to him.'

Richard persisted. 'If she is to be married to Guy d'Abbeville, then she will scarcely become mistress to another man.'

'I do not believe that this is a love match.' Thrusting his glass from him, Villiers looked with annoyance at Richard Beauchamp. 'Even if she does not become his mistress, we must contrive to make it appear so. With enough doubt in his mind, d'Abbeville will act the part we plan for him. He regards us all as his friends; it should be a simple matter. And if the little Rochefoucourt makes any difficulties—why, my friends, we know what to do. We use the methods that we have used in the past. I assure you that Marie Besneval will help us. And, unless I am much mistaken, so will Madame de Maintenon.' Seeing that his fellow plotters were looking at him with bewildered incredulity, he laughed again. 'Oh, not in bringing down the King—they must never know of that! But you know what jealous women are like! And they are jealous of the lovely little Rochefoucourt. Yes, they will aid us.'

Still smarting from the insult he had received at the hands of Charles Villiers, Gaston watched them leave the inn, determined that next time they dined there he would try to overhear as much of their conversation as he could. They were plotting, of that he was more convinced than ever.

In happy ignorance that she was to be used in a game of power and intrigue, Teresa began to love life at Court. So many compliments on her new gowns! So many invitations to join this party at the music evening, or that party for cards, that she sang, danced and feasted her days, the darling of Court society. Henri Deschamps, an admiring smile on his face as he watched her attempts to master horse-riding, spoke impulsively. 'Teresa, you are as graceful in the saddle as you are in the ballroom. I do not wonder that half Versailles is at your feet.'

Blushing rosily, she allowed Henri to help her dismount and turned a glowing face to him. 'Are they really, Henri? I have begun to wonder. For it seems to me that it has all happened so suddenly.' Frowning slightly, she wrinkled her nose in a manner that Henri found increasingly delightful, as if in puzzled thought. Henri's compliment was sincere, and for that reason she valued it, for she had often thought in the past few days that compliments rose too easily to the lips of courtiers and their ladies. Increasingly she had found herself doubting the truth of the honeyed words she heard daily. Momentarily, cynicism flitted across her face, and the lovely sparkling eyes darkened.

She is beginning to see through life in Versailles, Henri thought sadly. Finding that he wished to protect her, he hastened to reassure her that, indeed, Versailles loved her.

'If you say it is so, then I believe you.' Sunny humour restored, she could talk of the firework display they were to witness that evening and the gown she intended to wear.

Despite his honourable motive in wishing to reassure and protect his new friend, whose infectious gaiety was like a breath of fresh air, Henri was troubled. The sort of attention and acclaim that Versailles presently bestowed upon Teresa was usually reserved for very important people. While Teresa was pretty—beautiful, even—and vivacious, and her company enlivened the most boring functions, she was hardly an important person. Her mother had been connected to the Queen, her father, an unimportant member of the aristocracy, had been a worthy man; but personages such as Madame de Maintenon, the Marquise de Montespan, the haughty Richard Beauchamp and arrogant Charles Villiers all sought her company. Uneasily aware that this was unusual, Henri wondered if they could know that Teresa was about to become betrothed to Guy d'Abbeville. Would that account for her sudden popularity? It might, he conceded. But doubts, uneasy suspicions, persisted in his mind. Could he ask Guy? No, he had the feeling that Guy had regretted his confidences about the proposed marriage and was reluctant to discuss matters with him. That the people for whom Guy had no affection and little respect should accord this girl the attention they normally reserved for the King's new mistress disturbed Henri greatly. But, he reasoned, if he could see that, then surely Guy must see it also? However unwilling a bridegroom he was, his good name, and that of his future bride, meant a great deal to him, and he must act if he thought the matter serious.

Teresa's activities had not gone unnoticed by the Duc. With mounting cynicism he observed her fulfilling what he believed to be her foolish ambitions, and determined to halt her giddy flights if they should threaten his consequence in any way. That his interference might be welcome or unwelcome to Teresa personally troubled him not at all.

He did her an unwitting injustice, for she was slowly learning wisdom without acquiring cynicism. Her Duc compared favourably with most men she had so far met at Court. While she could never lose her heart to him—she was convinced of that—she was learning to respect him. That he could be an amusing companion she had observed several times when meeting him at various Court functions; that his company was universally desired pleased her. Of her approaching marriage she tried not to think at all—life at Versailles might not be very sincere, but it was fun. If she pleased the King, the marriage might not take place for a very long time. Recognising that he had meant what he said about hating the Court and wishing to return to his estates, she knew that once he had obtained permission to live permanently in Provence once more he would attend his King as little as possible. Dreading the thought of marriage to a man who loathed and despised her, she thought instead of how pleasant life would be with the affectionate and undemanding Henri. Pleasant, yes; exciting, no.

Walking back across the gardens to the palace, Henri and Teresa were laughing and talking nonsense when they encountered the Duc. Bowing with exaggerated gallantry, he begged leave to accompany them. 'For it seems that I must be at one with the world who has chosen to make Mademoiselle Rochefoucourt a favourite.'

'I was not aware that you wished to be at one with the world of Versailles, Duc,' she responded tartly, flushing at the ill-concealed mockery in his voice and manner. All Versailles appeared to love her, adulation was sweet to her—only the Duc, mocking and cynical, refused her what the Court granted unreservedly.

'You will escort Teresa back to the palace, Guy. I must change my clothes—I attend the King at hawking in less than an hour.' Stammering a little, for he recognised the signs and knew that, beneath the air of mocking gallantry, the Duc was angry, Henri decided to take leave of the pair.

'Since I came expressly to find her, I shall be delighted.'

The Duc had come expressly to find her! For some reason Teresa felt elated when she heard those words. With the exception of an occasional visit to the Queen, of whom the Duc was clearly fond, he never sought her company. Perhaps he was beginning to revise his unfavourable opinion of her. His next words dispelled any illusions she might cherish.

'It has come to my notice that you are to sup with Madame de Maintenon this evening, before attending the King's firework display. You will send your regrets and tell her that you are unable to accept her invitation.' These curt words were spoken without once looking at her.

Incensed, and conscious of his great height, Teresa stopped walking and looked up at him. 'How dare you? If Madame de Maintenon chooses to honour me with an invitation, then of course I shall accept, and with pleasure!' she added defiantly as his brow darkened and eyes hardened. In fact, she had not finally accepted the invitation, which was more like a summons, for there had been something in the manner of the governess which she could not like...

The Queen had not required her for duties, and she had spent an hour or two with the Princesse d'Elbeuf, receiving instruction on what it was proper to wear upon certain occasions. 'Not that you need a great deal of advice, for you have excellent taste, as your friend, Marie Besneval, has been telling us. How very ornamental you are, my dear.' Teresa suppressed a smile on hearing these words; she was always amused by the vague, kindly Princesse's odd speech. In private, she and Marie laughed at the Princesse, although Teresa was not always as amused as she pretended by Marie's cruel mimicry. 'The King does not attend mass this evening, so I dare say that few will be at the chapel. Do you go?'

Although the Princesse had not really been interested, Teresa guessed accurately, in whether she attended mass or not, she felt a tiny stab of remorse. For these days she only attended her devotions if she wished to see other members of the Court, or be seen. However, the afternoon was stifling and the chapel would be cool.

'Yes, I do go,' she told the Princesse. 'That is, if you have quite finished,' she added politely.

'Yes, quite finished. Run along.' The Princesse was amiable and vague in her dismissal.

Few attended mass, and she only recognised the black-clad form of Madame de Maintenon. As she prayed, Teresa became aware that she was the object of Madame's scrutiny. Surprised, she exchanged a glance and was shocked to see malevolence in the dark brown eyes staring at her from beneath the heavy lace mantilla. How stupid she was! Mentally, Teresa shook herself, and turned her attention back to the priest on the flower-laden altar. It must have been a trick of the light—the flickering candle-light and the incense had combined to make her imagine that look. On the few occasions she had met Madame de Maintenon, she had received an impression of utter reserve and slow dignity. The governess, at over forty, was greatly removed from Teresa in age; she was known to be a woman of serious mind and piety. With absolutely nothing in common, they could consequently have had no opportunity for disagreement. So she must have imagined that look, she told herself again. But the chill feeling persisted. Try as she might, she could recall no occasion when she might have offended the governess.

To her great surprise, Madame de Maintenon followed her from the chapel and walked with her a little way.

'The evening is still very fine, *mademoiselle*. Would you care to walk by the canal, for I feel that it would be delightfully cool now.' Her voice was quiet and melodious, her expression grave.

'Yes, that is most kind of you, *madame*.' Teresa found that her voice was breathless, but her fears were subsiding. How could she have thought that such a woman could direct malevolence towards anyone?

It was pleasant beside the canal—birds sang in the trees, and the gently lapping water made an attractive accompaniment to the swishing of Madame de Maintenon's black silk gown. They walked some way in silence, and Teresa's uneasy fears began to return, for she felt that there was some purpose to this apparently aimless stroll.

'You have made an impression at Court, *mademoiselle*. The King likes you. He admires you. Do you admire the King?'

How was she to answer? This woman was governess to the children of the King and his official mistress, the rival of her Queen. Hesitating, she looked shyly at the governess, trying to read the intent behind the quietly worded question.

'Everyone must admire the King,' she responded as diplomatically as she could.

A tiny smile relieved the heavy features of her companion. 'Exactly so. A very wise answer. We should be very happy for you to sup with us this evening. That would please the King. You may come to my private apartments at eight.'

For some unaccountable reason, Teresa did not wish to accept the invitation, but it sounded as though it might be a summons from the King. Dare she refuse? Madame de Maintenon had said 'we'. Did she mean the King and Madame?

'I am not sure if Her Majesty requires me this evening,' she murmured. 'I shall have to ask Princesse d'Elbeuf.'

'Naturally, you must request permission.' Madame's smile was now pronounced; it did not make her more attractive. 'We shall expect you at eight o'clock.'

Without waiting for a reply, Madame turned her footsteps back to the palace and talked of other matters on their return. Clearly she did not expect Teresa to refuse the invitation . . .

Now, however, commanded by the Duc *not* to accept, she felt herself possessed of a great desire to do so.

'I am afraid that is out of the question, Duc. I go this evening. I believe,' she tossed her head defiantly, 'that the King desires my presence.'

If she had hoped to make an impression upon him, she could not have chosen a better method. Alarmingly grim, he reminded her of that afternoon in the room of the convent. On that occasion he had said that he would rather go to the Bastille than marry her. If he had repelled her then, he thoroughly frightened her now. What sort of husband would he be? Not kind, her mind told her swiftly. One part of her longed to tell him about her unease concerning Madame and her invitation; another part—the part uppermost now—rebelled at the peremptory order. He might consider her stupid and frivolous, but he should soon discover that he could not order her about as though he owned her.

The very moment those thoughts entered her head, she was assailed by the unpleasant thought that that was at the root of her fears. Married to the Duc, she would be completely in his power. To be loved by such a man would be wonderful; but to be married to him without love would be terrible. In their case it was so much worse, for he hated her. Shuddering, she tried not to contemplate the future, for it was bleak indeed.

His lip curled, and contempt marred his fine features. 'So, the King desires your presence. How successful you are! Is this not all you hoped for when you came to Court?' Contempt changed to a sterner purpose. Taking her wrist in a cruel grasp, he bent his head closer to hers so that she was conscious of his nearness. 'Tomorrow evening our betrothal is to be announced. You will then dance to my tune. In the meantime, I do not wish my future wife to be an intimate of Madame de Maintenon. You will please me by refusing this invitation.'

If he had used words of kindness, if he had only implored her, or even explained himself, she might have been tempted to yield to her own inclinations and refuse the invitation. Now her resolve strengthened.

'I have no wish to please you.' Adopting Marie's coquettish air, she once more tossed her head. 'I would rather please the King.'

In his heart he understood what had been going on in her mind; if he was honest with himself, he knew perfectly well that she had no idea of the whisperings concerning Madame de Maintenon, and if she had heard them she had certainly not understood. That she feared him in some way hurt him. Conscious that he had made no attempt to win her, or make the thought of marriage in any way agreeable, he could scarcely blame her for wishing to enjoy herself. But that she should choose such people as Villiers, Beauchamp, Maintenon and even Montespan for her companions, spoke ill of her judgement.

He began to think that she had some inherent flaw in her make-up, hitherto unsuspected by him, and was conscious of a feeling of disappointment. Better by far to have a foolish wife than an evil one. That Marie Besneval, with whom he had been forming a deeper friendship than he had realised, should appear to support her actively in her new friendships surprised him greatly. For Marie understood the world of Versailles so much better than this naïve girl.

Stepping back and releasing her wrist, he stared down at her with anger and contempt in his dark eyes, and spoke. 'If you will not do this for my sake, will you not refuse for the sake of the Queen? I cannot think that you should wish to repay her kindness to you by consorting with her enemies.'

Teresa was appalled. These pleasant, charming people, the enemies of the Queen? What ridiculous nonsense! Why, they were all devoted to the Queen. If he had hoped to move her with that argument, he was much mistaken. Also, she much disliked the imputation that she would ever be disloyal to Queen Maria Teresa. He was so obsessed with hating the Court, and the desire to return to his stupid estates, that he thought everyone must be guilty of some plot. Well, he should soon discover that she was made of very different material. Marriage to him might mean that he could control her actions, but he should never control her thoughts.

By the time she was ready to go to supper, Teresa's customary good humour was quite restored. In her finest looks, and conscious that the rose silk gown over a flowered underskirt admirably complimented her flawless complexion and fair hair, her eyes glowed luminously; all she needed to complete her present happiness was the admiration of a particular man.

Taking a fold of the delicate material and lifting it, she held out her foot to study the satin shoes with jewel-covered heels, and smiled when she recalled suggesting once that she venture to walk to Versailles in such dainty wear.

Madame's apartment was ablaze with candle-light, and despite the warmth of the evening a huge fire burned in the marble fireplace. The effect was overpowering, and Teresa experienced a sudden longing for fresh air. Madame de Maintenon approached, both hands outstretched and a smile of welcome creasing her face.

'I am so glad you are able to be here, you are a charming ornament for my little room.'

Allowing Madame to lead her to a small red brocade sofa, Teresa thought with irritation that that was the second time someone had referred to her as an ornament. While she could acquit the kindly Princesse d'Elbeuf of any malice, she was unsure of Madame de Maintenon's motive. And as for ornamenting such a room as this! The sumptuous furnishings took her breath away; there was a great quantity of heavy gilt mirrors, tables large and small, all supporting masses of flowers and carved figures. Comparing this room to the quiet refinement of the Duc's house in the town of Versailles, she thought it cluttered and overly bright. The carpets were too deep, the sofa too soft, the heat intense, the air heavy. Accepting a glass of white wine, she made an effort to appear interested in the conversation of her hostess. Dressed all in black, Madame's sallow skin looked darker than usual, and rich rubies flashed on her hands and at her throat.

'So, I was saying to the King that you would be sure to amuse him with some music after dinner. For you know how fond of music he is.'

'I could never play anything that would please the King!' Teresa was horrified at the prospect of entertaining him. If she had been careless in the pursuit of her studies at the convent, she had been quite neglectful of her study of music.

'You could please the King in other ways, Teresa Rochefoucourt. You cannot be blind to the fact that he finds you a delightful companion.'

Madame de Maintenon was not smiling now, but her eyes were sly and secretive. Watching her, Teresa was puzzled by the new expression.

'I cannot pretend to understand you, Madame. How can the King claim to find me a delightful companion when he has only spoken to me once or twice? I know what it is,' she began to smile, her fears and ridiculous fancies receding. 'You are trying to make me feel at my ease, and are flattering me. Everyone has been so kind to me, paying me the most outrageous compliments. I can assure you, Madame, I am not so innocent as to believe all of them, but I accept that they are paid in a spirit of kindness.'

The supper, which was served by a fleet of quiet women, also clad in black, was delicious. Seated at a small, round table some distance from the fire, Teresa began to feel more comfortable, and could begin to appreciate that the large apartment had some very attractive features. The white panelling which lined the walls was painted with a variety of exotic birds, with bright plumage of gorgeous colours. Madame was an excellent hostess and, with a variety of amusing stories and witty observations, soon had Teresa laughing merrily and exchanging her own anecdotes.

The last course had been cleared away and Teresa had declined to drink more wine, feeling just a trifle lightheaded. Indeed, her concentration was beginning to waver, but it was such a deliciously heady feeling that she ceased to worry. It was refreshing to talk about things rather than people, for she had begun to weary of the ceaseless gossip about people at Court; it was often unkind, and even cruel.

'I am privy to the King's confidence and understand that I must wish you happy.' On seeing the merry expression disappear suddenly from her young companion's face, Madame was immediately solicitous. 'Does the thought of marriage with the Duc not fill you with rapture?'

'I...that is...I am not sure.' Teresa could not confide in this woman, for she was close to the King. Yet she could not pretend to a joy she did not feel—her nature was too open and honest for that.

'If the thought of marriage with the Duc does not please you, you would find the King very much your friend,' Madame de Maintenon whispered softly, so softly that Teresa was not quite sure that she had spoken.

'I am not precisely sure,' she played for time. 'I do not really know the Duc that well.'

'Do I understand that you do not wish to marry him?' Madame was more insistent.

'I am not sure,' Teresa confessed with a feeling that she was being disloyal to him—yet he had done nothing to earn her loyalty, she consoled herself.

Madame de Maintenon began to look secretive again. 'There are ways to discover these things. Ways that have existed for generations, I know of these ways.'

So serious was her tone, so solemn was her face, that Teresa believed her instantly, yet she could not be sure that she understood.

'Do you mean witchcraft, *madame*?' she breathed fearfully.

'What a stupid name to give it!' Madame tossed back her thick, dark hair, and there was a new expression in her dark eyes, fierce and arrogant. 'The gift of fore-seeing the future has been in my family, secretly, for generations. I have always believed that the gift comes from God—He created all things, so where else should I have obtained my great power? You would like to know if you will marry your Duc, and if you do marry him, whether you will be happy. Well, that we can find out.'

Teresa experienced a moment of pure terror as she witnessed the dull, pious governess turn into a powerful, arrogant woman who had unknown gifts and longed for great things. A moment later she felt as though she must have been once more mistaken, for now Madame spoke silkily.

'It is a little game I play—it amuses my friends, quite harmless. Come, take another glass of wine and we shall indulge ourselves with a little unexceptionable enter-tainment for half an hour, until the King joins us.'

Thrusting out a hand, Teresa would have refused the wine, but the black-clad servant was at her elbow again. From where had the woman appeared? For Teresa was quite sure that she had not observed the woman coming through the door from the servant quarters. As she sipped from the tiny glass, she realised that she was not drinking wine, but some thick, sweet liquid which made her feel very strange. Fanciful notions began to crowd into her mind. The servant looked vaguely familiar—she reminded Teresa of Madame de Thiange; the other ser-vants, although she had paid little attention to them, bore resemblance to many of the women of the Court. How very strange!

When she tried to rise, her legs felt leaden and her
limbs heavy and clumsy, although her mind was startlingly clear. Madame's face began to waver and seemed
to float before her; the expression of piety had given
way to an unholy glee. Evil moved through the overheated room, as real as the sound of a creaking door to
her right. Puzzled and confused, she tried desperately
to focus her mind on the door—if it was a servant, as
surely it must be, she would beg to be escorted back to
her own apartment. But the door remained shut, and to
her horror she saw that it was a concealed door in the
panelling that was opening, through which came a slim
figure dressed as a nun.

As the nun approached her, she saw that the hands
holding a silver bowl were covered in jewels. This was
no nun! The bowl, containing an aromatic mixture, was
placed on the table before Teresa. As someone pushed
her face down to the bowl, she saw from the corner of
her eye that several nunlike figures glided into the room
and stood in a silent circle around the table.

The fumes from the bowl rose upwards, and almost
choked her at first. She tried to twist her head away, but
firm hands pushed her face back over the bowl. After
a few minutes the sensation was pleasant; she felt herself
drifting into a twilight world. The face of Madame de
Maintenon appeared, flabby and kindly, her eyes large
and vacant, like a cow chewing the cud on a hot summer
day.

'Tell me what you see!' A voice hissed in her ear, but
it seemed to come from another world.

Madame's face receded and muddy water, slime and
rotting vegetation began to swirl before her eyes—green,
dark brown, then the water began to clear. The sky was
blue, and the sun was shining on the King's gondola as
it glided up the canal near the palace. In another gondola
musicians played, as though for a wedding feast. Instinctively she knew it was for a wedding feast, the
wedding of someone who was desperately unhappy. So
strange. Was it symbolic? No. Wait. There was the
Marquise de Montespan's voice. Her vision shifted and

she saw the Marquise in the shadows, wringing her hands and weeping as she watched the King hand Madame de Maintenon, gorgeously attired into the royal gondola.

'Madame de Maintenon enters the King's gondola,' Teresa whispered.

The sunlight faded, there were chill bitter winds, and black and purple mourning draped everywhere. Shivering, and trapped by her visions of the future, Teresa was unable to look away. With great sadness she knew that the mourning was for the Queen, and was surprised at her own grief, unaware that she would come to regard the Queen with such great love and affection. It could not be far into the future, for the King still retained the sensual good looks of his Bourbon heritage. Madame— no! The Marquise de Maintenon, appeared at his side, a little older, a little fuller of figure, an expression of tender pity on her face as she laid a hand on the King's bowed shoulder. Putting up a hand to touch hers, he murmured something to her.

'So, the King marries the Marquise de Maintenon,' she heard herself whisper.

Feeling that she could bear it no longer, she tried to cry out, but no sound came; attempting to close her eyes against these pictures of the future, she longed for something good and pure and strong, for she was sure that she had witnessed the consequences of a great evil. Instantly a picture of the Duc appeared, but he was receding into the distance. 'Guy, Guy!' She called out in anguish, but she could not hear the sound of her own voice.

Feeling that some miracle must have happened, for she was sitting on the red brocade sofa, her head resting against a broad shoulder, an arm protectively around her shoulder, she turned instinctively to return the embrace. 'Oh, Guy! I knew that you would come to me!' Lifting her face, a spurt of joy coursing through her, she prepared to tell him of her strange experience, all animosity towards him quite gone. But it was not the Duc who held her and looked down at her with such

carnal desire in his eyes, it was King Louis the Fourteenth, the Sun King!

Teresa regarded him with mounting horror; what had
happened to her? How did she come to be sitting with
the King on this sofa? Had she not been sitting at that
round dining-table with Madame de Maintenon a mere
moment ago? She had experienced a brief moment of
joyous relief when she had thought that the Duc held
her in his arms. If her peculiar vision had taught her
one thing, it was that the Duc alone of this corrupt and
power-hungry Court was a man, a trustworthy and
honest man.

How could she have been so blinded by the glitter and
false glamour that she had not realised this before? But
she knew it now. If she could marry the Duc, she would
have a man of worth and substance, a life of truth and
honour; they were qualities that did not exist in
Versailles. To search for them would be a vain and empty
search. With a longing to tell him of all these things, she
tried to tear herself away from that embrace. It was imperative that she find the Duc and speak to him
immediately.

'Come, my dear *mademoiselle*, do not turn away from
me.' The King's voice was vibrant with passion. 'When
I entered this room and found you in such distress, I
could not leave you. When you returned my embraces,
you made me feel how very empty and desolate my life
has been without you. Sunshine and a radiant spring,
the very essence and beauties of nature, are all confined
within your delightful body and enchanting face. Can I
dare hope that you can return even a tenth of my feeling
for you?' There was confidence in his voice. Had anyone
ever dared offer a rebuff to him?

How such flowery compliments would have pleased
her only this morning. How triumphantly she would have
boasted to Marie about her conquest of the King's heart.
What a fool she had been! The words uttered by the
King revolted her. That her own behaviour had invited
such remarks, and protestations of a passion she was
sure did not exist, disgusted her even more. Once more

she pulled away from the King's embrace, noticing that her tears had stained the lapels of his purple coat.

'You mistake, Your Majesty, I never intended that you think that I was in love with you...' Her voice trembled, and she felt that her knees must give way as she stood up.

Rising to stand beside her, Louis took her hands and raised them to his lips. 'I like your modesty, Teresa. It becomes you, I have wearied of forceful, demanding women.' His eyes burned with passion.

It was thus that Guy d'Abbeville found them as Madame de Maintenon ushered him into the apartment. Behind him, Teresa could see the Marquise de Montespan, her mouth snapping shut, her eyes glittering with rage, looking first at her and then at the King. For one wild moment she longed to rush to Guy and beg him to take her away from this overheated room and the atmosphere of corruption that still pervaded it. But the King was still holding her hands, the red brocade sofa lay between them—and the stony expression in the Duc's eyes created a far wider gulf than she had the knowledge or experience to bridge. With a flash of appalled insight, she saw how the scene must appear to him. She was alone with the King, he was holding her in an attitude of unmistakable intimacy, and, what was far worse, the Duc had forbidden her to keep the engagement. To annoy and defy him, she had boasted that the King desired her presence. How foolish she had been, for in that instant she felt that she had lost all that could have been most dear to her.

CHAPTER SIX

STEPPING over the threshold and walking around the sofa, the Duc stood beside Teresa, and she felt the comfort and support of his arm under hers. Bowing to the King, he spoke smoothly.

'I must thank you, sire, for looking after Mademoiselle Rochefoucourt in her sudden indisposition—it was most kind of you. Only this evening I was telling her that she should decline Madame's enchanting invitation, but it is very difficult to reason with a lady when she is determined to have her own way.'

The Duc's flow of words caused the atmosphere to lighten.

'Hah! How well we know that!' The King laughed, and most of his unease disappeared.

Teresa, a flush of mortification now making her cheeks as red as they had been white, kept her eyes steadfastly on the carpet. One part of her longed to escape this room, another revelled in the closeness with the Duc. Now that he was here, all her fears were receding; she felt secure and protected. Whatever must have been his feelings on discovering her in the King's arms, he was rescuing her from a situation of acute embarrassment, and she thanked him silently from the depths of a full heart. If only she had listened to him! Conscious that she owed him an explanation and apology, she longed to be alone with him. Unaware of what was being said, she directed a brief glance of entreaty up at him.

With a tiny nod of comprehension and reassurance, he increased the pressure of his fingers on her arm. It was the smallest gesture, but it meant so much to her that tears threatened to fall.

Somehow they managed to leave the King's presence with a measure of dignity and aplomb. However, once

94

out in the corridor her strength threatened to desert her and she could feel her knees shake.

'Guy... I want to explain,' she ventured.

'Not now,' he murmured quietly. 'We are being watched. Comport yourself as though nothing untoward had happened. Soon you will be within the safety of your own rooms.'

Once more she felt the calming influence of his words, and was reassured. At least he understood some of her feelings. For this she was grateful.

When he had entered Madame de Maintenon's apartments, it was as though a draught of clean, strong air and bright sunshine had dispelled the nightmare that she had endured.

It was not until they were in her own room that he finally spoke. 'Madame de Maintenon, knowing something of the relationship that exists between us—doubtless you told her—summoned me to attend you back to your apartments, as you appeared unwell. You knew that the King was to join you, and I am quite convinced that you feigned illness in order to create an opportunity to be alone with Louis. You are in excellent company, Teresa—many of the King's previous mistresses have used just such a trick. I arrived to find you in circumstances of intimacy. Tell me,' he asked abruptly, 'for how long had you been alone with him?'

'I am not sure,' she whispered miserably. 'For only a moment, I think. Madame de Maintenon gave me something to drink—it was unpleasant. I am not sure what happened to me, but I thought that it was you with me.'

Frowning deeply, he looked gravely at her. 'I want the truth, Teresa. You cannot expect me to believe that you mistook Louis for me.'

'When I drank that stuff in the glass, I think I became unconscious, for one moment I was sitting at the dining-table and the next I was on the sofa with the King. Please, believe me.' She looked piteously up at him and involuntarily moved closer to him, for she was still afraid of the memory of what had occurred. 'For I swear before God that I am speaking the truth.'

For a fleeting moment he responded to that appeal,
his hands reached out and briefly caressed her bare
shoulders, but as she moved into the safety of his embrace he pushed her away.

'I may tell you this, Teresa, and you would do well
to take note if you plan to become the King's mistress,
and hope between you to fool me into acting as a con-
venient and complacent shroud for your illicit affair—
you were never more mistaken. I told you before that I
preferred the Bastille to marriage with you. Well, you,
and Louis, can know now that I would die rather than
disgrace my name or my house.'

With the feel of his hands burning her shoulders, and
the insult he had just offered, she was confused as well
as frightened. Did he really think that she had plotted
to become the King's mistress? Could he imagine that
she was so base and unworthy that she would use her
marriage to him, the finest man in France, as a cover
for a guilty alliance with the Bourbon King? 'I said that
I thought it was you.' Again she whispered, tears threatening to overcome her.

'If it were not so damned tragic, I could laugh at that.
Have you forgotten, my dear Teresa, that you dread
marriage to one so old and boring as myself? I tell you
again that I will not be a complacent husband!'

Stung by his manner and insults, she retorted swiftly,
'It is strange, is it not, that men cannot stomach the
thought of giving to women the freedom they demand
as a right for themselves?'

'If it is freedom you want, my dear,' he sneered at
her, 'then this diabolical marriage need never take place.
Before God! I thought it bad enough to be saddled with
a stupid wife, but to be tied to a woman who expects
freedom! I tell you I cannot bear it.'

Teresa had matured in the last few hours; recognising,
in part, his worth, she deeply pitied him. She had not
contrived at being alone with the King, yet it must have
seemed so to him. Madame de Maintenon had played a
part well—had she intended that to be the outcome of
the evening? Surely not? For what had she to gain by

such duplicity? She had said that they would play a little game—a little game in which she could find out whether or not she would marry the Duc. In her vision, she had known that a marriage had taken place— a marriage between two desperately unhappy people. Fervently she hoped and prayed that it was not her own marriage, for now she did desire this marriage—but she also desired happiness. There was an intensity in the scrutiny to which Guy subjected her. 'You told me that Madame de Maintenon gave you something to drink, and you thought you were unconscious afterwards. Can you tell me exactly what happened?'

The still quiet of her room, so restful, was at such variance with the painful emotions evoked by the recollection of the evening that she found it difficult to speak. Had she imagined what had occurred? Certainly her imagination must have played tricks on her when she had thought that the women dressed as nuns had been women of the Court. That must be so, otherwise the truth was too hideous to be faced.

What was the truth? Had she been used as a tool in some enactment of the black arts? Had her fear of Madame de Maintenon led her to believe that she had used her in such a way. Was it not more likely that she had drunk a little too much wine and misunderstood Madame de Maintenon? It was true that she had spoken of some gift from God—surely that could not be bad? Did she mean the power of prayer? So many questions remained unanswered. Above all remained the overpowering sense of evil, and the knowledge that the Duc was a good man, a man above all others at Versailles.

One thing she had not imagined—the King had held her in his arms and spoken to her of love. Holding her hands, he had assumed an attitude of loverlike possession, and that scene had been witnessed by the Duc! Whatever could she tell him, for she was loath to speak of the things she had seen when under the influence of the potion that Madame de Maintenon had given her? The thought that the Queen would die and be replaced by Madame de Maintenon was painful in the extreme.

She experienced a real longing to confide in the Duc, sure that he could help her, but unsure that he would, if he knew the truth.

'Madame de Maintenon and I had some supper, we talked for a while, and then she said that she knew of a little game we could play—a game to find out about the future——'

'Great heavens! She surely did not involve you in that?' Leaping to his feet in a swift, violent motion, he went to the window, fists clenched, then whirled about to face her. Towering over her, his face shadowed, he spoke with angry vehemence. 'And you agreed! Were you quite mad? Had you learnt so little at the convent that you were willing to deal with the devil at the first opportunity?'

'You do not understand—she told me that she had a special gift, a gift from God.' Afraid of him, she persisted in her efforts to make him understand.

'And you believed her?' he snapped angrily.

'At the time, yes. Now I no longer believe in anything or anybody.' Except you, she longed to say, but in the face of his fury and wrath she kept silent.

'And then you became unconscious?' he was cynical.

Beginning to resent his attitude, for her experience had been both shocking and unpleasant, she, too, stood and looked up at him. 'No. Someone brought a bowl of liquid—it was after I drank the potion—my head felt odd, and I could not stand or move. My head was pushed over the bowl, and I saw pictures in the water. The Marquise de Montespan was weeping, Madame de Maintenon was a Marquise and being helped into the King's gondola, then the Queen was dead and the King was marrying Madame de Maintenon.' In her terse account, she did not tell of the wedding or the person who was desperately unhappy, for now she was sure that it was the Duc. Did he love Marie Besneval so very much that marriage to her became increasingly unbearable? Of course it did, had he not said so many times?

Her extreme pallor and the darkening of her eyes spoke more eloquently of the shock she had received than any

words she uttered. Anger stirred in him that she had been
used in this way.

'And why did you think that the King was me?' As
he had spoken in a more gentle tone than used previously, she was encouraged to be more open with him.

'Because you appeared, reaching out to me. I knew
in that moment that you were entirely good, and that I
had misjudged you. It was dreadful, I was calling for
you, but no sound came...' Putting up her hands, she
covered her face, convulsed by a hysterical sobbing.

Unable to resist her tears, and aware for the first time
of some of her horror and revulsion, he gathered her
into his arms and attempted to quell the rising hysteria.

'Come, Teresa, dry your tears. We must talk, you and
I. For when the King announces our betrothal I wish to
present a happy face to the Court; it is important for
both of us that we appear united.'

Resuming his seat, the brief, glorious intimacy over,
he pushed her gently back to her chair. That moment
had meant nothing to him, it was no more than the action
of a man comforting a child, yet to her it had been like
finding a safe haven after a storm. So strong were the
emotions roused in her—perhaps it was the effects of
her momentary hysteria, for she had never imagined she
could put the episode into words—that she found herself
shy about looking at him, afraid that her new emotions
would show on her face.

The Duc had been acutely conscious of her nearness;
if she had begun to intrigue him before, he now found
himself not all averse to her changed emotions. Cyni-
cally, he wondered if her changed heart was not the consequence of that shocking experience, and when the ill-
effects of it had worn away, so would she revert to being
a silly, spoiled darling of the Court. That the King should
find her desirable surprised him not at all; Teresa
Rochefoucourt was very beautiful. But in marriage he
wanted a great deal more than a pretty face—he wanted
a companion, someone whom he could love. In that
moment he believed that he could come to love her.

Reaching out, he took her hand, surprised to find that it trembled in his.

'Did the King make love to you?' Striving to make his voice light, he failed miserably.

Imps of mischief danced in her eyes, a smile curved her mouth. 'He said some very silly things.' Tilting her head, smiling through her lashes, she was coquettish without intent, and he found himself smiling in response. 'If I were to tell you, you would accuse me of boasting of my royal conquests, and say that I achieved my heart's desire.'

Laughing with her, and looking much younger, she wondered how she had ever thought him old.

'Tell me about my future home—I long to hear all about it.'

Withdrawing his hand from hers, he rose and began to pace about the room. Turning in her chair, she watched his face lose its mask of cynicism and become animated. 'It is the most beautiful place on earth, Teresa. I love it, and always shall, above all other things.'

Above me? She had not known that she could be jealous, but now she discovered the power of that destructive emotion. Fool! Of course he did not love her, but, she vowed to herself, I will make him love me.

'My sister and her husband look after the affairs of the estate, but I would sooner look after things myself. Twenty-six farms, a couple of villages and three churches are a lot to manage. What can I say? The land is the loveliest on earth, the climate is warm and sunny, the people are the best in the world. There is everything there that a man could desire: work, occupation, hunting, shooting, fishing.' Returning to the chair he had vacated, he did not sit, but, resting his hands on its back, stared broodingly out over the gardens spread below. 'You cannot imagine what hell it is to be trapped here.'

'It will all be different after we are married,' she ventured timidly. He had hardly painted a picture of a life that was attractive to her, for how could she be châtelaine to what was clearly an estate of vast proportions? If he loved her it might be easy, but he did not love her.

What was his sister like? Her mind immediately conjured a vision of a woman like him, strong and independent, or his aunt, the Abbesse, equally masterful and determined. Would she not despise her new sister-in-law?

Pulling her to her feet, he swung her round, a glow of admiration in his dark eyes. 'It *will* be different—it will be wonderful to return with my beautiful wife.'

Happiness sang through her veins, making her eyes sparkle and her lips part in joyful expectancy. Setting her down, and placing his hands on her shoulders, he looked deeply into her eyes. 'We do not love each other, Teresa, but at least we no longer hate each other. It is enough to begin with, for once I am at home again I shall be happy.' The pressure of his hands on her shoulders began to increase, and slowly he began to stroke her shoulders and neck until his hands cupped her face. For a wild moment she thought he was going to kiss her, and her lids lowered and her blush deepened; time seemed suspended and she was scarcely aware of breathing. 'Do not fear that I shall force myself upon you, for I know that you are not yet ready for my lovemaking.'

Disappointment made her almost cry out, but he had said 'We do not love each other.' How could she tell him that she did love him? This kind and tender person of the past half-hour was a revelation to her, a revelation that she could love until the end of time. Did he mean that his love for Marie Besneval must die before he could love her? Or was the prospect of returning to Provence so happy that he could regard her with tolerance? She did not care—he had held her in his arms, he had said that it would be wonderful to return with his beautiful wife. It was a better beginning than she had dared hope. Somehow or another she would earn his love and affection, make him proud of her.

It was difficult to give voice to words when he still held her face cupped in both his hands and looked deeply into her eyes, with an expression that was darkening to intensity. Unawakened, she did not recognise it as the kindling of physical desire, and mistook it for returning anger.

'Please, do not worry that I shall not be a comfortable wife, Guy.' It gave her intense pleasure to speak his name, and her voice trembled a little. 'I mean to study and read and learn all about the things that interest you, so that I shall be able to talk to you of sensible matters.' Unconsciously, she had put up her hands to cover his, her eyes so full of love that his heart gave a skip of pure joy. 'I shall model myself on the Queen.'

'Heaven forbid! I am not sure that I wish for any but a silly, frivolous girl straight from the convent.'

This time she could not mistake the darkening in his eyes for anger, and as his lips moved to cover hers her response was all that a deeply passionate man could desire.

Afraid that his ardour might frighten her, he gently drew away from her and released her with extreme reluctance. Teaching her to love would be a delightful task, for there was passion and fire in her. But not yet—she must become accustomed to him, and he to her. Lurking in the back of his mind, for he had become cynical and disillusioned in Versailles, he wished to make quite sure that the King did not plan to make Teresa his mistress. Now, he wanted her body, but he also wished to love her spirit and society. Louis had the power to make women love him—his royal rank and his charm combined to make him fascinating. Teresa's revelations about Madame de Maintenon's future had shocked and disturbed Guy, for he had good reason to suppose that she might at least become the King's mistress. But his wife? Much though he wished to punish her, he realised that he must tread warily; he was constantly in the shadow of the Bastille, and Madame de Maintenon must not think that she had gained an enemy in him.

Beneath his deliberations about his own future, he was seriously alarmed for Teresa's sake. That her vision of the future had shocked her, she understood; but that she was in terrible danger, she had not comprehended. For a long time he had suspected that Madame de Main-

tenon had been scheming for power; it was rumoured
that many women, and even some men, at Court had
taken part in satanic rites. Contempt for their vanity and
folly was his usual response to such news; but when he
observed such disparate bedmates as Charles Villiers and
Madame de Maintenon in deep and earnest conversation in the corner of the chapel, his suspicions were
aroused. Both were intelligent and power-hungry, a
dangerous combination in the Court of the Sun King.

Teresa had been used as a medium by de Maintenon
and her cronies; soon others would—must—hear of it.
That she might be used again by other Court factions
was possible. If he could marry her and get her away to
the safety of Provence, she would be saved. Would Louis
agree to that? Louis was enamoured of her, he had seen
that on the evening of the dinner, but would he pursue
her as a quarry?

Shreds of cynicism still clouded Guy's mind. Teresa
might imagine herself in love with him at the moment;
in her fright, her mind had turned to him as a possible
saviour, but that was not love. She was ready to be
awakened—having become an object of desire, she was
ready to desire, but none of these things were love. It
was still possible that she and Louis had formed some
plan between them—a plan whereby she would become
his mistress. It was increasingly rumoured that the King
had wearied of his mistress's temperamental outbursts,
but that he should be contemplating taking Madame de
Maintenon—a woman older than himself, of stout body
and no particular beauty—as a mistress was too fantastic to believe.

Increasingly, he found that he cared very much about
Teresa's feelings. That she should pretend eagerness for
this marriage in order to bluff him, hurt him unbearably. Could he have mistaken the glow in her eyes?
It was not feigned—she had no power of artifice; if she
was untutored and ignorant, she was also delightfully
direct and spontaneous.

She was watching him anxiously, trying to read his
thoughts, and he smiled down at her. 'We must make

do together, Teresa.' The thought of her reading and writing and improving herself every day in order to impress him had touched him very deeply, but he did not say this, in case she might think that he was teasing her. Most of the women with whom he had had affairs over the past dozen years had all been older than himself, agreeable and experienced companions. With very young girls he had always been a trifle impatient—their giggles irritated him, their ignorance exasperated him. It occurred to him then that Teresa laughed, not giggled; when told something, she learned quickly.

An empty ache when he withdrew from her, a feeling that his thoughts concerned her, yet not favourably, all confused Teresa. Wisely she did not ask, fearing that he would tell her that he loved Marie. That he liked her and wished to make a success of their coming marriage should be enough for now.

The great ballroom of Versailles was lighted with thousands of candles; flowers in great containers were banked in corners and depicted various forest scenes. Trestle tables groaned beneath the weight of the food piled high—pastries and trifles—the Versailles chefs had worked all the week for this Friday evening—and bowls of fruit punch and wine. At the King's little reception there were already several hundred people drifting about, exchanging smiles and salutations, eyes constantly straying from a companion to see who would next arrive and enliven the already glittering throng.

Peeping through the doorway through which she would enter with the royal party, Teresa saw a mass of silks, velvets, brocades, satin, lace and jewels all move and glitter to the accompaniment of the orchestra. She saw Marie, lovely and radiant in a gown of amber brocade, her skin creamy and thick, dark hair piled up on her head. It was a style out of the ordinary and looked charming. Flirting with her fan, her large, dark eyes were lustrous, and a coquettish smile curved her lips. She's beautiful, thought Teresa miserably. How on earth can I compete with her? I know that Guy must love her, for Henri Deschamps and Richard Beauchamp are enchanted with her. Charles Villiers, distinguished in dark blue brocade, was paying charming court to an elderly Comtesse, who, obviously delighted, rapped his knuckles with her fan every so often, and punctuated her conversation with roguish glances.

The musicians kept looking anxiously at the great double doors through which the King and Queen would enter—as royal musicians, their only desire was to please their royal master. The Marquise de Montespan, a confection of white brocade and knots of pink ribbon, tapped her foot angrily, aware that a mere month ago the musicians would have considered pleasing her as important as pleasing the king. The perfumed, painted, exquisite Court who surrounded her had diminished in number, and she gave vent to her wrath by passing a number of spiteful, vindictive remarks about the absentees. If the titters and exclamations of admiration from her Court did little to mollify her wounded feelings, she had the supreme satisfaction of knowing that she was the loveliest and the best-dressed woman in the ballroom. That was, until Teresa Rochefoucourt made her entrance in the wake of the King and Queen, with her fingers resting lightly on the arm of the Duc d'Abbeville.

The courtiers and their ladies created a warm, perfumed wave as they parted into a broad avenue of bright colour, bowing and curtsying deeply to welcome their King and Queen. As each man straightened up and his lady rose in billowing grace, eyes were turned and fixed on Teresa, who seemed to float down the ballroom. Shining eyes, flawless complexion, and the smile of a girl in love, she epitomised the ideal of feminine youth and beauty. With tiny, almost imperceptible nods, she acknowledged the presence of her friends. Every so often, and simultaneously, she and the Duc would look at each other and exchange a shared, intimate glance as though in love. Engaged thus, the Duc did not notice that the King and Queen had halted their stately progress in order to talk to a couple the King had not seen for some while. The Duc would have collided into his

King, an unforgivable breach of Court etiquette, if Teresa had not given his arm a sharp nip. Recovering his position quickly, he looked down at Teresa to discover her in the act of putting up a hand to her mouth to conceal a mischievous smile, to which he responded with a rueful grin.

None of this was lost on those who watched every action and glance avidly, with emotions that varied from tolerant amusement to vexation and despair.

The royal couple took their seats on the dais overlooking the ballroom, and smiled benignly at their noble subjects. Teresa stood with the Duc behind the royal chairs and looked out over the crowded ballroom. As the King rose, very much the grand monarch, hands extended to address his audience, all movement seemed suspended. Every eye was on the King, in expressions of carefully schooled friendship and adulation.

'My good friends, and loyal subjects! My Queen and I give you all blessing, and bid you welcome to this little reception.' After pausing to allow time for the polite laughter with which this sally was received, he proceeded, beaming amiably. The King was disposed to be in a good humour; everyone must, therefore, be in a good humour. 'I wish to announce that the forthcoming betrothal of Guy Denis d'Abbeville of the Chateau d'Abbeville of Arles in Provence to Maria Teresa Rochefoucourt, god-daughter of Queen Maria Teresa, will take place in the royal chapel on Saturday of next week. This betrothal has our blessing.'

Teresa saw that the careful expressions faltered for a moment, and a ripple of surprise, cupidity and envy flitted over several faces, to be quickly masked.

Taking Teresa's hand, the King led her forward, and, with an inclination of the head, invited Guy to step forward. His gesture was one of friendship, but his fond smiles and hand-patting were all for Teresa. 'I believe that we must not agree to too hasty a wedding, for we do not wish to lose this jewel of Versailles too quickly.' Moistening his lips, eyes devouring her until she felt hot with embarrassment, he continued, 'Although I am sure that the Duc will wish to carry her away to his estates before long.' In response to a look of silent entreaty from his Queen, he slightly altered his tone. 'So you may all prepare for the disappointment we must face when they take their leave, which will probably be very soon. There can be none more disappointed than myself that we cannot persuade this pearl of loveliness to remain among us, for there would be none more welcome.' This last was pronounced in accents of roguish gallantry, but few were taken in, for Louis had made it very clear that, if she were willing, he would take Teresa as his next mistress.

The lovely Marquise de Montespan, long nails curled into soft white palms, endured the covertly malicious looks cast in her direction. Vowing that she would not be publicly humiliated, as years earlier she and Louis had thus publicly humiliated the Queen, who now occupied her place beside him on the dais, she determined that she would contrive to oust Teresa's pretensions, and win back her royal lover, the father of her children.

With a wave of his hand, Louis indicated that the dancing might commence, and turned his attention to the party on the dais. There was an immediate buzz of conversation—heads nodded vigorously, eyes wide with delightful speculation, faces animated. What food for gossip! Courtiers and their ladies, who had exchanged not half a dozen words in as many months, found that they had much to say, and took more pleasure in each other's company as a consequence.

'May I join with my husband in adding my felicitations for your future? I cannot tell you what a great joy it is to me to see you both together and so very happy.' The Queen's lustrous eyes glowed with warmth as they rested on Louis. 'It reminds me of those early days when I first came here from Spain. How very happy I was.' She paused, and added more quietly, 'And still am.'

Much moved, Louis patted her shoulder. 'You always give me reason to think that you are the most excellent of women, but tonight I must think myself the most unworthy of husbands.'

'Never that, dear heart, never.' The Queen looked at her unfaithful husband with all the loving adoration of a young bride, and he accepted it as his due.

The Duc was used to these intimate exchanges, for the King lived much of his daily life in the public eye, and his every action was carried out under the close scrutiny of dozens of people. But to Teresa this was an unpleasant revelation—her innocence did not protect her from the knowledge that the King's too evident admiration had placed them all in an acutely uncomfortable position. She felt humble surprise at the Queen's love, still, for her husband. Did love really endure? True love must. Did she have that sort of love for the Duc? Yes, she decided, she did. Her love would endure, because it was strong, and based on an increasingly firmer foundation.

'We shall have a great festivity to mark this betrothal—a really spectacular festivity. All shall say that they have never seen anything so fine, or so grand.' Throwing out his chest, Louis became absorbed in happy dreams of grandeur.

'Have you forgotten that the Austrians are arriving next week? It will be an opportunity to impress them,' reminded his Queen.

'Tch! It does not suit me to be receiving them. I could wish that I were elsewhere.' Pouting, Louis was forced back to reality.

Another reality was at that moment descending upon him. It was the custom for the Queen to withdraw once the signal had been given for the dancing to commence. Then Louis would summon the intimates of his party about him, and they would chat for a while before leaving the ballroom. The talk was generally of an inconsequential nature, as Louis meticulously attended to affairs of state each morning. This evening was a slight exception, for besides the Duc and Teresa there were a few others in the royal party. The Queen, deviating from her normal custom, had not withdrawn as usual, but in remaining to talk with the party had been screened from the view of those in the ballroom by those who stood about the royal couple. The Marquise de Montespan usually joined her royal lover when the Queen left the company, and, believing that she had, the lovely Athénaïs, enraged by the jibes of her supposed friends, had pushed her way on to the dais.

It had been painful to watch the King with Teresa, painful to endure the mocking sympathy that had been extended to her.

'Did you see that simpering fool Rochefoucourt?' she snapped angrily at Marie Besneval. 'And the way the King looked at her with such doting fondness. Lord! I was nearly sick, it was such a sight.'

A tall, thin Princesse, sumptuously clad in crimson silk, who had slanting, spiteful eyes, and had cherished hopes of an offer from the Duc, tittered angrily. 'But she did well to capture a Duc; her father was only a very minor member of the nobility. My family certainly never recognised him.'

Marie Besneval was beginning to tire of these vicious comments. Finding that her pride and not her heart had been wounded, she saw that if the Duc was not yet in love with Teresa he was in a fair way to becoming so very soon. No matter what wiles she used, she had always known instinctively that when such a man fell in love it would be forever. If his love died or left him, it would make no difference, for he was not the sort to ever love another. In a curious way she had been proud of Teresa tonight; she had entered the ballroom in the royal wake, aware as she must have been that all eyes were on her and that she was the subject of conjecture and speculation, yet she had conducted herself like a Duchesse. There was grace and dignity in her every movement and gesture, yet without a trace of haughtiness.

It was with some relief that Marie allowed Henri Deschamps to claim her hand for the pavan. The slow, stately dance suited her present mood, and Henri was an excellent dancer. His light conversation and innocuous remarks exactly suited her humour; she had no wish to discuss the betrothal that was uppermost in every mind and on every wagging tongue tonight. As though guessing these thoughts, Henri tactfully talked about everything else.

'Would you care to walk on the terrace, Marie? The air is quite stifling in here.' Keeping his voice carefully neutral and friendly produced exactly the right response in his capricious love.

'I would love to, Henri. I am greatly fatigued.'

Placing a gentle arm beneath her elbow, he just managed not to leap for joy as he led her on to a terrace awash with the last bronze rays of the setting sun.

When the King's mistress edged her way on to the dais, she saw at once that the Queen was still present, and realised her mistake. A tiny frozen silence greeted her presence, but she put her chin up, for she was determined to fight for her position. Louis loathed breaches of etiquette; formal manners, pomp and ceremony were the breath of life to him, and all must follow his lead.

'I trust I see you in good health, Marquise.' The Queen accompanied her words with her slow, sweet smile.

Curtsying deeply to the Queen, but with her eyes on the King, the Marquise responded mechanically. 'Quite well, Your Majesty.' She had planned to take her place beside her lover, but his Queen's presence prevented that, so she was led into her second mistake of the evening. Moving back, she stood beside Teresa. The similarity in dress did not make for a similarity in appearance, it accentuated the contrasts between them. Between youth and age, there must always be an unfavourable comparison; the flaunting attraction of a beautiful, experienced woman becomes tainted beside the dewy charm of an innocent girl. Thus observed and spoke the assembled Court as they watched with glee the tableau on the dais.

Casting a glance of contempt at them, Teresa saw clearly for the first time the greedy, cruel stupidity of the ambitious who surrounded the King. Only too well did she now see why her Duc should wish to escape to the clean air and freedom of his own lands. When the

Queen had given her kindly greeting, Teresa could have
applauded her godmother's kindness and tact. Seeing
that the dancers were watching them with smirks and
occasional laughs, she vowed that she would give no
cause to add to their cruel glee, well aware that many
who now enjoyed the Marquise's discomfiture had
courted her favour only a few weeks ago.

Her own mother had been a figure of the distant past,
and in those few tense moments Teresa identified with
her and felt close to her as never before. She could
understand her mother's longing to leave the Court, this
scene of corruption, once she was in love. Teresa longed
to say something to ease the renewed tension. She did
not in the least hold the King's mistress responsible for
the actions of her governess. King Louis's lips were beginning to twitch with annoyance, and the courtiers and
ladies who formed their party were beginning to stir
uncomfortably.

'I know that you come to tell the King about the
dreadful fate which almost overtook him, Marquise.'
Teresa's eyes twinkled and a mischievous smile curved
her mouth. 'But it was really all your fault.' With many
embellishments, she recounted how the Duc had almost
collided with the King, ending with an unaffected smile
to the Marquise. 'And all because he was lost in admiration of *you*. I was very envious, I assure you, for I
thought until that moment that after the Queen I was
sure to be the finest lady in Versailles. But when I saw
the Duc staring at you, I knew that I was not.'

Her infectious gaiety bubbled over into a little chuckle,
and when the King chose to be amused and laughed
heartily they all joined in. It immediately relieved the
tension, and some other light topics of conversation were
introduced. Everyone generally approved of Teresa's
swift comprehension of a difficult situation and her
adroit handling of it. The Marquise was so far recovered
in composure to suggest that the gown she intended to
wear for the forthcoming visit of the Austrian delegation would be even finer, her eyes anxiously on the
King's face.

With an expression of annoyed indecision on his face, the King waved the lace handkerchief he was holding in a fussy, quick gesture.

'I am not sure that we will be in Versailles for the visit, for the Queen will no doubt wish to visit her godchild's new home. We shall all prevail upon your hospitality,' he briefly glanced at the Duc, 'to inspect it. It will give me a chance to see something of my realm—I have not been out of Versailles for some little while. But no doubt that your gown will be all you hope it to be.'

Snubbed, but more kindly than she could have hoped under the circumstances, the Marquise chose to withdraw from the dais when the Queen rose to depart with her ladies.

Teresa and the Duc went to join the dancers, who parted before them with only slightly less ceremony than they had afforded the King and Queen.

'It is not the moment to kiss you, my darling, but if we were alone together I would express my gratitude in such terms that you would be in no doubt as to my feelings. To be going home! Even for a short visit. It is a miracle. Come dance with me, my little darling wife-to-be.'

CHAPTER SEVEN

'I HATE her! I hate her! I want her crushed!' The King's mistress paused her stormy perambulations to grind the diamond-studded heel of her shoe into the soft white carpet. She looked at Charles Villiers again, eyes glittering with rage. 'You stay silent, Charles. Have you nothing to say?'

'Nothing that will bring you comfort, my fair Athénaïs. But if it is revenge you want...' He allowed his drawling voice to trail away and awaited a reaction. It was instantaneous.

'I do! You cannot know how much. That I should be grateful to that little upstart. You saw how she did it!'

Charles Villiers did see how she had done it, and had silently applauded the social grace which had extricated the royal party, not to mention the Marquise de Montespan herself, from a potentially disastrous situation.

'And the King wants to pay a royal visit to the Duc's estates! How often have you known him to visit anyone? He is terrified to stir outside Versailles in case he loses his throne. Now, because a chit of seventeen smiles at him, he fancies himself a boy again. My God, he is forty. Foolish forty!' She laughed angrily. Eyes narrowing, she looked at Charles fully. 'You said that you knew how I could be revenged on her. How? I would do anything—anything!'

'I happen to have a piece of information that should interest you very much, but,' he held up a slim white finger, 'I want something in return.'

'Naturally, who does not?' Her response was bitter. 'What do you want in return?' Thrusting forward her scarcely covered bosom, and allowing her hips to sway a fraction, she allowed her lips to quiver in a way that

113

used to drive the King to distraction. 'I can be very generous.'

Laughing easily, he lay back in his chair. 'Save your charms for the King—I presume that behind all your anger you want him back? You had better keep a cold bed for the time being, if that is your ultimate desire. Kings are notoriously cruel to fickle mistresses; keep your strong feelings for revenge, it can be a very satisfying reward.' Knowing that Montespan's race was run, he had no intention of telling her so, but was content to use her in his game of power; she was so enraged that she would do anything. But he had no intention of telling her what his plans were—women could not be trusted. One satisfying night in bed, and their pillow-mate became the recipient of their most intimate confidences.

'Your little enemy was a participant in a most interesting little ceremony held by your governess.'

Gasping with outraged disbelief, Athénaïs rounded on him. 'You lie! That holy turnip engaged in black magic? I presume that is what you are saying?'

'That is precisely what I am saying. Rumours, for once, were correct. The medium she used—and, yes, do not look so incredulous, my dear, she does have considerable powers—was your little enemy. I believe that whatever the little Rochefoucourt was able to tell her has kept the smile on her face ever since.'

'What I would give to find out,' she breathed.

'That is not important. What is of importance is that she was present. I doubt her Duc knows of it, for surely she would not dare to tell him? In any case, if it became known her credit would be quite destroyed, and I believe that she would do anything to protect herself and her future husband. You see! I have delivered her into your hands.' There was a gloating satisfaction in his voice.

'You offer me no proof.' Sharp and businesslike, her clever brain was conceiving a plan quite different from his. She wished to destroy Teresa completely.

'Oh, there were witnesses. How else should I have known? The names of those present need not trouble you, bar one—Marie Besneval.'

The pronouncement of that name riveted Athénaïs de Montespan to the spot, and into her whitened cheeks came two angry spots of colour. 'I will make her suffer, also. I shall destroy all my enemies.'

Taking his leave, he could not help smiling maliciously to himself. If that were the case, she would have to destroy all the Court—himself included.

So much seemed to have happened to Teresa that each time she returned to the convent at Villepreux she was surprised that it remained unchanged. The unvarying routine of each day, the murmur of prayers, the quiet ringing of the chapel bell, the air of purposeful content that reigned. How conscious she was of it all.

'You have grown very fashionable, Teresa,' acknowledged the Abbesse. 'The last time you were here with Guy I remarked that, also. How is my nephew?'

A soft blush stained her cheeks and she smiled shyly. 'Very well, Abbesse. Our betrothal was announced last night. It was a very splendid occasion.'

A nun entered the Abbesse's room and deposited a tray of coffee and cakes on the table. This was an honour indeed!

'You seem happier about the marriage than when we last talked.' The Abbesse smiled as she poured coffee.

'I am,' replied Teresa simply. 'I never thought that I could learn to love Guy. It seemed impossible a few weeks ago...' Her voice trailed away and she became silent.

Without appearing to do so, the nun had been studying her visitor closely, and frowned slightly. 'I fear that something troubles you, my child.'

'No, nothing,' Teresa denied quickly. 'I am all delight at the thought of my marriage. If I could win Guy's love, then I would be the happiest girl in France.'

Handing her a cup of coffee, the nun persisted. 'I think there is some cause for disquiet. You are not as you used to be, Teresa.'

So concerned did the nun seem, that Teresa found herself telling her about the dreadful events in the apartment of Madame de Maintenon, only omitting the

King's lovemaking. She was quite convinced that the Abbesse would never understand.

For a few moments the nun remained silent, as though deep in thought, and Teresa wondered if she had guessed or even heard about the King's conduct.

'A few years ago a similar scene was enacted—the young people in the palace thought that it would relieve the monotony of their days. Ah, yes,' she smiled. 'You think that convent life is monotonous, but there are many at Court who find it equally tedious. At least our life here is full of purpose.'

'I am aware of that Abbesse,' returned Teresa.

'Of course you are, child. But I digress. After one such episode a close friend of Guy's committed suicide.' She was silent for a long moment, and Teresa had a sense of nameless and unsaid horrors. 'It made him aware that life at Court could be, if one allowed, a wicked existence. Out of folly is sometimes bred evil. It had a salutary effect on my nephew, for he grew to be more sensible and caring as a result of that experience.'

That Guy could ever have been involved in the black arts had not previously occurred to Teresa, and she took her leave of the Abbesse in a much disquietened frame of mind.

'Marie, is he not the most wonderful man? Am I not the most fortunate girl in France? Now that you have told me your wonderful news, I can speak freely to you. You are wondering how I came to change so rapidly,' Teresa halted her raptures, unsure how to go on, for she was sure that Marie could not have been one of the women in the apartment of Madame de Maintenon; still, she was loath to recall the events of that night. 'It is enough to say that I had an experience which changed my mind.'

Marie blushed, glad that Teresa did not speak of an evening of which she was increasingly ashamed.

'Are you quite sure that you have no more feelings for the Duc? That you are in love with Henri?' Teresa looked shyly at her friend.

'Love? I do not know about love!' Marie could still be impatient with Teresa. 'If you mean, am I in rapture, then, no, I am not. If you mean, am I glad that I accepted his proposal of marriage, then yes, I am. We shall deal well together.'

'I wonder if the Duc would permit you and Henri to join our party to Provence, for I should dearly love your company, and I know that the Duc is very fond of Henri. Think what fun we could have! Say that you will come.'

Marie's conscience began to trouble her—in the face of such real friendship and unaffected spontaneity, she felt uneasily that if her part in the attempts to bring about Teresa's downfall should be known, then she would indeed have lost a valuable friend. Also, the prospect of a visit away from Versailles appealed to her very much; that such a visit would be spent in the company of the King and Queen was irresistible. 'I would love to come, thank you.'

'Well, Teresa? You are in glowing spirits, as always. Do I take it that it is my company that has you in such fine form?' The Duc smiled down at his future wife, eyes glinting as they rested on her.

'Of course! Also the prospect of riding in the park with you. I am anxious to show off my new prowess— Henri has been a very good teacher, as you will see.'

Despite the heat of the previous days, this was a cool, rather blustery day. The horses, heads snatching against the bits, clearly longed to gallop across the parkland and into the forest.

Intent upon exhibiting her skill, now that they were mounted and moving across the green, Teresa had little thought for conversation. To her surprise, she had mastered the equestrian arts quite easily, and, once she had overcome her initial nervousness, had proved a competent horsewoman.

'When we are in Provence, I shall show you some of the finest stretches of gallops that you are likely to see in the world.'

With his head thrown back, enjoying the outdoors, Teresa thought him so handsome that it was like a

physical ache. But his remark about Provence reminded
her that she had to tell him about the invitation that she
had extended to Marie. Biting her lip, she decided that
this would be as good a time as any to tell him. Marie
had thought that the invitation was given from motives
of pure friendship, but Teresa, too, was learning some
artifice. If she could see Marie and the Duc against the
background of his own home, she could then decide if
he still loved her. Glad she might be that Marie had accepted Henri's offer of marriage, but she doubted very
much if Marie would have accepted it unless she was
quite sure that the Duc's own marriage was to take place.
Yet she had told Teresa once with confidence that she
and the Duc loved each other.

'Guy, there is something I must tell you, although,'
she gave a shaky little laugh, 'I am sure that you will
not mind.'

There was a hint of iron in his eyes, a slight frown to
mar his countenance. 'Another confession, my love?'

'No, no. Nothing of the sort. It is just that I have
invited Marie to accompany us. I thought it would make
a good number for our little party. And she is my only
real friend in Versailles.' She had added the last quickly,
for she saw a look of thoughtful abstraction replace the
frown.

A moment later it was gone, and he was laughing
easily. 'You have assumed the duties of châtelaine very
quickly, my love. Of course I have no objection. I trust
that you wish me to extend the invitation to Henri?'

In happy accord the ride proceeded; the horses had
been trotting quickly through the forest, but were allowed to slow down as they encountered a leafy path
which led to a sheltered glade. The blustery wind only
stirred the branches here, for they were deep in the forest;
the air held a pronounced chill and the light was muted.
Glancing with some alarm at the Duc, Teresa wondered
if he felt as she did that there was an atmosphere of
menace everywhere. Goodness! She shook herself mentally. Whatever was coming over her? In the Duc's
company she should feel safe—had she not decided that?

Looking at this handsome profile with its clear features and firm line of mouth and jaw, she fancied there was a saturnine expression in his dark eyes. Perhaps it was the way he frowned; she could not be sure. The feeling of menace persisted, and she began to glance about uneasily. On her rides with Henri and Marie and others, she had noticed that they usually followed the route taken by the King when hunting, and kept to broad paths and wide thoroughfares.

Reigning in, he dismounted and in silence looped his rein around a tree stump before assisting her to dismount. As he reached up to help her, there was an unfathomable expression in his eyes, and she recalled that on one occasion she had thought that he had the power to frighten her. Shivering, she slid from her horse's back and into his arms. Briefly he held her against his chest, and she felt her shiver of alarm turn to a thrill of physical desire. Taking her hand, he led her through a clump of trees which opened out on to a small clearing.

To her surprise, there was a small house in the middle of the clearing. At first she thought it must be a woodman's cottage, but then realised that it was larger than a cottage, and its style and proportions were vaguely familiar. With an unpleasant jolt she saw that it was a smaller version of the Duc's house in the town of Versailles. With firmly shut doors and tightly shuttered windows, it had a closed, secretive air. There was something distinctly unpleasant about the house, and, shivering again, she felt the stirring of evil move through the undergrowth and waver about the house.

'Why do you shiver and look so frightened?' His voice was deep, but behind the reassurance there was a note of interrogation.

'I am not sure. There is something about this place that I cannot like.'

'Have you ever been here before?' Interrogation, distinctly now, and tension.

'No, never. And I do not think I would like to come here again.' Her hand tightened in his. 'Take me away from here, Guy. Now.'

Not obeying her insistent demand immediately, he put an arm around her shoulders, pulling her round to face him. Putting a hand under her chin, he looked full into her eyes, but there was nothing of the lover in his serious, intent look. 'If anyone should attempt to bring you here—refuse to come. If you are tricked into coming to this place, you must give me your solemn promise that you will not enter that house. Or I assure you, my dear Teresa, that however afraid you are now, I shall give you greater reason to fear.'

Releasing her, he returned to the horses and she followed, her mind in a whirl of fantastic speculation. As they rode back to the palace in silence, she thought over the curious episode that had started out so light-heartedly and ended on such a serious note. Was that his house? Was it a house that he used for assignations with Marie Besneval? What was in the house that he feared she would find out about? Curiosity began to penetrate her alarm. Without giving her any reason for forbidding her the house, he had told her that he would make her afraid if she entered. Had he the right under such circumstances to demand her solemn promise that she would not enter the house? Assuming that she would give the promise, he had not waited for her reply. That irritated her.

He was escorting her back to her apartments, for she had to attend the Queen, when they met Marie in one of the many galleries near the Queen's apartments. In the dull light which flooded the gallery from the many long windows, her skin looked sallow, and she wore an anxious, strained expression as she listened intently to the conversation of Charles Villiers and Richard Beauchamp. So absorbed was she in listening that she was unaware of the approach of the Duc and Teresa, and visibly started when Teresa addressed her.

'I am sorry if I gave you a fright.' Teresa was puzzled by her friend's manner and demeanour.

'You did not frighten me in the least,' lied Marie. 'I had not expected to see you. Should you not be in attendance on the Queen? I believe that she expects you.'

Speaking sharply and darting a wary eye at the Duc, her manner suddenly became brittle and artificial. 'I would ask your escort to Versailles, Duc. I presume that you return to your own house immediately.' With a shrill little laugh, she continued, 'But, of course, as I am not betrothed to you, I can scarcely be seen in your company alone—unlike Teresa.'

His face inscrutable, the Duc replied quietly, 'Neither is Teresa—yet. Certainly I will give you escort, for I believe that your friend Madame de Thiange wished to visit her attorney. Will you not join us for an early dinner, Villiers? Beauchamp? I should enjoy a comfortable talk with you.' A wary hope flickered in Marie's eyes, and her two companions looked surprised and gratified. 'I shall escort this young lady back to her apartment, and meet you in the main courtyard.'

Bowing ceremoniously to Marie, and less formally to Villiers and Beauchamp, the Duc walked away with Teresa. Warring feelings battled in her breast. On previous occasions she had felt that the Duc did not like her to associate with the personable Charles Villiers or the charming Richard Beauchamp, although they appeared to be his friends, so she was pleased to see that she had been mistaken. That something other than mere courtesies had been exchanged between himself and Marie, she was convinced. Had love sharpened her wits, or made her blind with jealousy? She could not decide. All she did know was that when the Duc raised her hand to his lips in parting salutation at the door of her apartment, she snatched it away, saying pettishly, 'I am sure I do not wish to keep you from such a pleasurable assignation, my lord Duc.' Going into her apartment, and closing the door with something suspiciously like a bang, she did not observe the Duc's lips twitch into amusement.

Stripping off her riding habit, and washing hastily, she thought furiously over the curious events of the past couple of hours. She changed into a gown of pale lilac, with an underdress of flowered silk. She could make little sense of all that had occurred—only that there was some

relationship existing between Marie and the Duc. There
was little time for reasonable thought, for the Queen
expected her at any moment. If only there was someone
in whom she could confide! She dared not voice to the
Queen the terrible suspicions that were growing in her
mind. Briefly she thought of Henri Deschamps, but dismissed him as a confidant, for he was to marry Marie.
Not being of the Duc's high rank, he did not need to
gain royal approval for the marriage—they might be
married at any time. Besides, she was not yet used to
men, and, while she enjoyed their company, she did not
stand upon such easy terms of friendship, as did Marie.

Patting the last charming curl into place, she felt ready
to leave for the Queen's apartments. She must hurry—
if the King and Queen did not share much in taste and
inclination, they shared a love of punctuality.

As she left the apartment a small page almost collided
with her.

'My mistress bids you take a dish of coffee with her
when you have done with the Queen.' Breathless, and
pulling at crumpled hose, he looked a comic sight.

'I should be delighted, I am sure, but—' She did not
have time to finish her sentence, for he was departing
with as much haste as he had arrived. 'Wait! I do not
know who is your mistress.'

Stopping his run with a slight skid, he turned and
called, 'The Marquise de Montespan,' and hurried
around the corner before Teresa could once more recall
him.

Why should she not accept? Because she had reason
to dislike the governess, there was no reason to be equally
suspicious of the mistress. The Queen had spoken kindly
to her, and the Marquise had seemed grateful to her on
the dais—perhaps she wished to thank her privately. It
would be churlish and mean to refuse. After all, had not
the Duc taken Marie to dinner? Did he not expressly
invite her?

Also there was the question of that curious little house,
a smaller replica of his own Versailles house, in the forest.
Without explaining why, he had commanded her never

to go there, and, should she be tricked into going into the forest, on no account must she enter the house. If the Duc knew that she was likely to be tricked, then he must know the identity of those likely to perpetrate such an action. These thoughts did nothing to add to her happiness.

'Your reading has improved, Teresa,' the Queen complimented her. 'I do so love the sound of your voice; it is very clear and sweet.' After listening to her reading for some time, while she quietly sewed, the Queen eventually stopped her. 'Perhaps you would be good enough to look at the list over there on the table near the window? My ladies have helped me prepare a list of those suitable to be asked to your betrothal ceremony. You can tell me if there is anyone you would particularly like to be invited, and I can tell you if the person is suitable, for we do not open the gates to the people of the town until much later in the evening.'

Teresa gasped when she saw that the list contained the names of the most notable families and houses of France—besides princes and their princesses, there was every other rank of the aristocracy, even princes of the church. Her eyebrows raised and her mouth forming into a rounded surprise, she saw that the name of the Marquise de Montespan appeared.

'You look surprised, Teresa. What is the cause?' enquired the Queen gently.

Teresa blushed in confusion, for she had not wished to appear to question any person on the list, as to do so was to question the Queen's choice. 'It surprises me to see the name of the Marquise de Montespan on the list . . . she is——'

'The King's official mistress,' the Queen finished her sentence for her. 'And as such she must have a place on any Court list.' With her grave, sweet look tinged with compassion, the Queen continued, 'She is much to be pitied, and I do pity her, the poor creature. For, while I remain the King's wife and my position is secure, a mistress can only hold her position for as long as she holds the King's attention. The reign of a Queen is for all her life; the reign of a mistress is brief, and usually ends unhappily.'

Teresa had never considered the matter in that light before, and saw that the Queen was right. 'Just before I left my apartment to come here today, a page of the Marquise was sent to ask me to take a dish of coffee with her. Would you object if I attended?' It was with relief that Teresa was able to ask for this permission, which felt more in the nature of a confession.

'One must always keep appointments, Teresa.' There was gentle reproof in the Queen's voice. 'If there is ever doubt, then the invitation should not be accepted in the first place.' Carefully studying the embroidery, which was a new altar cloth for the royal chapel, the Queen continued, 'you will be able to tell me if the Marquise enjoys her customary good health. I believe that she has not been quite well since her last confinement.'

'Confinement? Do you mean that she has only recently had another child?' Why she should have been astonished, she could not tell, for the Marquise had already borne the King several children. But that he should be willing to abandon his mistress so quickly, and at such a time, nauseated her.

As though guessing her thoughts, the Queen repeated quietly, 'The Marquise is much to be pitied.'

What was the Duc doing now? Teresa wondered as she left the Queen and made her way to the other end of the palace, to the apartments of the Marquise. Deep in thought, she barely noticed the lovely sculptures, paintings and furniture that she passed, and was only conscious of a blur of gold, shining mirrors and ornate carvings. Like the apartment of the governess, it was all overpowering. The apartments of the King's mistress were a lovely contrast, being large, airy, full of light and delicate colour, warm without being stifling, and fragrant from the many bowls of pot-pourri.

The page who answered her knock led her to a small chamber off the large room into which she had been shown. A statue of the Blessed Virgin reposed on a marble table, surrounded by lighted candles; before this

statue knelt the Marquise, dressed in celestial blue, head
bent, praying. Remaining thus for several moments, as
though unaware of Teresa's presence, she blessed herself,
then rose and, backing away from her little altar, turned
to greet Teresa.

'Greetings, Mademoiselle Rochefoucourt. You find
me at prayer; I had not been expecting you for another
while, and I always pray at this time.'

So youthfully fresh was her lovely complexion, so
sparkling her beautiful eyes, so trim her figure, that it
was difficult to remember that this woman had borne
the King several children and was almost as old as him.
There was a sweet, childlike appeal in her smile as she
asked Teresa to accompany her to the nursery, as she
begged leave to show off her new baby. How could Louis
treat this poor woman and this dear little baby so
shamelessly? thought Teresa as she bent over the crib
and looked at the chubby-faced baby, deeply asleep, a
pink fist curled, little mouth puckered. Experiencing
a longing to hold the baby, she would have asked the
Marquise, but already the woman had turned away, a
smile, doubtless of maternal pride, on her face. Reluc-
tantly, Teresa straightened up. The baby looked adorable,
and smelt of peaches, and she wondered what her child,
the child she would bear the Duc, would be like. How
much she had changed! Marvelling at such a change, she
was pleased to discover that she no longer hungered for
pretty clothes and diversions in quite the same way as
she had a few weeks ago.

'What a lovely baby. How happy you must be!' Teresa
burst out with unfeigned envy.

'That is our seventh child, and Louis thinks all our
children adorable.' The Marquise looked demure in her
celestial blue.

Teresa began to think that the stories she had heard
about the Marquise's gambling, her wild extravagances,
her open contempt for anybody she did not like, must
surely be exaggerated. Instead of the images conjured
up by the unkind gossips, she had found a pretty, domestic woman, as pious as the Queen, and doting over her

baby. Perhaps this was the confidante she had been searching for? Would she dare confide in the King's mistress, and seek her advice?

Following her into the large *salon*, and sitting opposite her on a comfortable velvet sofa, Teresa observed again the youthful features of Athénaïs de Montespan. She seemed to radiate goodness and purity, and Teresa was reassured about the rightness of her presence here—also, the Queen knew and approved of it. Accepting a sweetmeat from the little silver dish on a table at her elbow, she prepared for the Marquise to speak first.

Leaning forward confidentially, the Marquise's lovely face assumed a very serious expression. 'You may wonder that I have summoned you this afternoon, for I know that you serve the Queen. But I have had some disturbing intelligence, and wish to ask you about it. For you must know that the Queen and I have the King's welfare very much at heart, and would do anything to protect his good name.'

Alarmed at her ominously serious tone, Teresa was doubly impressed by her mentioning that, like the Queen, she had Louis's welfare at heart. 'What have you heard, Marquise?' she asked, with a good deal of trepidation.

'That you took part in a ceremony of black magic, in order to discover the events of the future,' the Marquise told her bluntly.

Deathly pale, and feeling as though someone had hit her very hard in the stomach, Teresa gasped, as though for air.

'You did, did you not?' Gentle words and sympathy touched chords of new understanding in Teresa's maturing consciousness.

'Yes, but I did not know what it was about! It was not until afterwards...I swear, Marquise, that I did not participate knowingly in such a ceremony. I thought it a game. Madame de Main——' Abruptly she stopped, unable to tell this kind and beautiful woman that it was her own governess who had administered the potion to her and used her in the ceremony.

Putting a hand to her mouth, her lovely eyes full of distress, Athénaïs de Montespan gasped. 'Never tell me that it was Madame de Maintenon! I cannot believe that I have been so betrayed. It is more terrible than I thought. The King will be vastly displeased, and, as the betrothed of the Duc d'Abbeville, you have placed your Duc in great danger. If he is lucky, he will go to the Bastille; if not, he will be executed.' Covering her face with her hands, she appeared to weep all the while, watching the appalled consternation make Teresa's shocked white face a mask of terror.

'What can I do?' she whispered eventually.

'I do not know.' Spreading her hands and shrugging helplessly, the Marquise appeared to be considering the matter. 'You could confess all to the King and beg his forgiveness.'

Anguished, Teresa cried out, 'But that places Guy, the Duc, in danger!'

'That is true. Sincerely do I beg that you tell me no more of this terrible matter, or I shall feel that, in honour, I have to tell His Majesty about it. Believe me, *mademoiselle*, I had expected that you would tell me this was all a nonsense. Then I thought all I had to do was to tell you to be more careful of the company which you kept; but now...' Again she spread her hands and shrugged.

Such advice had Teresa only recently received from the Duc; so much did the King's mistress appear to have in common with those she loved and respected that Teresa decided she must be a thoroughly good woman.

'I think I might have a solution to your problems. My confessor is due to arrive quite soon—he is a priest from the town of Versailles, and I could perhaps ask him to hear your confession. Then you could ask his advice. I know that he will give you sound counsel. But I beg that you tell me nothing.'

Presently, after some strained conversation about herself and the Duc, and affairs of the Court, the Marquise's confessor arrived—a distinguished, middle-aged man of quiet demeanour and aristocratic manners.

If he was surprised that the Marquise should ask him to hear Teresa's confession, he did not betray it.

'I should be honoured, *mademoiselle*. If you would care to come to the Church of the Redemption in the Avenue du Vieux Versailles, tomorrow afternoon...?'

'I think that *mademoiselle* would like you to hear her confession today, father. She is to become betrothed on Saturday, and will have many things to do tomorrow.' The Marquise indicated the small room where she had her altar. 'You could be private in there.'

The priest bore a strong resemblance to the much older man who said mass at the convent. Teresa told him this, and asked if they were related.

'Père Dubois is my uncle, a most worthy man,' he responded quietly. Inclining his silver head, and folding his hands in prayer, he bade Teresa kneel before the little altar. 'I shall hear your confession now, *mademoiselle*.'

As the priest incanted the words of the blessing, Teresa felt immeasurably reassured. It was also easier to make this particular confession facing the altar rather than the priest, for how would such a holy and distinguished man view what she had to say?

'Before I can give you absolution, *mademoiselle*,' he said quietly and unemotionally when she had finished, 'I believe that you must tell me of all the circumstances leading to your betrothal, for if matters were honourable, then you would not have been tempted into seeking ungodly means to discover your future.'

Haltingly, she related all the circumstances leading up to her betrothal. Hardly daring to look around at first, when she had told him everything, she eventually forced herself to look at the priest, now seated at a small table near the window, deep in thought.

'As a penance, for I must hold you culpable, you must set down in writing all that you have related to me under seal of the confessional. It will be locked away in the Church of the Redemption, and on my death I shall give orders for it to be burned. In the meantime I shall keep it as a reminder to you that you have transgressed the laws of God and man, and if I should hear that you are tempted to revert to your previous ungodly pursuits, then I shall remind you that under the seal of the confessional you vowed to forsake them. For I shall ask you to set down your willingness to renounce all dealings with Satan.'

Crossing to the doorway, he summoned a page and asked him to bring writing materials as they were needed urgently. Of the Marquise, there was no sign. Placing the writing materials on the table, he bade Teresa sit at the table and commence her writing. Besides practice with her reading, Teresa had also been writing whenever she had moments between her duties to the Queen and the various social events that she frequented. Now she could write quickly and proficiently. She was about to write her renunciation when the priest, who had been hovering behind her and watching her still somewhat painstaking efforts, detained her hand.

'Will you affix your signature to what you have written, *mademoiselle*? Then, on this separate piece of paper, you may renounce your sins. That is the proper way to write such a thing. There, that is right. Now, if you please, your renunciation.' He took up the confession and, reading it through briefly, folded it and put it in his pocket. 'Ah, I see that you have finished. Good. Now, if you will kneel again, I will pronounce absolution.'

It was with a feeling of profound relief that Teresa received the absolution. It had been good to unburden herself to someone as wise as the priest, and she felt her spirit lighten. How fortunate that he had happened to be visiting the Marquise on the very afternoon that she, too, had been a visitor! She was fortunate indeed.

Some moments later the Marquise floated into the room, a vision of maternal pride and loveliness as she carried her baby in her arms. 'Père Dubois, I bring my little baby for you to bless.' A trimly clad nursery-maid hovered in the background. '*Mademoiselle* I know, will excuse us. Thank you so much for your very pleasant company. Do say that you will come to see me again, very soon. Look! Baby has taken a great liking to you—

see the way he smiles! Give him a little kiss before you go.'

In the face of so pretty but comprehensive a dismissal Teresa could scarcely have stayed, even if she had wanted to. Bending to kiss the baby's deliciously soft cheek, she experienced again the strong desire to pick it up and cuddle it. Soon, perhaps very soon, she might have a baby of her own. Departing with these happy thoughts, she tripped lightly across the palace to her own apartments.

'Do pronounce blessing on my baby, Père Dubois. You see how good a baby I have—am I not a fortunate woman?'

The blessing completed, the Marquise handed the baby back to the waiting nursery-maid and summoned the page to bring wine and cakes. Murmuring quiet commonplaces, they nibbled cakes and sipped wine. Starting suddenly, the Marquise noticed that a lilac reticule lay on the table by the sofa. Calling over her page, who was standing near the door, she handed him the reticule. 'Run after *mademoiselle*, quickly, for she has left this reticule behind.'

As the door closed behind the page, the Marquise dropped her gentle manner and regarded the priest with eyes that gleamed with excited speculation. 'Well, Père Dubois, what do you have to report?'

Raising his eyebrows, his aristocratic face haughty and disdainful, he looked displeased. 'Would you have me break the seal of the confessional, Marquise?'

Rising swiftly and going to sit beside him on the sofa, she placed one arm around his shoulders and began to lightly caress his face. She was all feminine softness, yielding body and perfect complexion, and he was no proof against her wiles: with a wicked smile erasing his dignified expression, he took her wrist and lightly kissed it.

'I will give you the confession.' He stood up. 'I warn you, you will not like it, but do not vent your anger on me, my pretty, for I know you of old. Just remember

that it was you who wished to know of these matters.'
Handing her Teresa's confession, he prepared to depart.

Snatching the piece of paper from him, the Marquise
began to scan the lines eagerly. A sardonic smile twisted
his features as he watched her expression change from
almost childish glee to chagrin, then finally to a con-
torted rage. 'She lies! She lies!'

As his wicked smile faded into lines of dissolution,
Père Dubois said, 'No, she does not. That was obtained
under what she believed to be the seal of the confessional. There are still some left, my vicious little
Athénaïs, who are uncorrupted, and that girl is one of
them.'

Her anger made the Marquise's voice come in a
strangled whisper. 'She shall die for this. There will be
no wedding, for I vow that there will be no bride.'

CHAPTER EIGHT

GASTON rubbed his hands with glee as a heavily laden travelling carriage drew up outside his inn; a liveried servant leapt down and demanded from a waiter if this was Gaston's. A heavily rouged face peered irritably from the interior of the vehicle, and beside her sat a vision of loveliness that almost took Gaston's breath away. Stifling an urge to rush out and greet these visitors, he waited. Fine feathers, he had learned, did not always make fine birds. Grandiose they might be, with a couple of carriages behind carrying the servants and baggage, and with clothes and jewels that would pay a King's ransom, but that did not mean that they could or would pay his bill. Having tired of listening to his nephew, a page to Montespan, relating all the latest Court gossip, he decided that he would stroll out in a few minutes and see what they wanted.

'But, Uncle, you have not heard the best bit. You recall Père Dubois...'

But the visitors had mentioned the name of the Duc d'Abbeville, a powerful name indeed—powerful enough to move Gaston from his gleeful contemplation of them to wish them enter his humble abode.

'Later, boy, later. You see that I have illustrious guests.' Two minutes later, bowing from the waist, he was ushering a very tired old lady and a very radiant young one into his best private parlour.

'You are Gaston after whom this appalling hovel is named?' the elder demanded in a querulous voice, addressing some spot between his eyes. 'Bring me some tea. No food, I cannot possibly eat anything. The roads from Provence are simply dreadful; I am sure that every bone in my body is broken. You may offer my daughter something, and send your wife to attend her. No, no,

132

this parlour will not do at all, there is not a comfortable chair—and is that dust on that table?' Pausing this alarming recital to fix her gimlet eye on him, he rather felt that between the eyes had, after all, been preferable. She looked meaningfully and dreadfully at the offending table.

Running over to the table, Gaston dusted it with his long white apron.

'You may change that apron before you attend on us again. Adelaïde, sit down and stop fidgeting about. Where is my maid? Lazy creature.' She addressed thus a spare little woman, who was toiling in with mountains of dressing-cases, jewel-cases, rugs, pillows and cushions. 'Really, Sophie, must you make such a song and dance over everything?'

Removing the loose coat of light silk that she wore over her heavy brocade gown, she handed it to the wretchedly laden Sophie, who had to drop a cushion and rug hastily in order to accept it. 'Have you received a message from the Duc?' She whirled about to admonish a young guard who had travelled with them. 'What does he say? Does he expect us? Why is he not here?'

As the guard had not yet had time to depart with the message summoning the Duc to the presence of the Duchesse Marie-Victoire San Rémy, he could hardly be expected to have returned with an answer. Duchesses of the order of Marie-Victoire were not deterred by such trivial considerations, and she looked without pity at the gulping young man, who fled before her fierce glare.

'I think, Mama, that you would find this chair tolerably comfortable. Do try it, it is far more comfortable than that one.' The vision pointed to a fine chair with a soft seat and straight back. 'That is the one I am going to take.'

Without a word, only a snort of some sort, the Duchesse immediately took the other chair, and the vision's eyes twinkled in amusement.

Phew! thought Gaston. At least one of them is not going to be impossible to please.

Adelaïde, Comtesse Souvré was, at twenty-six, in the very flower of her loveliness. Even at sixteen, when the Duc d'Abbeville had fancied himself so desperately in love with her, she had been a remarkably pretty girl. It was a tribute to the fierce, mercenary, demanding Duchesse Marie-Victoire that she had not forced her youngest, and by far best-loved, daughter into a marriage with the wealthy Duc, their nearest neighbour. Instead, she had permitted her to marry her childhood sweetheart, Albert St Quentin, Comte Souvré, close friend of the Duc and later his companion on military campaigns. Although the marriage had never been blessed with children, it had been blissfully happy until the Comte's death, a year earlier, on the Dutch campaign. That the Duc had made valiant but unavailing efforts to save his friend was widely known, although he never spoke of them.

The wily old Duchesse, unable to relinquish the dream of seeing her daughter become Duchesse d'Abbeville, and leader of all society in Provence, had waited until her year of mourning was over, then declared that they would sojourn at Versailles for a few months.

Eyes twinkling with amusement, Adelaïde had smiled affectionately at her transparent mother. 'Dear Mama, are you still hoping to promote a match between myself and Guy? I assure you it will not do, for I am sure that we have nothing in common any more. His was a youthful infatuation——'

Mama interupted her, snapping, 'Did he not go to rack and ruin with grief? I am sure I must have heard a dozen times that he fought duel after duel in an effort to get himself killed, tried to dissipate his fortune, and ran after every married woman who would have him. And there were plenty, by all accounts.'

Settling herself more comfortably in her chair, and watching her parent with loving eyes, the younger woman smiled gently. 'I cannot help thinking that he only did what pleased him, for you know he was always headstrong. Albert always told me that he was the best of friends, and the most intrepid of soldiers. As you know, my Albert did not always like his military duty—indeed, he often said that if it had not been for Guy, he would not have had any fun at all away from me.'

'Well, I dare say that we may have received exaggerated accounts. As to your thinking that I wish to promote a match between yourself and this reprobate, you are mightily forward! I never thought of such a thing,' lied the Duchesse brazenly. 'You might marry where you choose, if you've a mind to.'

'I shall, Mama. Now, let us not talk of this matter any more, for I wish to enjoy myself while I am here. Perhaps the Duc will not be able to accommodate us. It might be as well to ask the patron——'

'Not accommodate us?' screeched the Duchesse. 'After we have been jolted over hundreds of miles of miserable excuses for roads! Of course, he will be pleased and honoured to accommodate us. He has a house here— what use can a single man have for a house, pray, if not to accommodate his friends?'

Adelaïde reflected that it was just as well that the rumours concerning the Duc were probably greatly exaggerated, or she could think of several good reasons why he could not accommodate them. The arrival of Gaston, followed by what appeared to be his entire staff, brought them fuel for the fire, loaded trays containing every sort of genteel refreshment, and several bottles of red and white wine.

The Duchesse started to cough in a greatly affected manner before the first stick had been kindled, waved away three parts of the food, declaring it to be barbaric and inedible, and accepted a glass of wine with a look of acute suffering. Soft moans replaced the querulous voice, and she did, Adelaïde noticed, begin to look very fatigued. Closing her eyes, she leaned her head against the high wooden back of her chair. Sophie, attempting to place a cushion behind her head, was berated for her pains.

Adelaïde murmured to Gaston, 'Perhaps you have a room where the Duchesse could lie down——'

'Not in this hovel!' rudely interrupted her mama, very much awake all of a sudden. 'I cannot be expected to lie in a bed inhabited by the riff-raff of Versailles—not even to gratify your whims, Adelaïde.'

Bowing until his nose scraped the floor, Gaston uttered, 'I assure Her Eminence that only the very highest rank of person is permitted——'

'I am not Your Eminence, and, barring the royal family, there is not a higher rank than mine in France. Be gone, you sleek rascal, with your smiling face and villainous ways!'

Gaston, with his anything-but-smiling face, withdrew and sent out a waiter to enquire if the Duchesse's guard had found the Duc at home. For all his shrewdness, Gaston was not a villain—he was as honest a man as was likely to be found keeping an inn in Versailles. Nevertheless, he decided that he should add a few *livres* to the Duchesse's bill to account for her rudeness. Great pains had been taken over the hasty repast prepared for the Duchesse—not to pander to her high rank, but because she had claimed the notice of the Duc d'Abbeville. With relief, he saw that the Duc himself was striding into the inn. Hurrying forward, he almost forgot to bow, so great was his relief.

Grinning, the Duc patted Gaston on the shoulder. 'Giving you a difficult time, is she, Gaston? Do not worry, my friend, I am here to spirit her away; for unless she has changed very much, she has turned the place upside down and driven you all to despair.' Pausing by the door to the best parlour, he grinned again, sympathetically. 'I shall settle the Duchesse's account, and do not forget to add a few *livres* for the trouble that she has doubtless caused you. No, do not announce me, for I am not sure what sort of reception I shall get.'

As he returned to his supervision of the dining-rooms and kitchens, Gaston could not help thinking, as he had thought on many other occasions, that the Duc represented all that was finest about the aristocracy; there was an openness about him, a willingness to understand his inferiors and treat them with dignity and respect, and, above all, an ability to extend the hand of friendship to all. At that moment Gaston had not felt as though he were an innkeeper, despised by the aristocracy, often treated little better than a dog, despite the fineness of his inn and the superb food and service he offered—he had felt like a man, for the Duc had exchanged a perfect and amused understanding with him. I would serve him, and gladly, thought Gaston, and not count the cost. His dignity restored, his demeanour now calm and unflustered, Gaston explained to his ruffled wife that an accurate bill would be made up for the Duchesse, with no extras added.

'If you're in that good a humour, you can serve those people—aristos I will not call them—who are demanding your finest dinner. They are in the private room on the first floor—the one at the back of the house. And, priest or no priest, I do not like Père Dubois.' Shuddering, she hurried away while Gaston, forgetting about the Duc and the Duchesse, began to rack his brains, trying to recall where he had heard mention of Père Dubois before. Someone had been telling him something. Oh, well, he thought, it was probably of no significance.

Holding Adelaïde's hand for a long moment, the Duc looked into her calmly smiling face, where unshadowed friendliness blossomed like a breath of fresh air, and remarked again, 'You have grown lovelier, Adelaïde. I will not ask you both if you enjoyed your journey, for I am sure that it was most uncomfortable.' Kissing both her cheeks, as he had previously saluted her mother, he added, 'I cannot tell you how very welcome you both are to Versailles——'

'It is for Louis to welcome us to Versailles, popinjay, not you.' Marie-Victoire was not ill-pleased by the reunion between the pair—if there was nothing loverlike in Guy's demeanour, he was clearly delighted to see them both. She could have wished that the welcome he gave her daughter was more distinguished than the one given to herself. As it was, she must suppose that he had acquired some Court manners, and she liked him for it.

Despite her display of ill temper, she was glad that the
Duc wished them to remove to his own house immediately, for she did wish to lie in a comfortable bed and
sleep away the fatigues of the journey. There would be
time to propose the match dear to her heart later.

The gown that Teresa thought she would wear for her
betrothal ceremony was the gown that she had worn to
the King's reception on the evening that he had announced the betrothal.

'I think not, Teresa,' the Princesse d'Elbeuf explained. 'Rarely is the same gown worn twice at
Versailles. It would be proper to wear something that
befits your approaching station. You could wear the underdress—that is really beautiful—and perhaps an overdress of silver?' Circling Teresa, she inclined her head,
deep in thought. 'Do you know that your little Celeste
is really a very good dressmaker? Why do you not ask
her opinion?' Nodding happily at her suggestion, she
smiled her kind, vague smile. 'You could go this afternoon—a page will accompany you. The Queen has a
music lesson this afternoon, and will not need you to
read to her. Although after your betrothal you will be
expected to be present when she receives the duchesses
and cardinals each evening. You might think of ordering
some gowns suitable for that.'

Summoning a page, she bade him accompany Teresa
into the town and wait for her outside Celeste's establishment until she should have finished. 'And do not
think to slip off into one of the inns, or I shall hear of
it and have you punished. I charge you most strictly to
escort *mademoiselle* there and back.'

The page, a lanky boy of good family, nodded sulkily.
Squiring *mademoiselle* to the dressmaker's was not his
idea of an afternoon's sport, but when the Princesse
d'Elbeuf was not fussing amiably about the Queen's
quarters she could be very sharp-witted indeed, and never
failed to report any transgressions. Supposing that he
would be required to carry any number of parcels and
boxes, he hoped that he did not meet any of his fellow
pages, who would doubtless make game of him. Still,

he liked Mademoiselle Rochefoucourt—she had a merry smile and graceful ways, and she always remembered to speak to pages with kindness, thanking them for any small service performed, unlike many others he could name, who thought of pages as servants. They were the *nouveaux* who knew no better.

Teresa's friendly manner and infectious good spirits soon caused the page to lose any lingering shyness he had of her.

'I am fourteen,' he replied in answer to her query. 'My family sent me to Versailles a couple of years ago, when I was twelve.'

'Do you enjoy life at Court? It must be very dull when you are too young to attend the balls and banquets,' she commiserated.

'It will be very dull when I *do* attend,' he said feelingly. 'You can have no idea of how boring it is to stand beside a buffet all evening, helping to serve food. We have a much better time in Versailles town.'

'Do you serve the Queen?' Teresa could not recall seeing the boy very often.

Revolted, he replied instantaneously, 'Lord! No! Pages serve the King. But I delivered a message to the Queen's apartments, and when old d'Elbeuf—oops! Sorry, *mademoiselle*. Please do not report me, I meant no discourtesy, but the Princesse d'Elbeuf can be a holy terror.'

Teresa tried to disentangle this speech and conjure up a vision of the Princesse as a holy terror, and dissolved into chuckles. 'Do not worry, master page, I shall not report you—although you do the poor Princesse a disservice, for she is the kindest of souls.'

They had fallen into an easy and companionable way of talking, and Celeste's establishment was soon reached without either being conscious of the passage of time.

'I shall wait here for you, *mademoiselle*,' the page told her, all the while looking not at Celeste's doorway, but longingly up the street to where a group of pages had entered Gaston's.

Taking pity on him, Teresa spoke quickly. 'If you would like to go and buy a glass of wine,' she fiddled about in her reticule for some money, 'I expect I shall be at least an hour.' Thrusting the money into his hand, she did not wait for thanks, but hurried up the stairs to Celeste's room of business.

An hour later both young women were highly satisfied with their business. Teresa had agreed to Celeste's suggestion of an overdress of lace upon lace, layered in a lovely confection.

'You are so slender, *mademoiselle*, that it will look divine. You will look like a flower from the fields—nature will not be able to compare with you.' Clasping her hands, the girl allowed her eyes to travel heavenward, as though lost in this thought.

'I see that you have not wasted much time in learning some of the more foolishly extravagant phrases of Versailles. I am almost disappointed in you, Celeste.' Teresa was surprised to find that she spoke rather tartly, and forgot that a few weeks ago she would have found nothing extraordinary or displeasing in such a remark.

Dismayed, Celeste flushed and stammered an apology. 'Pray, forgive me, *mademoiselle*, if I seemed to exaggerate, but I feel that it is true. Everyone praises me for my fine dressing of you, and they crave that I make them exactly the same sort of clothes. Even the Marquise de Montespan desired only this morning that I make her an exact replica of some of your gowns—is that not an honour?'

Vague doubts about the Marquise greeted this innocent pronouncement, although Teresa was aware that she ought to feel flattered.

'But your friend, Mademoiselle Besneval, told her not to worry, for she would tell her just which gown to have copied. But truly, I was not exaggerating, for it is *you* who make my poor gowns. When you wear something, you do so with joy—it makes each gown come to life.' Seeing that Teresa appeared deep in thought and was not really listening, Celeste hesitated, feeling that she had said something displeasing, but could not imagine what. 'When do you require this gown, *mademoiselle*?

It is more intricate than any other I have made for you, the lace will need to be——'

Cutting short her sentence, Teresa looked at Celeste in astonishment. 'Why, it is for Saturday, of course—for my betrothal ceremony. Forgive me, Celeste, but you must have understood that.'

'Your betrothal? But I thought that there was to be no betrothal,' Celeste stammered, looking mystified.

'What can you mean? Make yourself plain!' Teresa spoke sharply, for she had had enough of mysteries.

'But . . . Mademoiselle Besneval and the Marquise de Montespan . . . I am sure that they said that there was to be no betrothal.' Biting her lip and looking thoroughly apprehensive in the face of Teresa's blank amazement, she continued. 'This morning, when they were here, I heard them talking. They said, very clearly, that there was to be no marriage between you and the Duc. If there is to be no marriage, then what point is there in having a betrothal, *mademoiselle*?'

Concealing the mingled alarm and anger, Teresa managed to smile at Celeste. 'I expect they were talking of someone else. You misunderstood, did you not?' Gathering up her things, and looking again at the patterns that Celeste had drawn, she tried desperately to gather her confused thoughts.

'Oh, no! I am sure that——'

She did not allow the dressmaker to finish, but looked at her very steadily. 'I am sure that you were mistaken, and that you will not repeat what you have heard, for I assure you that it is untrue.' But can I assure myself that it is untrue? she asked herself. Feeling quite unable to face the street, she went to the window, trying to steady her voice and nerves, for the words had given her a very unpleasant shock.

'Does this window open? I would like to see if the page who is to escort me back to the palace is here yet, for I do not wish to wait about in the street.'

Flying to the window, Celeste tugged at it, glad to perform this small service, for she had seen shock and then dismay register on *mademoiselle's* face. Cursing herself, she vowed that in future she would pay more attention to the advice given her by her estimable mother, who had told her never to repeat anything she heard. Cultivating discretion was as important as cultivating her craft; she must never forget. Never, she vowed, would she forget that again. In later years, when she became one of the most famed dressmakers in all France, picking her own clientele, she was to become as renowned for her discreet nature as her great skill.

Peering down into the street, glad of some air to cool her hot cheeks, Teresa looked for her errant page. No sign of him, she thought with exasperation—perhaps the Princesse d'Elbeuf was right to be so strict with all the underlings. Craning her neck to look along the street to the inn, she received another shock that almost caused her to topple from the window. The Duc was emerging from the inn, looking strikingly handsome in a coat of deep burgundy, with a long waistcoat of dark cream brocade, soft leather riding-boots covered shapely legs, and he was smiling and laughing in a way that made her heart turn over.

Looking completely relaxed and unaffectedly happy, he was gazing down into the face of a truly beautiful woman, doe-eyed and with a complexion of damask. Never, thought Teresa miserably, had he smiled at her like that; never had he looked so happy or gay in her company. Who was the raven-haired beauty who leant on his arm with such familiarity? Closing her eyes against the sight which gave her a stab of pain so real that she put her hand to her bosom, as though to quell it, she withdrew from the window, and therefore did not see the Duc turn with equally happy courtesy to an older and far less lovely lady, whom he handed tenderly into the waiting carriage.

Leaning against the window-sill, she felt blood pounding in her head, and the pain of jealousy and betrayal tear her apart. Strange emotions, devastating and painful, filled her, and she had no weapons with which to fight them. Who was the woman? Was she one of the women that he took to that little house in the forest?

Certain that she had never been present at Court, Teresa decided that she must be one of the women of the town that Marie and Charles Villiers often spoke of so slightingly.

Many courtiers, anxious not to incur the King's displeasure by involving themselves in light love affairs in Court, kept women in the town. It was all very discreet, for such women were never permitted to enter the palace. That the Duc should have such a woman appalled her; yet, she said sternly to herself, why should she be so surprised? Why should she have imagined that he had not needs like other men? He had made it plain that he could not tolerate the thought of marriage with her—she was young and stupid. This woman was nearer his own age, and looked as though she had his affection as well as his interest.

Was that why the Marquise de Montespan and Marie had avowed that she would not marry the Duc? Recalling the little scene in the gallery, when they had met Marie and Charles Villiers with Richard Beauchamp, Marie had said that unbetrothed, she could not venture alone with the Duc. He had replied that he and Teresa were not yet betrothed. For some reason she had remembered that remark. Now, a thousand small disquiets and misgivings merged into a well of fear that he would not want her, that something would happen to prevent the betrothal.

'Would *mademoiselle* like me to fetch her a glass of wine?' Celeste had become alarmed at the pale face and agonised expression. What on earth had she seen that had caused it? Curiously, she went to the window and looked out. Nothing there to cause such alarm, and was that not a Versailles page standing at her door? 'Are you well enough to leave, *mademoiselle*? Your page awaits you. Or would you prefer to sit a while and have some wine?'

Gathering her emotions together, Teresa made a supreme effort at normality; she even managed a tiny smile. 'I am quite all right. Thank you for your consideration, Celeste, but I should like to leave now.' Drawing a deep breath, steadying her voice, she tried to sound light-hearted. 'You will send the gown to the palace by Friday, will you not? For I will wish that any alterations to be made are made on that day. I wish to look my best for my betrothal ceremony.'

The page leapt to attention as she stepped out into the street. The air felt humid now, rather than cool, as though a storm was brewing. Perhaps it was the headache which had begun to throb behind her eyes, or perhaps it was her imagination, but she thought that she saw a distant flash of lightning. That the page had spent his time drinking wine was obvious from his flushed, grinning face, and she was obliged to bite back a stinging remark. It was unfair to offer him friendship when she was in sunny humour and withdraw it because life was now bleak in all its aspects.

'Are we close to the Avenue du Vieux Versailles?' she asked the page, who had begun to lope along beside her in an effort to match her hurrying, agitated footsteps.

Women! he thought disgustedly. An hour ago, she had been a cheerful companion, now she had a face of thunder. Probably her dressmaker had not got her gown ready, and she was ready to murder someone. Oh, well, better humour her. The Avenue du Vieux Versailles was where her Duc had his house—she probably wished to take shelter there, for, unless he was much mistaken, there was a mighty storm brewing and they would never reach the palace without getting drenched. The Duc was a great favourite among the pages—he would always give them a chance to exhibit their newly learned skills in fencing or hawking, without making them feel as though they were raw and clumsy, unlike some others he could mention.

Guiding her across the street, he turned first down one street and then into another, until they reached a quieter part of the town, where all the houses had been finished and where the air of refinement was pronounced. They had almost reached the Duc's house, but she appeared not to notice for her head was bent as though in deep abstraction. Seeing that she was about to pass by the courtyard which separated the house from the Avenue, he took her arm and led her into the Duc's Versailles domain. Raising her head for the first time, she saw with swift, alarmed comprehension that they stood before the Duc's house. Turning a look of amazed enquiry on the nonplussed page, she said, 'We are at the Duc's house! Why did you bring me here? I wished to go to the Church of the Redemption.'

At the back of her mind she must have known that the Duc's house was situated here. Was that why she had felt a sudden need to come here? In her mind she thought of the comfort and counsel that Père Dubois could give her: of course, argued her heart, you really came here to see if the Duc had brought his mistress here, did you not?

'Church of the Redemption? What church? I do not know of any church here. You must mean the Church of The Holy Family, but it is at the other side of the street that we left over there.' He pointed back in the direction from which they had come.

Her brain reeled. 'You must be mistaken. There *is* a church here, I know there is. Let us find it!' Suspicions too horrible to contemplate began to assail her frightened mind. Maintenon, Marie, Montespan—like a dull, dread rhythm the names echoed again and again through her brain. The air was heavy and the light faded quickly. The page stirred uneasily beside her, turning to go. A sudden flash of lightning illuminated the sky and the scene within the room to the left of the front door of the Duc's house. The Duc, *her* Duc, stood there, and in his arms was the lovely, doe-eyed creature he had escorted from the inn.

A roll of thunder directly overhead made the page jump, but Teresa was too numb with pain and shock to care. The creature wound plump, loving arms around his neck, and he bent his dark head to hers. A sheet of rain fell with such violence that she recoiled, but mercifully it obliterated that dreadful sight. Impossible now to see him kissing another, although she knew the feel and taste of his mouth and wondered that the tumult of emotions his touch had caused were still with her, mingling with her pain and shock. Blindly, she turned and ran from the courtyard. She would never, ever again allow him to touch her, but that thought brought no comfort, either.

CHAPTER NINE

'I NEVER had the chance to thank you for all you did for my Albert, Guy.' Adelaïde smiled mistily up at the Duc. 'I know that you never talk of it, but it was very important to me to know that he died with such a very old and valued friend beside him.'

Putting his arms around her, for it seemed the natural thing to do, he spoke quietly. 'Your husband died a soldier's death, Adelaïde. It was my privilege to be with him. He spoke of you all the time, said that he wished you to marry again.' Smiling into her eyes, with a slightly rueful twinkle, he continued, 'He suggested that I might marry you. But I do not think that idea would appeal to either of us, *hein*?'

'Of course it would not, although it is certainly in Mama's mind.' She chuckled. 'The idea of another marriage appeals to me. I was happy with Albert, and I believe that if one is happy in marriage, one expects always to be happy in marriage. But not you and I, my dear.'

'As a matter of fact, I have not yet had time to give you news—I am to be betrothed on Saturday. It was all very sudden, thrust on me by strange circumstances...' He gave a small shrug.

Quickly comprehending that there was some mystery, she looked anxious. 'Are you happy, Guy?'

A warm glow in his eyes, a curious little smile on his lips, he replied, 'I believe that I am going to be the happiest man in the world, Adelaïde.'

Warmth and relief rushed through her tender, romantic being, and, putting up her hands, she embraced him and kissed him on either cheek. 'Then I am happy for you, for, unless I am mistaken, you are in love?' she queried, a gentle smile on her full mouth.

147

Returning her affectionate salutation, he released her. 'I think I am, Adelaïde.' He grinned boyishly. 'And with the most unlikely girl in the world. She is seventeen, a merry little scamp, bent upon enjoyment, always in some scrape or other, and if she had any notion of the behaviour expected of a duchesse I should be as pleased as I was delighted.'

'This is wonderful! That is the very wife for you, Guy. You are too used to having your own way. Every woman you meet tries so hard to impress you that you take everything for granted.'

Drawing the curtains against the storm, and summoning a servant to make up the fire, he regarded his friend thoughtfully.

'You are all very well informed in Provence,' he remarked drily.

Laughing, she responded with a twinkle. 'That you are called the Wicked Duc is known the length and breadth of France. Come,' she patted the sofa beside her, 'tell me all about your scamp, for I long to hear all about my new neighbour.'

'I have been thinking that you may be of some help to me,' he began slowly.

'Naturally, I should be delighted.'

'The doubts I have about her—this is strictly between ourselves—is that she is inclined to keep the wrong company.'

Thick, dark eyebrows rose in disdained surprise. 'Good heavens, Guy! Never tell me she is bourgeoise!'

With an impatient gesture, he dismissed this suggestion. 'No, she is well-born. But she has this exasperating habit of believing anyone who will pay her an extravagant compliment.'

Concealing a smile, Adelaïde attempted to speak gravely. 'But, my dear friend, all women respond to compliments. I see what it is—you have grown old in your conceit, and have not set out to woo her.'

With a shade of reserve crossing his darkly handsome features, he stared into the rekindled fire. 'She actually said that she did not wish to marry me because I was too old and too boring.' Grinning ruefully, he glanced at his companion. 'Can you imagine what that did to my self-esteem? I have always cherished the idea that the sort of girl I marry would not require pretty, artificial compliments, but would take me for myself alone.' There was self-mockery in his voice, and she was touched, despite her rising irritation, that such a clever man, such a success with women of all ages, could be so stupidly blind.

'It seems to me, Guy, that Mama could not have chosen a better time to visit Versailles, for I can see that I am meant to be immensely useful to you.'

The page hurrying after Teresa thought that she had gone mad. Here it was pouring from the heavens, they were already soaked, *mademoiselle's* silk dress was clinging to its swaying hoops, her thick bunches of curls were plastered to her head, and her soft shoes were already waterlogged, but still she maintained that crazy run.

'There must be a church here. There must,' she repeated again and again.

Wearily, he paused. 'I tell you, *mademoiselle*, that there is not. You have run up and down this avenue a dozen times, and must have seen for yourself that there is no church.'

While he could understand her distress—for he, too, had seen the Duc kissing that woman, and he pitied Teresa—it was pointless to run about in the rain-sodden streets, getting drenched. Already the streets were turning to rivers of mud, there appeared no cessation of the cloudburst, it was cold, and he could feel the rain penetrate to his skin. A page was expected to act correctly on all occasions, but Louis's father had omitted, when writing the detailed instructions governing the behaviour and education of pages, to mention just what a hapless page should do with a demented woman in a rainstorm. He was seriously contemplating going back to the Duc's house to beg his assistance when deliverance, in the shape of Charles Villiers, appeared. Like most of the pages, he disliked Villiers' smooth, cruel tongue, but he was prepared to set aside his dislike, seeing that the man had stopped his carriage and was assisting *mademoiselle* into it.

'Are you escorting this lady?' he asked the page.

'Yes, sir. We were returning to the palace, but we got rather wet——'

'I can see that, my good fool. As you are so soaked already, a little more rain will do you no harm. You may walk, or run, back to the palace. I am sure that the exercise will do you good. There is no need to report that you failed to protect *mademoiselle* adequately, for doubtless she will be warm and dry and restored to the Queen before you have even reached the palace.'

Cursing him silently, the page bowed his thanks and started to walk through the sheeting rain to the palace, glad that, at any rate, *mademoiselle* was rescued.

Inside the coach, Marie Besneval was wrapping Teresa in a fur cloak and murmuring words of soothing comfort, while exchanging glances of amazement with Charles Villiers. It was obvious to both that her distress had a cause far beyond the soaking she had received, for through the raindrops hysterical tears coursed down her cheeks.

'There, there, *chérie*, do not weep. Can you not tell me what is wrong with you? I am your dear friend, and would so much like to help you.'

Teresa forgot that she had heard the most disturbing news of Marie only half an hour ago, forgot that Marie had declared herself in love with the Duc, yet was preparing to imminently marry another; she could think only of the comfort brought by Marie's words. 'I hate him! I hate him!' she blurted out hysterically. 'He has betrayed me. I will never marry him, never!' There was such vehement conviction in her voice that she amazed her hearers, who began to exchange looks of guarded hope.

'Charles, it is not possible that we take her back in this condition—it would cause too much comment. We shall make a little diversion, and Teresa can dry herself and be more composed. Later we shall return.' Nodding meaningfully, and holding his glance for a long moment, she returned to her soothing of the distressed girl.

'So quickly?' he murmured quietly, so that only Marie caught his words.

Nodding again, this time with determination, she replied, 'Yes, today. It must be done today.'

Banging on the roof, he gave the coachman fresh orders, and sat back on his seat opposite them, a satisfied smile playing about his mouth, a speculative gleam kindling his blue eyes. From time to time he passed his tongue over his lips, as though in pleasurable anticipation of some dark and secret treat in store for him.

When the coach stopped the rain was still driving in torrents, so Teresa could not see where they were, and when Marie bundled her from the coach into a dark porchway she had no idea where they were. For a wild instant she thought that they must be in the forest, but dismissed the idea as preposterous. Marie unlocked the door of the house, which appeared to be deserted, and they entered; Charles Villiers did not follow immediately, for he was giving fresh orders to the coachman, who lumbered off into the gloom and rain.

While Marie pushed Teresa into a small bedroom, Charles Villiers set about the task of kindling a fire. Shivering, Teresa looked about the small room. It was richly furnished, and there seemed to be a great quantity of religious objects. This reassured her, for she had had a moment of ridiculous doubt when entering the house. They were probably on the outskirts of the town—she could not tell how long they had been in the coach, she was too distressed.

Now, cold and wet, she was glad that Marie was assisting her from her soaked garments. It was necessary, of course, to take everything off, for every stitch she wore was soaked through, but she felt a qualm of apprehension, for Charles Villiers was on the other side of the door, in that large room into which they had stepped. She had the impression that they were the sole occupants of the house. Vigorously towelling her naked body, she felt life begin to flow again in her frozen veins. How strange that there were no servants, for whoever owned this house was clearly of the class and financial means to keep a staff. The bedposts were carved with birds and animals, vines and flowers; the wall coverings were made of silk, and the tasselled curtains were of heavy wine-coloured velvet. Feeling her feet sink into a deep carpet, she glanced down to find that the floor was covered with thick white fur—unimagined luxury!

Bending over a carved chest of antique design, Marie lifted its lid and took out a folded white garment. Shaking it out, she handed it to Teresa. It was a thin white gown, very straight and simple of design—rather like a nightgown, although made of much thinner and finer material. As she slipped it over her head its soft folds caressed her body, and Teresa shivered with delight, for it felt warm.

'I shall go and make you a *tisane*, for you are chilled to the bone, and I am very much afraid that you have taken a cold.' Taking up Teresa's wet clothes, she opened the door.

Involuntarily, Teresa put up her hands to shield her body, for Charles Villiers was in the next room, she recalled. What had startled her more than that was the realisation that Marie had hardly spoken since they had entered the house. She had probably allowed Teresa time to collect her scattered wits, but now Teresa realised that the house was abnormally silent. Even the lighting of the fire had been accomplished with the minimum of sound. It reminded her of the convent, where the nuns would rise very early in the morning to go to the chapel to pray. Very occasionally she had also risen and crept silently to the chapel in the hour before dawn, yet that little journey for the purpose of prayer had been accompanied by the silent flutterings of the order; the air moved. Here it seemed to be as still as the grave. There was something wrong about this house, she thought to herself. Something that was not normal.

How foolish you are being, Teresa! she told herself sharply. You have had a great shock and, moreover, have been drenched and chilled with the rainstorm. Was it still raining? She could hear nothing, and the curtains were shut tight across the window, Marie had lit candles, and the light flickered around the room, yet the glow held no warmth, none of the accustomed comfort that candle-light normally brought.

Returning with a cup of steaming brew, Marie set it down on a table near the bed. Bending once more over the still-open carved chest, she produced a thick, fleecy cloak and draped it over Teresa's shoulders. Huddling into its warmth, Teresa sat on the edge of the bed, digging her bare feet into the fleecy snugness of the fur floor covering. Holding the proffered cup with both hands, she put it to her lips. It was delicious, with an aroma of oranges; the taste was sweet and heady.

She had almost finished the *tisane* when vague echoes of remembrance teased her brain. Where had she tasted that drink before? Was it on the occasion that the Queen had had a headache, and she had obliged to fetch her a *tisane* from the Queen's own kitchen? No. No, that had tasted of raspberries. With a slight questioning look directed at Marie, she began to frown. Could it be the same sort of drink that Madame de Maintenon had given her? Languor began to steal through her body. The bed felt soft. She longed to lie down and sleep.

'Marie, I feel so tired. Would you mind very much if I slept?'

Marie was all concern. 'You have had a very nasty afternoon, *chérie*, and you will feel much better directly; you must not sleep now. Wrap the cloak around you, and come and see the lovely fire that Charles has made. As soon as your clothes are dry, you must return to the palace. It would not be wise to sleep here.'

Striving to remember everything that had happened before when she had supped with Madame de Maintenon, Teresa was certain that the *tisane* that Marie had made for her was the very same, although not so thick and syrupy. Incautiously, she had drunk almost all of it. That she was in acute danger she did not doubt. That this was no ordinary house, she was now aware.

Under the influence of the potion, part of her memory cleared, and she now saw that Marie had been one of the so-called nuns. Her instinctive wish to acquit Marie had blinded her to that. Celeste's words returned, with a new and horrifying meaning. But what part did Charles Villiers play in all this? Surely he was a friend of the Duc? An ugly pattern began to form as the pieces of the picture began to fit together in her mind.

Was this the Duc's house? The one in the forest? That would account for the lack of servants and the lack of noise. Had he planned that she should die? Was that why Marie had been so certain that she would never marry the Duc? In honour, he could not withdraw from the betrothal, yet he really loved Marie and wished to marry her. Perhaps Marie had only accepted Henri's proposal in order to create a diversion from her true purpose.

Now Teresa felt an acute sensation of physical danger, although, curiously, the potion had given her a feeling of complete relaxation. Whatever happened next, she must not allow them to see that she was in any way suspicious. If she had been a gullible little fool to believe in their demonstrations of affection and friendship, then she only had herself to blame. Whatever happened she must stay awake and keep alert. Allowing her anger to grow, for that seemed an antidote against the potion, she thought of the invitation she had given to Marie to stay with them in Provence. While seeming to be glad, Marie must have laughed at her behind her hand!

'How kind of Charles,' she managed to say, while feigning to be much more sleepy than she actually was. 'I shall come out in a moment. Do go and thank him for me, and tell him how very grateful I am that he rescued me today.'

Looking uncertain, Marie hesitated, as though she would urge Teresa to come out of the bedroom. 'Perhaps you could rest for a few minutes; we shall not be ready yet.' Forcing a smile to her lips, her eyes still watchful, she quickly amended, 'That is, your clothes will not be dry for some time.'

'Is my gown quite ruined?' Teresa did not feel that she could too readily abandon her role of childish frivolity.

'No. I am sure that once it is washed and pressed it will be as new.'

How false she sounded! Why did she not ask her what she had been doing in the Avenue du Vieux Versailles? Surely that would have been quite a normal question to ask someone who had been discovered wandering distractedly in the street? No, obviously Marie had much more important matters on her mind. What did they have to wait for? What did they have to get ready? If only she could persuade her to leave the room, Teresa thought frantically, she would investigate the possibility of escape. Marie moved to the door and, opening it, had some whispered conversation with Charles Villiers. Teresa was sure that she heard him say, 'She must not sleep.' Why must she not sleep? Then more conversation, and Marie returned, shaking her head.

'It would be better if you came out to the fire; Charles is very much afraid that you will catch a bad chill.' Attempting to smile in her old coquettish way, and failing miserably, she continued, 'Think what your Duc would say if he thought that we had allowed you to become ill.'

That hypocrisy nearly turned her stomach, and, putting up a hand to her mouth, Teresa managed to gulp, 'Quick! A bowl! I am going to be sick!'

In a flash Marie had gone, an expression of extreme trepidation on her face. Quickly rising from her improvised seat on the bed, Teresa ran to the window and pulled aside the curtains. In dismay she looked at the shutters securely excluding the light and a way of escape, for these were the sort with the bars on the outside. How very unfortunate. Now she was sure that she was in the Duc's house, for she recalled that she had seen the shutters, and noticed that the bars were all in place on every window. No escape was possible from the window. She would have to try to get out through the door. It should be easy, there was only Marie and Charles Villiers.

Somehow she must try to get as close as possible to the front door.

Going to the door, she put her hand out to open it, intending to go into the large room and say that she felt much better and would like to sit by the fire, when she heard Marie speaking in an urgent voice.

'You must not hurt her! I will not have her hurt. Do you understand?' There was a soft, unpleasant laugh from Charles Villiers. 'Squeamish, Marie? I had not suspected such womanly concern from you.'

'What if the Duc should find out?' Marie sounded frightened.

'My good friend the Duc d'Abbeville will know all about this day's work by tomorrow morning. I want him to find out.'

'I do not understand you at all,' muttered Marie.

And neither do I, thought Teresa in despair. All her reasonings were overset, for if Marie was not party to this escapade, then what was she doing here? Marie was worried that the Duc would find out; find out what? Charles Villiers had said that he wished the Duc to know what was going on. It was all so confusing. Who was that woman that the Duc had held in his arms? His mistress? thought Teresa savagely. He probably brings her here. Glancing at the bed that a moment ago she had thought so comfortable, she saw that this was where he probably brought her, and found that she could not contemplate the thought without feeling a torrent of jealousy and rage. Comfortable! It was the most hideous bed that she had ever seen. Why, even those carvings were all wrong!

Taking the candle from the table beside the bed, she held it closer to the carvings. Intertwined in the fruit, flowers and leaves were animal figures—monkeys with the faces of babies, but with such evil expressions that she recoiled, as though stung. Into her mind flashed the fruitless search for the Church of the Redemption and the hideous fears and suspicions that had made havoc of her thoughts ever since. The lovely domestic picture of the Marquise de Montespan faded and merged into the pious respectability of the priest. A priest without a ministry. It had all been a fraud; she had been duped.

With sickened fright, she recalled that she had signed a confession—a confession that would incriminate the Duc. To what purpose would these people use that confession? The Duc, the Queen, and she, Teresa would all be discredited. One tiny piece of knowledge, a little piece of information, caused joy to spurt through the black fog—the Duc did not know of her presence here. That he was to be informed meant that he was not party to whatever was going to happen here.

Her joy gave her courage. They must think her incredibly stupid! How very easily she had allowed herself to be led into this trap. But somehow she must find a way out. Her confused thoughts could be sorted out later. Charles Villiers had said that the Duc should know all about the affair in the morning—was she to be kept here overnight? Villiers, she determined, would tell the Duc nothing! She would seek him out herself and demand explanations. It was imperative that she did not allow her muddled emotions to blind her to the truth. If the Duc was involved with these people, and had a mistress in Versailles, she wanted to know about it.

Her features schooled into a semblance of gaiety, Marie opened the door and faltered only slightly as she spoke to Teresa. 'I see that you do not need this bowl now, you look much recovered. Were you coming out to join us?' She was a trifle suspicious, obviously wondering if Teresa had overheard her hasty consultation with Charles Villiers.

'Yes, I was. I feel so much better now. That *tisane* has restored me wonderfully. But I am cold and would like to warm myself.' Stepping past Marie, who looked apprehensive despite all her efforts, she went out to face Charles Villiers.

A huge fire burned brightly in the hearth, illuminating what was a much larger room than she had at first supposed from her brief glimpse on entering; but then there was only the fading light from the outside to show a comfortably furnished apartment. It seemed as though this was a central room, and several others opened off it. Of a flight of stairs there was no sign; she had thought that she might make an excuse to get up-stairs and climb out of a window, but that route of escape was denied her.

With his hands behind his back, smiling urbanely, Charles Villiers invited her to sit on a high thronelike chair beside the fire. It was rather like the chairs that Their Majesties used on the dais in the great ballroom of the palace. With a jolt, which she managed to conceal, she saw that all the furniture resembled that reserved for Their Majesties' exclusive use in the palace. Stifling her repugnance, for she had always liked Charles Villiers, and believed that in his heart there was a special place for her, she smiled in response and took the offered chair.

The chair was so high that her feet didn't quite reach the ground, and, holding them out to the blaze, she began to feel a threatening lethargy overcome her. Perhaps it would be well if she feigned sleep. She could then ob-serve everything that occurred, and watch for a chance to get out of the house. In one corner of the room there was a curious table. It was higher than an ordinary table and looked more like—what? She could not for the moment recollect—the *tisane* had fuddled her wits and her memory, so that ordinary memory would not function, and the things she was able to think about only concerned events that she wished to put from her mind, but they kept returning with startlingly unpleasant clarity: Madame de Maintenon, Père Dubois, the Duc's anger on hearing from his aunt, the Abbesse, that he would have to marry her. If the Abbesse had not been an aunt of the Duc, she would already have appealed to her for help and guidance. How nearly she had been tempted to confide in the Marquise de Montespan! Of course, she thought with dull despair, Père Dubois must by now have given her details of the confession. Perhaps not—perhaps she had been mistaken in thinking that he had said the Avenue du Vieux Versailles. Knowing that that was where the Duc lived, perhaps she had thought only of that address.

Hope flared briefly, but she was too muddled to think clearly. In the background Marie was moving about, taking things from cupboards and chests, laying them on the small table beside the large, high table. It was too much of an effort to turn her head, and, in any case, she did not wish to alert Charles Villiers that she was suspicious.

'I have not thanked you for your kindness, Charles.' Coaxing her features into a sleepy smile, she looked up into his face. How strange that she had never noticed that he was so much older than she was; always the soul of wit and courtesy, he had seemed curiously ageless. There were strange lights in his blue eyes as he looked down at her—a gloating look.

'It was a divine pleasure to be in the fortunate position of rescuing you, Teresa. You can never know what exquisite pleasure it gave me. May I betray curiosity and ask you what you were doing there?'

'I had been with my dressmaker, and when the rain started I was seeking shelter.' There was something hypnotic in the stare he gave her. Words became increasingly difficult to utter; it was as though he looked past her mind and into her soul. Summoning her courage, she continued. 'I had some thought of returning to Celeste's, but somehow mistook my direction, and then the rain was blinding, and . . .'

Pursing his lips, he tilted back his head as though considering the truth of her statement. 'Just so. That would be how it happened.' Looking down at her again, this time his stare more intent, so that she found it difficult to look away, and was only dimly conscious of Marie laying things out on the table in some disturbingly familiar pattern, he spoke. 'You were telling us in the carriage that you hated someone. Who was it? For you must know that we are all extraordinarily fond of you, and would wish to punish anyone who caused you distress.'

With a supreme effort she managed not to show her alarm; there was deadly intent beneath the surface courtesy of the words. 'My foolish page—he led me in the wrong direction, and my gown, as you can see, is quite ruined. But I beg you will not punish him—he is but a boy, and I am sure that he thought he was in the right direction at the time.' To her credit, she even appeared light-hearted.

There was a muffled knock on the door—three times—a pause, then the knock was repeated. Charles Villiers went to answer the summons. As soon as his back was turned Teresa turned to Marie, about to beg her assistance. The words froze on her lips as she saw with horror that Marie had been preparing, on the small table, an altar. It contained black candles, and the crucifix, large and with a beautifully carved figure of Christ, was inverted. Marie, as though reading her mind, shook her head, her face a mask of piteous, frightened appeal. If Teresa was a prisoner here, then so, too, was Marie.

Prisoner! Why had she thought of that? Why had she not asked to leave? Because Charles Villiers wanted her for some despicable purpose of the black arts, replied the logical part of her brain. Dread lay at the pit of her stomach; a lost hope faded into dust. Père Dubois came into the room, shaking the rain from his long cape, setting his rain-soaked hat on a receptacle near the door—looking at her with the same gloating expression she had caught in Charles Villiers' eyes a few moments earlier.

'Are the others here?' He spoke to Charles Villiers without taking his eyes from Teresa.

'Not yet, but I have summoned them—they are on their way. We should be ready to begin in half-an-hour.'

Walking to the fire and spreading his long, thin hands gratefully before its cheerful blaze, he smiled thinly. 'Good. Then let us have a glass of wine. What pleasant weather we have for our little enterprise, Charles.' Through the shutters they could all hear that the wind had risen to a long, wailing moan—the roaring of wind through a mighty mass of trees was unmistakable.

'How nice to see you again, Père Dubois. You have not chosen a good day to travel—or do you seek shelter, like us?' Teresa marvelled that she was able to speak so normally.

The priest was in the act of accepting a glass of wine from Charles Villiers. His hand stilled for a fraction of a second, and he looked from beneath his brows at her, as though seeking intent behind her innocent words.

'You may not be aware that this is something in the nature of a homecoming for me, *mademoiselle*.' What an ideal tool for their purpose, he thought exultantly. Was it possible that she was unaware of what was about to happen? Had she not guessed the significance of the altar now being prepared? So much the better. 'Charles, you do not offer *mademoiselle* a glass of wine. How very remiss of you. You must think us tardy hosts, Teresa. I may call you Teresa, may I not?'

There were three more muffled knocks on the door, and with baited breath she waited for the next three knocks—it must be some sort of signal. As Charles Villiers went to open the door yet again, the priest poured some wine into a glass and handed it to her. Over its rim she saw the Marquise de Montespan enter the room and sweep into its centre, followed by Richard Beauchamp and several men and women of the Court whose appearance was familiar to her, but whose names eluded her at that moment. Despite their rain-sodden appearance, they exuded the vitality of suppressed excitement.

Teresa realised that the room had a spacious appearance because the centre of it had been cleared of furniture. Apart from the thronelike chair on which she was sitting, every other item of furniture was pushed against the walls, revealing a chalk circle drawn on the floor.

Removing her hat, and pulling off her gloves, the Marquise looked questioningly at Teresa and then at the priest.

'*Mademoiselle* is delighted to be with us, Athénaïs. She has professed her delight at being able to shelter here. Are we not all fortunate?'

A ripple of mirth ran among the group of people, who were similarly engaged in divesting themselves of wet outergarments and taking glasses of wine from Charles Villiers. Of Marie there was no sign.

Handing her empty glass to someone standing near her chair, Teresa pretended to be very sleepy. Allowing her eyelids to droop shut, she made much play of the pretence of striving to stay awake. A buzz of conversation ran around the room; it seemed full of excited talk and bursts of stifled laughter. Tilting her head back, she closed her eyes almost shut, then, controlling her breathing to feign sleep, Teresa allowed her mouth to fall slightly open. It did not, in fact, require much effort, for she felt fully the effects of the potion and the glass of wine. Whatever happened, she must not fall asleep; she must stay awake. Whatever chance she had had of escape before now, it would require every bit of wit and ingenuity to escape from a room containing at least a dozen people—all of whom seemed bent upon some purpose involving her person. That a black mass was about to take place was now beyond doubt.

Wine was being poured freely into glasses, more logs were added to the fire, and an atmosphere of unbridled glee, corrupt and impure, permeated the room. The careful Court masks were gradually replaced by lewd expressions, as the men and women exchanged pleasantries that brought a blush to Teresa's cheeks. Desperately she hoped that anyone watching her would assume that it was the heat of the fire—so intense was the heat that she had to still herself from flinching.

An incense burner was lighted and suspended by its long chains from a hook on the ceiling. Pungent incense mingled with wood-smoke—how that smell evoked, powerfully, earlier memories of mass in the convent chapel. Happy and innocent days when, bored with the tedious repetition of the mass, she would day-dream—day-dream of the time when she might be allowed to come to the palace of Versailles. The great palace of the Sun King, where she would meet and captivate the Wicked Duc, where all her tomorrows would fuse into the glorious fulfilment of girlhood dreams.

'When the others return we shall get ourselves ready, Villiers.'

'Can we not leave her? She is asleep. I have your garment ready.'

One minute, thought Teresa, that is all I need. Just one minute, and I shall be gone from this place.

Hope was dashed by the priest's reply. 'Better that someone should stay with her; it is vital that she be present, if only half-conscious, for the invocation of the spell.'

Spell! What was this? Was she to be subjected to the same torment as she had endured at the supper of Madame de Maintenon? Knowing that she could not bear it, she almost cried out; for she knew that her own future was terribly bleak, and dreaded to catch another glimpse of what could only be her humiliated unhappiness.

'Can you trust Marie Besneval?'

'Assuredly, Dubois. The fair Marie dare not disobey me now, or she loses all hope of a marriage with Deschamps.' He gave an unpleasant laugh, soft and sinister. 'Although the little fool still believes, I think, that the Duc will marry her.'

'Then she does not know what we plan?' The priest was amused. 'That we plan to put Rochefoucourt's body in the Duc's house and have him accused of her murder? No, she does not even guess. She actually fears that we may hurt her little friend, although I marvel that she has the effrontery to change her opinion so swiftly, for I could have sworn that a mere week ago she would have welcomed such a plan for her rival.' Sneering in the direction of the room into which the women had disappeared, he continued, 'women are so very unreliable.'

Following his glance, Dubois nodded. 'That is what makes them such excellent accomplices. Always they must commit some little indiscretion, and it plays absurdly on their weak minds. In order to avoid detection, they will usually agree to almost anything. Montespan is different—I almost admire her, for she knows what she wants, and will use any means to attain it. Though why she should have conceived such a violent hatred for the little Rochefoucourt is beyond my comprehension.'

Throwing back his head, his smile more like a grimace, Villiers laughed again. 'She feared that the King was about to transfer his attention there, and, to make matters worse, she was obliged to appear grateful to her for rescuing her from a very unpleasant predicament in the ballroom.'

'Not being permitted to enter the palace openly, I could hardly be expected to know of that.' There were undercurrents of bitterness in the priest's voice.

'That will soon be remedied, my friend. D'Abbeville will be faced with threat of exposure. He will be accused, or at least implicated, in the death of his betrothed—her confession gives him some cause; he can then join us, or take responsibility. He loves his position too much to give it up. He will join us; I am confident. Then, when we have taken power, you will come to Versailles as a Cardinal. How will you like that?'

'Very much,' purred the priest. 'Although how you will achieve that, I am not sure—a defrocked priest is hard to reinstate. And d'Abbeville? How will you deal with him afterwards?'

'Him?' Villiers spoke carelessly. 'He will be disposed of. I have a fancy for his estates—Provence has long been a favourite with me.'

Teresa's brain whirled and a sickening myriad of pictures swam before her eyes. The only thing she could hold on to was that in her vision in the apartment of Madame de Maintenon she had thought that a bridal had just occurred, and was convinced that it was the Duc, so at least he would be safe. Possessed of a sudden fierce desire to protect him, even if he had betrayed her with another woman, she determined to tell him of the plot against him. In revealing her own, albeit unwitting, part in the sordid affair, she must renounce all claims to marry him. If the Abbesse would have her, she must return and take the veil, for there was no other life open to her.

With eyes that sparkled with unnatural animation, and talking in high, excited voices, the men and women returned to the central room. They all wore black cloaks, and as they moved into the circle Teresa could see that they wore little beneath them. Deeply shocked, and closing her eyes against such a distasteful spectacle, she also tried to close her ears against their bawdy comments and hateful camaraderie.

After a few moments, there was absolute stillness in the room. She could hear them moving, and was lightly touched on the shoulder. So unexpected was the touch that she jumped, and her eyes flew open and looked with awe at the sight of the priest, clad entirely in black and holding an enormous sword in his hands, standing in the centre of the circle. There was something terrifying in his face—it held an expression of power, satanic and evil. Incanting loudly, the men and women stood back until they were in a ring at the extreme edge of the chalk circle.

Raising the sword high in the air, the priest held it motionless in a straight line above his head. Calling out in a high, unnatural voice, he began to invoke alien names. Circling and swaying, he began to describe the shape of a star in the incense-laden air, which was filled with the fever of the fanatic.

Teresa became conscious that she, too, almost began to chant, and thought for one wild moment that she would leave the suffocating heat of the fire and join the circle. Remember that you are the intended victim, she reminded herself. If anything happens to you, you condemn the Duc to death. To save him, you must save yourself. Think of something else, her frantic brain told her. Unbidden, the words of the first prayers that she had ever learned rose to her lips. As she murmured them now, they acted as a talisman against the evil in the room. Gradually her mind cleared and she lost the urge to join the circle.

The priest stepped out of the circle, having first laid down the great sword. The satanic disciples fell silent, assuming attitudes of torpor, their mouths hanging

slackly open, their eyes feverishly bright. They crowded
close to Teresa, uncaring that their cloaks swung open,
conscious only of their bestial delight. All eyes turned
to her, and she shrank back in her seat. But it seemed
that nothing was to happen yet, for a gold chalice was
taken from the altar and filled with wine. Passing it from
mouth to mouth, they drank deeply. Several times it was
refilled, and then Teresa noticed that Marie, swaying
drunkenly, was one of their number, her earlier trepidation now replaced by a look of such utter debauchery
that Teresa was shamed and sickened on behalf of her
erstwhile friend.

They were absorbed, and Teresa knew that her chance
to escape had come. Leaping to her feet, she seized a
tall black candle and, whirling about, thrust it into the
priest's face, then at his black vestments. Surprise registered, then an ugly snarl of anger, but he was powerless to do more, for his garments had begun to catch
fire. Fleeing to the door, Teresa had a momentary
glimpse of those in the circle. They watched her with
stupefied amazement. Did they really think she would
sit like a dumb little ninny and wait to be led like a lamb
to the slaughter-table? They would hardly follow her in
their present condition, and Dubois, his vestments in
flames, had work to do to save his skin.

Wrenching open the door, she pulled it shut behind
her as firmly as she could, and began to run. The forest—
for she had been right in supposing that she was in the
little house in the forest, though she no longer cared to
whom it belonged—gave vent to a mighty, primeval roar
as it again attempted to resist the great storm which
threatened its existence.

CHAPTER TEN

PULLING up the thin gown which clung to her like a second skin, Teresa ran through the forest. Dim grey light filtered through the branches which waved like giant, demented hands over her head. Wind tore through her hair, and the rain, still falling heavily, blinded her. Whatever happened, she must find the Duc and warn him that the King's life and his own were in the gravest danger from those plotting against them.

The path, only barely discernible, had turned into a slimy quagmire and she slipped and fell headlong several times. Not daring to stop and look to see if she was being pursued, she ran on and on, her breath coming now in gasps as the effects of the potion she had taken and the fright she had endured began to take a toll of her healthy young body. If they should catch her she would surely die, for she had no energy to resist, and no more energy to run.

The shrieking of the forest in livid, agonised life made it quite impossible to properly distinguish the sounds around her, but she fancied that she could hear footsteps drawing closer and closer. It could only be Père Dubois, of the fanatical ambition and the corrupted morals—surely no one else would have had time to dress. That they must find her and kill her, she knew to be true, for when she told of what she knew they would all be as good as committed to the Bastille, and would probably be executed.

Something caught at the back of the flimsy gown and held her fast; screaming in terror, she tore frantically away, sure that it was the priest. He would hardly waste time in carrying her back to complete that macabre ceremony—it was more likely that he would kill her here in the forest and carry her body to the Duc's house. Life suddenly became unbearably sweet, and she desired to live. With one final twist she was free, and, stooping to pick up a stick, she determined to fight for her life. There was no one there! Breathlessly, she looked about, her eyes straining against the gloom. Bushes waved restlessly, leaves and twigs blew up into her face, branches swayed and inclined as though they would reach down and sweep her away into their leafy, tormented heights, but she could not see the priest.

Looking down at the ground as though he might be crouched there waiting to spring up at her, she saw that a piece of her white gown was attached to a trailing branch. It was a branch that had caught against her dress and held her fast. There was no one there; she was not being pursued. Laughing weakly with hysterical relief, she bent and picked up the fragment of cloth and held it against her face, tears of pent-up anxiety running down her face.

Her relief was short-lived, for she could distinctly hear the sounds of a horse moving through the forest. Merciful heavens! Why had she not thought of that? Of course they had not walked to the house, they had travelled by carriage—although in her flight she had neither thought of nor seen any horses or carriages. One of the men, probably Villiers, for he had appeared to act the part of the lackey, must have saddled one of the horses and now she was being pursued by a man who could move through the forest with a speed which could far outstrip her exhausted efforts. Standing quite still, she reasoned that she had an advantage—she could take paths that horses could not enter. But, in plunging wildly, she had quite lost her bearings—she might wander for hours and never find her way back to the path which would lead her to the Duc's house. With little alternative, she again began to run, trying to find denser and denser parts of the forest in which she might find concealment.

Clasping the stick tightly in her hand, for it was her only weapon, Teresa darted to and fro, uncaring when trailing branches tore at her clothes and body, scratching her cheeks and arms so that she was unsure if blood or rain ran down them. Surely she must by now have evaded those pounding hoofs?

Surrounded by dense undergrowth, she stared about, fully alive to the feelings of a hunted animal. Never again, she vowed, would she hunt. On sunny days, in company with a great crowd of others, gaily clad and in high humour, she had followed the hunt. On the way back, carrying the kill of the day, its limp, bloodied body slumped over the back of a packhorse, they had sung and congratulated themselves. Often they had picnicked, lounging at their ease in shady arbours. Had the stag any of her desperate feelings? Did the hunted animal have this primitive longing to live?

If she stayed crouched in the dense undergrowth she would die of cold; she must keep moving. Pushing her way free, she began to limp along a defined pathway. Her feet were beginning to sting, and one ankle hurt her unbearably. Thinking her way was clear, she tried to hurry. There were lights in the distance—she could not tell if they were from the palace or the town, but either way they represented safety and normality. Behind her she heard the unmistakable beat of a horse's hoofs, and, throwing a terrified look over her shoulder, saw that a horse was bearing down on her.

'Guy! Guy!' she called out again and again, as though summoning some magical talisman to her aid. Her flight was useless, for a great, sweating horse slithered to a halt at her side. A rider leapt to the ground and began to pursue her. Without the energy to run on, and with only the frantic desire to save herself, she determined not to be taken without a fight. Strong hands clasped her shoulders and she whisked around, the stick clasped in her hand, and, raising it, dealt her assailant blow after blow full in the face. The stick was snatched from her hand, and her shoulders were being shaken, not ungently.

'Teresa! Teresa! It is me, Guy. You are safe from harm.' Pulling her into his arms, the Duc d'Abbeville caressed her for a moment.

Scarcely allowing herself to believe that it was really the Duc, she drew back and stared into his face. She saw dark eyes, arrogance, a firm mouth and chin. Collapsing into his arms, she allowed her emotions to overcome her and broke into wild sobs. Incoherently she tried to tell him what had happened, but he was kissing her and would not let her speak. Gradually she became calmer, and allowed him to wrap his cloak around her shivering body with loving hands.

'I am taking you home; you may tell me everything later. Do not try to talk now—you are overcome, and exhausted.' Thus quietly and gently he talked all the way back to his house. Sitting before him on the horse, she became conscious of his body pressed close to hers, of the lean muscularity and the enormous strength, of the gentleness of his arms as they held her securely. Safe, safe, safe, she thought over and over again as the horse moved through the forest, and she could feel the blessed beat of his heart and feel his face close to hers.

Deeply refreshed, she awoke to a glorious day. Remembrance instantly drove away the happy lethargy. Looking around the richly furnished bedchamber, she had not much thought for admiring the lovely wall tapestries or the elegantly carved furniture—or even for thinking that the room was decorated in her favourite shade of celestial blue. Sitting up, she discovered that she was wearing a finely embroidered nightgown—a woman's. To whom did it belong? Was it the property of his mistress? There were so many questions that he must answer. Was that house in the forest his property? If it was not, he at least knew of its existence and its purpose, for he had expressly warned her not to enter it. His aunt, the Abbesse, had told her that his close friend had committed suicide after some involvement with the black arts. Had the events taken place in that house?

They had spoken of forcing him to join them in a plot to overthrow Louis—they must have been sure that he would approve of their cause, and she had often seen him on the friendliest of terms with Marie Besneval, Charles Villiers and Richard Beauchamp. It was curious how they had all merged into one group—even the glorious Montespan—during that satanic rite. Convinced that such a circle would divulge their aims or purpose only to intimates, she felt that at one time he must have been one of their number. If all of these unpleasant speculations should prove to be unfounded, and in her heart she admitted that she hoped this would be the case, there remained the problem of the doe-eyed beauty.

The memory of her arms about his neck, and the loverlike manner in which he had bent his head to kiss her, remained imprinted in Teresa's mind. Wondering if he would come to see her, she got out of bed and crossed the expanse of floor to a large mirror on the wall. She was appalled at the sight which met her eyes: there were scratches on her face, just beginning to heal; her hair was wildly disordered, and the nightgown, which was much too large, gave her a small, waiflike appearance. Pale cheeks and darkly shadowed eyes added to this unlovely picture. It would never do to face the Duc with her accusations looking such a fright. Just why she felt it necessary to look as attractive as possible, she did not examine too closely.

A small chest, very modern in design and as beautifully carved and made as everything else in the bedchamber, reposed against the wall, sunlight drawing out the beauty of the woodgrain. Thinking it might contain a brush or comb, she pulled open the top drawer. No brush or comb, only a small painting in a gold frame. It was an unmistakable likeness of the doe-eyed beauty: creamy shoulders rose from a gown of dark red; a lovely throat and neck, surmounted by a face of exquisite sweetness, were framed by thick, dark hair. Across the bottom of the likeness were inscribed the words, 'My darling Adelaïde'.

Not caring any more about her appearance, Teresa fled back to the comfort of the bed and, burying herself in the pillows, wept without restraint. Here was something she could not combat! If she had had doubts about the love that the Duc supposedly bore Marie Besneval, and those doubts had been amply borne out by recent events, there could be no doubting this fresh evidence. No wonder he had spoken of 'other hopes'. Adelaïde—

detestable name, she hated it already—must have been his 'other hope'. Who was she? Men did lose their heads over their mistresses, and sometimes married them. That she was a trollop, Teresa was sure—otherwise, why had she not been presented at Court?

Without knocking, the Duc entered the bedchamber and paused on the threshold. He was deeply affected by the sight of the woebegone little figure sobbing so bitterly in that great bed. Assuming that her tears were a consequence of her dreadful experiences on the previous evening, he quickly hastened to comfort her. Pulling aside the bedclothes, he gathered her into his arms, and felt immediately an unexpected surge of physical longing so powerful that he was obliged to release her, afraid to add to her alarms, and certain that she would be in no mood to receive his passionate lovemaking.

When he had discovered Teresa was in danger, he had realised that he did love her—very much—and was surprised that love should have caught him unawares. Seeing Adelaïde again had probably had a great deal to do with it. Even after he had outgrown his hot, youthful infatuation for his lovely neighbour, recognising that in a limited society where a young man meets very few girls he is likely to make the first suitable girl a recipient of his budding desires, he had continued to fancy himself in love. Always at the back of his mind, whenever he had thought of a châtelaine for Abbeville, his thoughts had turned to a beautiful young woman with a plumply curvaceous body and a gentle smile. A woman well-read, of quiet disposition and few ambitions—other than to make her husband happy, and to administer her household.

At twenty he had fallen in love with sixteen, at thirty he had wished to fall in love with twenty-six; then Teresa had erupted into his life. By degrees, he had fallen in love with her without even realising it. When the page had come to his house and told him that Charles Villiers had taken her to the palace, he had been annoyed. Leaving Adelaïde and her mother, both of whom had wished to retire to bed after the exertions of their journey, he had set out for the palace, meaning to ask her why she had not sought his hospitality. Alarmed at her non-appearance, he had made enquiries and found that a messenger had arrived with summonses so urgent that Richard Beauchamp, Marie Besneval and several others had departed, driving out of Versailles in a howling gale.

Further enquiries had elicited the information that the Marquise de Montespan was not in her apartments, and would not be returning for a few hours. For several weeks he had had suspicions concerning Charles Villiers and Richard Beauchamp, and, while pretending to mis-understand their veiled comments about taking power from the monarchy, had cultivated their friendship. If he was to prove to the King that he was his loyal subject, then he must present him with the evidence of the others' culpability. From the very moment that Teresa had told him of the events in the apartment of Madame de Maintenon, he had been fully alive to the danger in which she stood. Cursing himself for a fool, he vowed that henceforth he would take the greatest care of her.

Supposing them to be at Gaston's, for it was a favour-ite haunt of theirs when they wished to plan secret business that they would not wish overheard at Versailles, he had ridden back into the town. Gaston was all apology.

'A large party from the palace? No, sir, there are only a few sheltering from the rain. You see over there, *monsieur* and his lady, lately arrived in Versailles—they keep telling me about their palace connections. Tcha! I do not believe them. That young buck, he is out of money, but I have taken pity on him, for he looks so sad that I believe that he must have lost his lady-love. Look, they all huddle around the fire as though they cannot bear to leave it.' All the while he had been talking, he had been darting looks at the anxious face of the Duc. There was something very much amiss. Dared he ask, dis-creetly of course, in what way he could serve the Duc?

'If your honour could tell me if there was anyone in particular that he was seeking, mayhap I could be of assistance,' he ventured finally.

'Do you mean that there *is* a party here? Tell me at once, for it is imperative that I know!' His harsh voice and thunderous expression convinced Gaston that this was some serious matter.

'Before God, I swear that there is not! I would tell you if there was anyone here. But I have ways of knowing things, things that others do not. Always in an establishment of this sort people are coming and going, talking and listening. Me, I listen and observe. I say nothing, but sometimes I wish to be of use to those, like yourself, who might need information.'

Brows drawn together in a deep frown, the Duc decided to trust Gaston. The man had spoken honestly. He had not talked of selling information. He had volunteered nothing. With each minute that passed, the Duc became more anxious. 'The young girl, to whom I am about to become betrothed——'

'A charming young lady, Mademoiselle Rochefoucourt.'

'—seems to have disappeared. Charles Villiers took her up in his carriage at about four of the clock this afternoon, supposedly to take her back to the palace. They have not arrived. I am anxious.'

That short, bald, final statement spoke volumes to Gaston. Men like the Duc did not feel anxiety or betray it, except on the most serious of occasions. That the Duc did not ask him to keep anything confidential, or threaten him with reprisals if he should talk, spoke highly of his judgement of men. Gaston was reinforced in his opinion that the Duc was a man above other men.

'About that, I do not know, but there is another matter.' Seeing that the Duc was about to become impatient, Gaston hastened to reassure him. 'I believe that it must pertain to Your Honour's affairs. My nephew is a page in the service of the Marquise.' There was no need to give her any other name—in Versailles, the King's mistress was universally known, in polite circles, as the Marquise. In less polite circles she had a variety of other, far less flattering ones. 'But I will let him tell you himself.

Please, wait here.' Hurrying away and calling loudly for Paul, he disappeared into the back region of the inn.

Paul proved to be a sharp-eyed, intelligent-looking boy of about twelve. With a face freshly scrubbed and hair newly combed, he stood stiffly before the Duc. 'I shouldn't tell you really, sir. The Marquise will be mad if she finds out, but I didn't think it right—that's why I told my uncle all about it.'

'Good boy,' approved Gaston, who stood behind him. 'But mind that you obey me, and tell not another soul.'

'I wouldn't dare, I would be in terrible trouble,' he averred frankly. 'Mademoiselle Rochefoucourt came to visit the Marquise the other day. She asked her to come— she sent me, I was to make sure that she came. But I knew something was wrong, because she put on a real show for your lady. Praying, she was when *mademoiselle* arrived. Then she brings her to see the baby and makes a great fuss. That's not how she usually is—she hardly sees the baby at all. The nursemaid, Bernadine, the girl from Burgundy——'

'Get on with it, lad. The Duc does not want the history of the Marquise's staff; he wants to know what happened,' his uncle admonished him.

'Well, after they had seen the baby and had some tea and——' Seeing his uncle's minatory eye on him, he rushed on with his narrative. 'Then they had a talk and *mademoiselle* was upset, and the Marquise called in Père Dubois——'

'Ye gods!' This time it was the Duc who interrupted him, and Gaston had the satisfaction of feeling that he had behaved correctly in summoning his nephew to the Duc's presence.

'And he heard *mademoiselle's* confession.' Paul quailed before the murderous look in the Duc's eyes, and looked beseechingly at his uncle.

Patting him on the shoulder, Gaston encouraged the boy. 'Carry on with your tale. The Duc does not hold you responsible for anything, but tell him you must.'

'Then he made her set it all down on paper. Oh, please, sir, don't look so angry; it was none of my doing. He just asked me to fetch the writing things.'

White about a hard mouth, the Duc felt as though he would like to take the Marquise's pretty throat in his bare hands and squeeze until life was extinguished from her body.

'They sent me on an errand, after *mademoiselle* with her reticule, but I didn't go straight away—I waited a bit, because I remembered then that Père Dubois was an unfrocked priest, and I couldn't understand why *mademoiselle* should want to make her confession to him. But I did hear him tell her that his church was in the Avenue du Vieux Versailles, and it was called the Church of the Redemption. Then he gave the confession to the Marquise. That's all I know, sir.'

'Thank you, Paul.' Taking a coin from his purse, he would have handed it to the boy, but Paul shook his head and refused.

'No, thank you, sir. I only told you because I thought it right, and because I like Mademoiselle Rochefoucourt. We all do.'

'That is a truly noble gesture, Paul. It is greatly appreciated.' Averting his eyes, and looking past the uncle and nephew, he remained lost in thought for a few moments. 'I believe that you may shortly be in need of a new employer, Paul. There is always a place for you in my house—just tell my steward that I have spoken to you.'

'Would today be too soon, sir?' Paul spoke eagerly.

'I believe you would get rather wet, and I would not wish to have someone in my household dying of a feverish chill. Tomorrow morning will do just as well.'

With a feeling of growing apprehension, the Duc thought that he knew just where Teresa was—in that house of Satan in the forest. If those devils had harmed her in any way, they would die, one by one.

Accepting a fresher and sturdier horse from Gaston, and a change of cloak, for his own was in a sorry state, he had set out for the forest. Long before he had reached the house, which was hidden among the trees, he had seen the frantically running figure, and judged by the time that she must have spent there that nothing very much had happened to her. But those villains had meant to use her as a means of getting at him; they should be punished for that. By what means had they tricked her into entering the house? Had they used her confession against her? Poor little Teresa, what could have been in her confession to cause her such alarm? When he had heard his name being called in that forest, he had felt a wild, possessive joy.

It had not been difficult to enter his house and carry her above stairs unseen. When he had taken off the fragments of her gown, he saw that she had only a few superficial scratches, and had not, as he had feared at one stage, been raped. Bathing her scratches, and putting her into a nightgown—one of Adelaïde's, whom he had been obliged to take into his confidence—had been easy, for she had fallen sound asleep long before they had reached the house in the Avenue du Vieux Versailles, and nothing would wake her.

Speaking in a tone that no woman had ever heard him use before, he begged Teresa to stop crying, adding, 'For it distresses me to see you so very unhappy. When you are quite rested, you may tell me what happened to you.'

The storm of weeping was already exhausted, and only an occasional hiccup came from the pillow. Conscious of his nearness, for he was sitting on her bed, Teresa longed to return again to the embrace which had made her pulse quicken and her breath catch in her throat. Despite the infinite tenderness in his deep voice, there was passionate desire in his eyes, to which her body was responding. One part of her longed to accuse him of having a sordid and secret affair with the doe-eyed girl, while the other, less rational Teresa wished that she did not have such a wretched appearance.

In his eyes she was more beautiful than ever—the shadows beneath her eyes gave them depth and brilliance, although he longed to coax the smile back to her perfectly shaped mouth. Noticing a tiny bruise on her chin, which had escaped his attention the evening before, he immediately expressed concern, touching the small wound with his fingertip.

'Poor Teresa, to be so used. You will have to wear that detestable powder for a day or two, my darling, until your wounds fade.'

If only he would upbraid her! Demand to know why she had disobeyed him and gone into the house in the forest! In anger, she could have asked him the thousand questions which tormented her mind; but his tender concern took away her will to question him, and only increased her desire for his caresses. Allowing his fingertip to travel to her mouth, he lightly traced its contours, and involuntarily she reached for him, pulling his head down to hers and giving herself up to the ecstasy of wonder in the mutual passions aroused by his urgent and demanding kiss.

Her body began to yield to the weight of his, and when he moved in order to pull aside the bedcovers completely she thought that he was withdrawing from her and cried out, pulling his mouth back to hers. Longing for the kiss to last forever, she became so aroused by the feel of his hands exploring her body that her blood turned to flame and she forgot her fears and suspicions, and admitted to herself that she did not care what this man was guilty of—she loved him, and wanted always to be at his side.

'No, my darling girl, do not allow me to go further with you.' There was a hoarseness in his voice and his brow was damp. Thrusting her back on to the pillow, he held her shoulders pinned so that she could not wind her arms around his neck and inflame his passions beyond control with her delightful response. As she looked up at him beseechingly, her eyes shadowed with desire, he was tempted to abandon his scruples and make love to her. 'We must be *married* on Saturday, not betrothed. I cannot wait any longer for you.'

With a throaty, breathless chuckle, she spoke lovingly. 'Cannot you wait longer? You fraud. I distinctly recall you saying that you would prefer the Bastille to marriage with me.'

'Did I really say that? What a fool I must have been; I would prefer the Bastille to a life spent without you.' Looking into each other's eyes, deeply and intensely, they silently exchanged mutual love; it was as though they had searched for something, and, having found it, were satisfied.

'I shall go to the King today and request his permission. No, I'll demand his consent to our marriage taking place on Saturday. I want the right to protect you from all harm. No, no, my love, do not speak.' Putting a finger on her lips, he quelled her sounds of distress, regretting that he had chosen that moment to remind her of her ordeal. But sooner or later it would have to be faced—they would have to talk about it. Later, he decided. He wanted the magic of this moment to last. Teresa would soon forget all the unpleasant things that had happened to her, he intended to make sure of that. Youth, abundant vitality, a joy of living and loving were all her gifts; they would assist the process of healing her mind and wounded spirit.

'What will people say about my presence in your house? Surely the Queen will be very angry; it is irregular. Heavens! Guy, I should have been on duty this morning.'

'Do not concern yourself about that. I shall have to tell the King something of what has happened, and I shall also inform the Queen. It will make hurtful hearing for them both, but it is my duty.'

Looking at him with painful intensity, she asked, 'Do you know what happened in that house in the forest, Guy?'

'I have a fair idea, as I know for what purpose that house is used.' Keeping his voice level and unemotional, he divulged nothing else; his memories concerning the house were too disagreeable.

His silence revived her fears—it was impossible to avoid unpleasant speculation. How could he know what took place in that evil house, unless he had been present? With absolute certainty she knew that no one was likely

to divulge their individual part in any of the rites or cer-
emonies that took place there.

'What is wrong? A shadow crossed your face. Tell
me, sweet life, for speaking of it will help exorcise your
fears.' How kind and loving he sounded, but could she
trust him?

'It is worse than you fear, Guy. For they plan to kill
the King, and when they had used you in their plot to
take power, they were going to kill you as well. They are
not your friends, I am afraid.'

He sneered derisively. 'They were never my friends,
nor I a friend to them. I have suspected their plots for
some time; I do not fear them.'

'Marie Besneval?' she queried shyly. 'She told me that
you and she would have been married if it had not been
for me.'

Dark eyebrows rose above gleaming eyes. 'Have I a
jealous little minx on my hands?' There was a delightfully teasing note in his voice.

'They were going to kill me, Guy, and bring my body
here. If you did not agree to join them, you were to be
accused of my murder,' she whispered, so quietly that
he had to bend his head to hear her.

'Who? Who said that? Whose plan was that? By God!
He shall die, this very day!' He was shaking her slightly,
and she saw the same murderous intent that had
frightened Paul, Gaston's nephew.

'Père Dubois and Charles Villiers, but I do not think
the others knew, for this was said when the others went
away to...to...' Flushed and embarrassed, she could
not continue.

The hands that held her shoulders became rigid, and
he controlled himself with great difficulty. 'You need
never fear that you will see either of those villains again,'
he ground out from between clenched teeth.

'Do not fight them, Guy. I am afraid that something
will happen to you.'

'A duel?' He was full of haughty disdain. 'That privilege I reserve for my equals—those curs deserve a
traitor's death, and they shall have it.' Giving a hoarse

cry, he buried his head against her breasts. 'My God! Teresa, you cannot know the agony of grief I would feel if your dead body were brought here. To know that I would never see your smile again, never hear the music of your voice or watch the joyous way a room is brighter and warmer when you enter it.'

Stroking his dark head, she felt a change in her emotions, a strange, new tenderness, like the feeling she had had when she had kissed the Marquise's baby. 'But I am here, Guy, alive and well. It is better that we both put the affair from our minds, do not fight duels and revive old wounds.' Some premonition that disaster was about to befall them impelled her to urge caution. 'It is not wise to seek revenge——'

Interrupting her without apology, he spoke savagely. 'Not revenge. Justice. There is a difference. You will have to tell me the names of those present.'

Frowning with an effort of remembrance, she gave him the names of those she had recognised; the others she found that she could describe, despite having been in a drugged state, so that he recognised them all.

Tapping her nose in a familiar and loving little gesture, he stood up, and she felt bereft as his warmth was withdrawn, and wished that he would return to her embrace. It was sweet to hear words of love, and sweeter still to return them. Marriage would bring an emotional freedom, entirely adult and private, where intimate thoughts and feelings could be expressed and shared. A few weeks ago she had dreaded the thought of marriage with him. Now, despite her reservations and misgivings, she longed for their union with an ardour to match his own.

'It will take me a few hours to complete my business at the palace, for this is a delicate affair, and one which I must handle with great diplomacy. You are not to be anxious while I am gone; you are well chaperoned here. There is a lady here, of unimpeachable respectability. I will give it out that you are here with her.' A little smile flickered for a moment, softening his rather hard features. 'No one will question the propriety of your stay, for I intend that you will remain here until we are married. I do not mean to let you out of my sight again.'

'Guy, my clothes, I shall . . .' she began anxiously, and then relaxed as he smiled.

'They shall be packed and brought here, today. For I am sure that you cannot have changed so very much.' A doubtful look crept into her eyes, and she looked questioning again.

'There was no criticism meant, goose! I like my little feather-head, so do not look so worried.'

On this amicable note they parted—he grim-faced and bent on more deadly errands than he would allow her to know, she to contemplate a suddenly blissful future, where no shadows of evil or menace could reach her.

A little maid scratched on the door and peered around it—a thin, frightened child, of about Teresa's age. The housekeeper, upon learning that they were to serve no less than three ladies—a Duchesse, a Comtesse, and the future Duchesse d'Abbeville—had swollen with pride and importance. To her had fallen the noble task of arranging for the housing of the ladies and their servants. No expense was to be spared. The Provençal servants were surly and indifferent, and spoke in such thick, guttural accents that she delighted in pretending to misunderstand them. Summoning her niece, Jeanne, she had impressed upon her the need to behave with the utmost circumspection, to wait on the youngest of the ladies, and never forget that this was the future Duchesse. She must report every household occurrence that should by accident have escaped her vigilance to her aunt. Poor little Jeanne, terrified at the great responsibility that had been thrust on her thin shoulders, was surprised to find that the lady she was to serve was so very young and had a merry smile.

'If you please, *mademoiselle*, I am Jeanne, and my aunt, the Duc's housekeeper, has sent me to wait on you.'

'Come in, please, Jeanne. You are the very person I most wish to see.'

Grateful, and much flattered, Jeanne advanced into the room with more confidence than she had entered.

Bullied at home, frightened and overawed by her aunt, entirely demolished by the gimlet stare of the old Duchesse and intimidated by the easy, knowledgeable manner of the young Comtesse, she found *mademoiselle* a refreshing change.

'How can I serve you, *mademoiselle*?' Jeanne bobbed a little curtsy.

Sitting up in bed, hands clasped around her knees, which were drawn up to her chin, Teresa looked enchanting. Eyes twinkling, she chuckled. 'Well, I think I need some things with which to wash and brush my hair. Then I must have some clothes, and then some food, for I am ravenously hungry.' Speaking with emphasis, she had allowed her eyes to roll heavenward, her expression so droll that Jeanne giggled.

'I could bring you some breakfast first, and then I could bring the washing things. I am not sure about clothes, but I think my aunt, the housekeeper, could ask the Comtesse for some clothes. Will that be all right?' Standing with her feet apart, hands unconsciously wringing her smart new apron into a crumpled rag, she looked very comical. But there was an expression of great honesty in her wide grey eyes, and Teresa took an immediate liking to her.

'That sounds splendid, Jeanne.'

When Jeanne had departed, Teresa thought that the Comtesse she had referred to must be the lady of unimpeachable respectability that the Duc had spoken of. Unimpeachable respectability, she mused—sounds very old. Nuns were of unimpeachable respectability. She wondered if the Comtesse was like a nun, and thought of how disapproving she would be if she knew that the Duc had kissed a young woman called Adelaïde in this very house, yesterday afternoon.

How to broach the subject with him? Many men kept mistresses—wives were supposed to accept their existence and say nothing about it. The Queen had to accept Louis's mistress, and yet remain a pure and dignified Queen of France. Intolerable! Teresa's anger was raised. And yet, despite all this, she loved the Duc. His prot-

estations of love had been real. He would have to be a
very clever man to have feigned each expression of
passion, each touch; his reactions had been the spontaneous arousal of physical desire, genuine, she believed.

Having breakfasted and washed, she sat still while
Jeanne, rather inexpertly, brushed her hair.

With a very red face and scared eyes, Jeanne tried to
disentangle the flaxen curls. 'I'm not used to this,
mademoiselle. I hope I'm not hurting you. My aunt—
sorry, the housekeeper—said that if I didn't give satisfaction, I'd be out the door, fast as winking.'

'The more you brush my hair, the better you will
become at it. As I am quite unused to a maid, I can
assure you that I would be terrified of a very experienced girl. I think you and I shall deal very well together.'

These words, promising future permanent and secure
employment as maid to the future Duchesse, operated
powerfully on Jeanne. 'Oh, *mademoiselle*, you'll never
regret it. Never!' she breathed fervently, her grey eyes
round with wonder.

Becoming more confident now, she achieved a passable
success with her efforts, and began to chat quite naturally to her new mistress. 'I'm surprised that you didn't
have no servant at the palace. From what Paul's been
saying, I thought the place was awash with them.'

'Is Paul your young man?' Teresa asked, amused at
the artless confidences being imparted.

'No fear, he's only a boy! He came from the palace
this very morning. Until yesterday he was a page in the
service of the Marquise.'

Chill crept into the sunny bedchamber; it entered into
Teresa. A dull, unreasoning fear took hold of her. 'Do
you mean the Marquise de Montespan?' She tried to
sound casual, but to her own ears her voice sounded
strained.

Noticing nothing unusual, Jeanne began to assist her
into the clothes that had been sent by the Comtesse.
'That's right. Only, of course, everyone knows that she's
the King's mistress. This underskirt is too loose—you
are more slender than the Comtesse—but once we have

put the other skirts on, it will not notice. How pretty this is.' She held out the turned-back skirt which was put on last. Intertwined with lace and ribbon, its delicate shades of blue became admirably her fair colouring. 'Now for the bodice. I shall have to lace it tightly, because it's also too big. Never mind, we shall contrive, as my aunt says.'

Teresa allowed Jeanne to prattle on as she dressed her, tightening the full skirts at the waist, lacing the bodice with ribbon so that it fitted snugly over her breasts and shoulders, giving her a dainty yet shapely appearance. 'Such a shame that your luggage all got mislaid—very careless, these carriage-boys are. Although, the way Paul talks, you would think that if you made a mistake in the service of the Marquise you were likely to get killed.'

That was exactly what was likely to happen, thought Teresa. If the Duc was not on friendly terms with the Marquise, why had he taken one of her servants? If Paul was the page who had come that day to summon her to the Marquise's apartments, and the boy who had fetched the writing materials when she had made her confession—— Appalled, she stood stock still. She had completely forgotten about that confession!

Seeing that her new mistress, for whom she already felt a slavish devotion, was white-faced and frightened, Jeanne fell silent, wondering if she had said something untoward. Her aunt had warned her about talking too much and being over-familiar.

'Have I said something, *mademoiselle*?' she demanded anxiously, and was obliged to repeat her question, for her mistress remained as though turned to stone.

'What? Oh, no, Jeanne, it was really nothing that you said.'

'Have I laced your bodice too tightly? I could loosen it for you.'

'No, it is not the bodice. This Paul—what manner of boy is he?'

Describing him, Jeanne added that she thought for all his boasts about the palace he was glad to be in the Duc's service. Apparently he was flattered that the Duc had offered him a job. What did he do? 'Well, nothing has really been fixed up for him yet. The steward was grumbling that, what with all the staff we suddenly have, he'll be hard put to it to find the boy anything to do. So if there are any errands you want run, just ask me, and I'll get Paul to go.'

Teresa had to see Paul—she had to see if this was the same boy who was present that day of the confession. 'As a matter of fact, there is a small commission. He could fetch a gown for me. Will you ask him to come up?' Teresa knew very well that since she had but ordered the gown on the previous day, it could not possibly be ready, but she needed some excuse to see the boy.

Looking uneasily around the bedchamber, Jeanne grimaced, twisting her apron in her hands. 'I don't know as I could ask him to come up here, *mademoiselle*.' Her brow cleared as she thought of the solution. 'Why don't you go down to the *salon*? The Comtesse will be there, and I can send him to you.'

'A very good idea, Jeanne. Thank you.'

The house was larger than she had supposed, for there seemed to be many rooms on a couple of floors. An air of quiet refinement dominated, and was pleasing and restful after her experience of the day before. It spoke of well-trained servants, order and discipline—things that would have made Teresa shrug impatiently only a short while before. Running ahead of her, Jeanne reached the door of the *salon* to which the Duc had brought her on the very first day she had met him. How very different were her sensations now! Then she had longed to get to the palace; now she longed to escape it.

Pushing open the door, Jeanne announced in suddenly portentous accents which made Teresa jump, 'Mademoiselle Rochefoucourt.' Going into the room with a smile of anticipation, for she was conscious that she was in the Comtesse's debt, having borrowed her clothes, Teresa stopped short, her smile fading. Rising from the sofa, a vision of confident beauty dressed in amber silk, jewels flashing at her throat and on her plump arms, was the subject of the painting—the doe-eyed woman who had received the Duc's kisses! Amazement must have registered on her face, rendering her stupidly speechless.

'You look surprised. Perhaps you had expected my mother, the Duchesse San Rémy, but she has not yet risen from her bed. I am Adelaïde, Comtesse Souvré, and you, I know, are Teresa.' Extending her hands, she took both Teresa's in hers and clasped them warmly. 'You must call me Adelaïde, for we are going to be the best of friends.' She had a sweet, musical voice, and an expression of great sweetness—her portrait had not done her justice. So, this was his darling Adelaïde!

This was no Versailles wench! This was a lady—a lady, moreover, who was a guest in this house. Had not she heard many, many times that the Duc guarded his privacy wonderfully and never entertained anybody? This must be a very special person. Of course she was very special— the Duc had her portrait, he had her person, very much at home here, in his house. Teresa had seen them kissing, like lovers.

All her joy subsided and disappeared, as though it had never been born. She could not, would not, be like the Queen and sit and smile and nod at his mistress, as though she did not care! It was too much to ask. How dared he kiss her and make love to her, and say that he was going to the palace to get the King's consent to their marriage, while all the time his mistress sat like a Queen in his *salon*? Doubt and suspicion began to return, and pushed away her happy anticipations. Not knowing how to respond to this greeting, she had looked away from Adelaïde, confused and unhappy.

Misunderstanding these looks, Adelaïde thought that they sprang from the natural embarrassment of her position. 'You must not be shy of me, Teresa. For Guy has told me all about you, and I promise that I shall stand as your friend.'

Guy! She called him Guy! So Guy had told Adelaïde all about her, had he? Well, he had not told her anything about Adelaïde. Was she meant to remain in ignorance?

Was there some reason why he could not marry this woman? Was his marriage to her meant to conceal an illicit affair? When he had thought that she returned the King's interest, he had told her roundly that he would never act the part of the complacent husband—was she meant to act the part of the complacent wife.

The door was pushed open, and Teresa saw that Jeanne had brought Paul to her. Looking shyly expectant, he awaited his orders. Dumbly, Teresa looked at him. It was the same page. There was no doubt about it. This page had been present when her confession had been made and written. Feeling trapped by some dreadful conspiracy, she looked about like a hunted animal, and wished with all her heart that she had never come to Versailles. There was no prospect of happiness now with the Duc; the thought of the coming marriage filled her with dread and fear.

CHAPTER ELEVEN

TERESA heard herself request the erstwhile page of the Marquise to go to the establishment of Celeste and enquire if her betrothal gown was ready. Even to her own ears, there was a strained note in her voice—indeed, she was barely able to talk above a whisper. With the departure of Paul she felt some diminution of the hostile forces against her, and was able to turn to the Comtesse with some degree of calm. At the back of her mind, she questioned again and again the Duc's actions. One did not take the servant of an enemy into one's employ. It could only mean that the Duc was on friendly terms with the woman who had formed part of the conspiracy to kill her. Is that why he wanted her here, under his own roof—so that he could keep a close watch on her?

'Why do you not come and sit down, Teresa, and talk to me, for I long to make your acquaintance?' Adelaïde's voice and manner were sweet and inviting.

I do not wish to make the acquaintance of my future husband's mistress, she thought unhappily. How he must have lied to me! He was obliged to offer me marriage or face the Bastille, but really he would have liked to marry this woman. Her thoughts in a private agony of jealousy and despair, she allowed herself to be seated beside the Comtesse Adelaïde, forcing herself to sternly quell the urge to blurt out her fears and suspicions.

'Do you know the Duc well?' she asked timidly.

'All my life,' replied the other serenely. 'Our estates in Provence are next door to one another. So when you and the Duc are married, we shall be neighbours.'

Anxiously scanning her face, to see what the Duc could see in it to make him write those words across the bottom of the portrait, she was unable to resist asking, 'So you must see him a great deal. How you must have missed him when he came to Court. Is that why you are here in Versailles?'

Comprehension began to dawn in Adelaïde's eyes. Sensing that Teresa was in some way jealous of her, she assumed that she must have heard of Guy's proposal of marriage. It had been much talked of at the time, and his every subsequent action was attributed to his disappointment in love. 'You heard, I am sure, that at one time Guy thought himself in love with me.' Her eyes twinkled ruefully. 'But you must know that he was only twenty at the time, and it was only an infatuation. The stories of his duelling and reckless behaviour were all much exaggerated: but you have been long enough at Versailles to know how people exaggerate and speculate upon the most trivial of things.'

Was being in love so trivial? Teresa did not think so. Being twenty did not mean that a person did not have the power to love or care about another—that was a stupid idea put about by those who had never felt the force of that strong emotion. Striving to recall just what she had heard from the boarders in the convent concerning the Duc, she was silent, a tiny frown creasing her brow. There was something about his having fought a duel with a man over his wife. Or had it been with someone else? As far as she could recall, he had fallen in love with a married woman. Surely this could not be the woman? Yet she had said that the Duc had fancied himself in love with her. 'Did the Duc fight a duel with your husband, Comtesse?'

'Do call me Adelaïde; all my friends do. No, of course he never fought a duel with Albert. Albert was his friend, his dear friend—he would never have fought with Albert. People are really very cruel and thoughtless to put such stories about.'

Despite her attempt at lightness, Teresa could sense undercurrents of bitterness, and was sorry for her blunt question. Trying to make amends, she attempted to sound more sociable. 'Does your husband accompany you on this visit?' The shadow which flitted momen-

tarily across Adelaïde's face told Teresa that she had
asked another inept question.

'Albert died last year, on the Dutch campaign. Guy
was with him at the end. I am so very glad of that. Now
that my mourning period is over, my mama thought it
a good idea if we came to Versailles. When I first learned
of Albert's death, I thought that I should never recover;
I truly believed it to be the end of the world. But time
is a great healer, everyone says so—and, for once,
everyone is right.'

Feeling humbled, Teresa warmed towards Adelaïde,
for her words concealed, she was sure, a great deal of
unhappiness and patient suffering, yet she had not
spoken one word of self-pity. But she could not help
thinking that Adelaïde and her mother stood upon good
enough terms with the Duc that they could claim his
hospitality, and she had seen the lovely Comtesse in his
arms. Whatever happened, she must never forget that.

'You will have to excuse me for an hour or so, for I
have to go and look at a house which is for hire. There
is not a square inch to be had in the palace, even though
my mother, the Duchesse San Rémy, has the right to
command some apartments there. But even if there were
some room in the palace, I know that she could never
stand the continual racket. Guy sent his steward to look
at some houses as soon as we arrived yesterday——'

'Was it only yesterday that you arrived?' Teresa did
not like to admit that she had seen the Comtesse emerging
from the inn on the Duc's arm, or that she had seen
them embrace. If Marie Besneval was vanquished from
the arena of love, she must be glad, although she was
obliged to admit now that Marie had little chance of
achieving her ambition of becoming the Duchesse
d'Abbeville. But the lovely young widow, the widow of
his old friend, the object of his youthful love, was quite
a different proposition. Why on earth did he not marry
her? Because he is obliged by circumstances to marry
you, she told herself sternly. While recognising that the
Duc had a right to be angry with her, and Adelaïde to
resent her, she could not hide from herself the fact that

she was desperately jealous and bitterly unhappy. Why had he made love so charmingly? Clearly he had not meant a word that he had said and his loving gestures had been feigned. She would not be fool enough to yield to him again! That was a most solemn vow that she meant to keep.

'I should be back in time for the midday repast; then I shall prepare to go to the palace, for the Duc has presented our credentials and we shall be expected to attend the King and Queen this evening—Mama at the Queen's six o'clock reception for the Duchesses and Cardinals, both of us later at the King's banquet.'

Fear darkened Teresa's eyes; she did not feel equal to facing the Court quite yet. 'Shall I be expected to attend?'

Patting her hand, Adelaïde spoke kindly but firmly. 'You must, Teresa. It is imperative that you conduct yourself with dignity and normality. If it is your custom to go to these functions and enjoy yourself, and the Duc tells me that you have a great capacity for enjoyment, then it is vital that you do so tonight. Speculation will be rife, for there have been evil doings. Do not cry, for I do not intend to ask you about them. But you must understand that everyone will be talking—it is the way of the society with which the King surrounds himself. We must all behave as though nothing has occurred. Recall that I said I would stand as your friend—I shall not break that promise. Knowing Guy, he will take his own measures to deal with the situation. We must not interfere. It may be that he will try to protect your name, I do not know. But once you are married and living in Provence, you need not return to the palace for some time; by then the scandal will have died down and there will be other things to talk about.'

Pulling her hand away from the other woman's, Teresa spoke angrily. 'You speak as though I was in some way at fault, Adelaïde. That is not fair!'

Without taking offence, Adelaïde spoke pityingly. 'It is the way of the Court to gossip. They are not concerned with innocence or guilt—this affair will bear all the trappings of a delicious little intrigue, and will be talked of constantly. You must bear yourself with the dignity of a Duchesse—say nothing, appear surprised if anyone should assume you know anything about it, and laugh if any should state positively that you do.'

It was sound advice, and she knew it, but could not bring herself to thank Adelaïde, even though she knew that she was being petty and ungrateful. None of this was the affair of the Comtesse, yet she had professed herself willing to stand as her friend throughout the inevitable unpleasantness that would come. If Teresa had thought her ordeal over when she had escaped from the house in the forest, she realised now that the worst was possibly yet to come.

'I have told Mama—she will be coming down now—that you are Guy's intended bride, and will be staying here until your wedding day. She does not know about anything else. You will have to excuse her atrocious manners, for they are simply appalling.' Adelaïde smiled affectionately, and Teresa thought she could detect a note of pride in her voice. 'But she has a heart of gold, as you will soon discover.'

Going to the door, she turned to speak once more. 'Be of good heart, Teresa. You are not without friends; remember that.'

Teresa was aware that she betrayed spite in thinking that Adelaïde must bear the Duc some remarkable degree of friendship if she was prepared to stand as friend to one at the centre of a sordid intrigue. Moreover, it was an intrigue which, if it became known to its fullest and ugliest extent, would shake to its very foundations the Court of Versailles.

Good manners prevented her from getting up and wandering about the house—shortly to be her own house, although she could feel no sense of ownership as yet—and exploring. Indeed, Adelaïde had seemed much more its mistress than she did. It was Adelaïde who had invited her to enter and sit, Adelaïde who had told her how she must conduct herself. Becoming bored and restless, she could almost wish that the terrifying mother of her rival would make her appearance.

A light tap on the door made her spin around with relief, but when Paul entered the room the sight of him brought back such a flood of unwelcome recollections that she turned from him in shame and disgust. That confession! Even if the Duc were to destroy everyone present at that ugly satanic rite, that wretched confession would still exist, and could do untold harm to both herself and especially the Duc. Why should she care? He had his mistress in the house—his darling Adelaïde, whom he had once loved, and probably still did. But a fierce desire to love and protect him arose in her, making her feelings contradictory and confused.

'I am sorry, *mademoiselle*, but Celeste says that since you only ordered the gown yesterday, it will not be ready until Friday at the earliest, and she asked me if it should be delivered here, so I told her yes. But, if you like, I can go and fetch it.' Remaining by the door, he watched her uncertainly, for she looked angry.

'No, that is all right. You need not fetch it. I expect Celeste will bring it herself, for she will wish to fit it on.' Without turning around, she continued, 'You seem to have changed your employer. Was that not rather sudden?'

Hoping that he would tell her that he had been dismissed, and that there had been a post available in the Duc's house, she waited. Knowing that as soon as one servant obtained good employment they usually tried to get as many of their family employed as possible, she hoped that this might prove to be the case with the page. With all her heart she wished to disabuse her mind of the vile suspicions that were growing with every moment.

'The Duc offered me employment, *mademoiselle*, and I was glad to accept.' Gaston had strictly forbidden him to speak of the events which had led up to his change of employment, and, although *mademoiselle* looked so unhappy at his words, mindful of his uncle's warning he did not volunteer any further explanation.

'Thank you, Paul,' she said quietly and, dismissed, he withdrew.

Lost in her unhappy thoughts, she did not hear the
door sweep open, and only became aware that she was
the subject of interested scrutiny when addressed by a
loud, querulous voice.

'And whom might you be? I was not informed that
we had visitors.'

Duchesse Marie-Victoire, her wrinkled face heavily
powdered and rouged, her hair dyed and curled like a
young girl's, surged to the sofa, all rustling silk and
sweeping train. Rising, for the Duchesse was far more
regal than the Queen, and dipping into a curtsy, Teresa
stared at the amazing old lady. Jewels shone brilliantly
at her withered throat, on her scrawny arms, and dangled
from her earlobes; bright, piercing eyes took in every
detail of Teresa's appearance. If she was aware that the
visitor was wearing a dress very similar in colour and
style to one owned by her daughter, she did not pass any
comment.

'I am staying here, Duchesse.' Teresa became more
alarmed at each passing moment, for the Duchesse continued to stare at her with such concentration that she
thought she must be able to see into her mind.

'What's this? Staying here? I don't understand this at
all. Guy said nothing about anyone staying here. There
is my daughter and myself, that is all. It is most incon-
siderate of him to fill the house with people when we
have chosen to make a visit. I cannot understand.' This
last was repeated several times with much head-shaking,
causing the youthful curls to bob wildly about the
ravaged face.

Looking at her rather doubtfully, Teresa spoke shyly.
'I do not think that he has filled the house with people,
Duchesse. You must know that I am about to become
betrothed to the Duc, and he thought that, as you were
here, it would be a good time for me to visit. Normally
I live in the palace. I am a lady-in-waiting to the Queen,
and have an apartment there in the Queen's section of
the palace.'

Whether the Duchesse understood this Teresa could
not be sure, for it appeared that the old lady had really

only comprehended the fact that Teresa and the Duc were about to become betrothed. As soon as that had been related to her, she had plumped heavily on to the nearest chair and stared anew, an expression of amazed belliger-ence in her glittering black eyes.

'This makes very sad hearing, *mademoiselle*,' she told Teresa. 'Very sad, indeed. You must know that my daughter, the Comtesse Souvré, and the Duc are very fond of each other. At one time, it was rumoured, he was so desperate for love of her that he almost killed the man she was going to marry. What do you think of that, *hein*?'

'That must have been a very difficult time for you,' Teresa responded politely, wondering if Adelaïde had been telling the truth.

'Difficult?' The Duchesse cackled with laughter. 'Aye, it was difficult. So, you have a fancy to be Madame la Duchesse, have you?' So rapidly was the question put to her that she had not time to prevaricate.

'Yes. I love the Duc,' she replied without hesitation. All the while her mind was racing with a thousand ques-tions; why had the Duchesse said that news of the be-trothal made very sad hearing? Of all people in France to choose as the recipient of such confidences relating to her own daughter, why choose herself? Teresa began to detest the mother almost as much as she detested the daughter. As though answering her unspoken thoughts, the Duchesse continued speaking.

'My object in bringing my daughter to Versailles was to promote a match between her and the Duc. You have seriously disrupted those plans.'

In other circumstances Teresa could have found much to amuse her in that arrogant pronouncement; already her lively sense of humour was being irresistibly tickled by the absurdity of the old lady's words. Or were they so very absurd? The reasoning part of her mind could not deny that she had already received much evidence that an attachment still existed—certainly on the Duc's side.

'Where *is* Guy? It is most unreasonable of him to be absent when he has guests. I cannot think what the modern generation are about. You are staying here, that is most irregular. Girls today are allowed far more freedom than we ever dreamed of in youth. My daughter, it seems, has vanished. Of servants, I have not seen a sign since early morning.'

That she had, from the moment of opening her eyes, set the house, her own and the Duc's servants into a continual flurry of activity was overlooked. The washing water had been too hot, then too cold; a fire in summer had been declared a wasteful extravagance, yet when it had been allowed to die down she had wondered at the Duc's meanness. Food had been abhorrent at the early hour of midday, but when a small collation had been brought to her bedchamber she had wondered if she would be obliged to either starve or eat in a common inn while staying with the Duc.

'I believe the Comtesse has gone to inspect a house——'

Rudely interrupting her, the Duchesse looked fiercely at Teresa. 'So, we are to be driven out, willy-nilly. I have had the most wretchedly uncomfortable journey, slept not a wink in that uncomfortable bed, and now, before I have time to draw breath, I must be bundled from this house!'

Teresa was somewhat nonplussed. With the resilience of youth, she was already recovering from her ordeal; confused and wary she might be about the Duc's feelings for her, but she was quite certain of her own heart, and with youthful confidence and optimism she determined that she would fight and win in this situation. But she could appreciate that a long journey, the disappointment of her hopes, and removal from the comfort of her own home must be very trying to the Duchesse.

'Would you like to walk around the town? It is a very fine morning, and I should be very pleased to accompany you,' she ventured.

'Do you wish to kill me? I cannot be expected to drag myself through a sea of mud to gratify your wish to go gadding about!' The Duchesse was fast becoming more and more querulous and difficult.

Biting back a smile, Teresa attempted another gambit. 'Perhaps you would like to play cards? The Queen is very fond of cards. Her favourite game is *hombre*, and I am used to playing, so that I am now quite good.'

Somewhat mollified by these attempts to amuse her, the Duchesse answered more mildly. 'I never play cards in the middle of the day; it is not done in my circles. But tell me, *mademoiselle*, what do you think of the Queen? You tell me that you are a lady-in-waiting to the Queen.'

'I am sincerely attached to the Queen. She is my god-mother, you know, and out of fondness for my late mother, who was also her lady-in-waiting, she allowed me to serve her.'

'What of that creature that Louis flaunts all over the place?' barked the Duchesse aggressively. 'I suppose you are sincerely attached to *her* as well?'

Distaste and reserve mingled in equal measure on Teresa's face. 'I cannot think that my opinion of the Marquise de Montespan can be of any interest to anyone.'

'You don't like her!' the old lady cackled with glee. 'Famous! I detest the trollop. It is infamous that such practices are encouraged at Court—the Queen being obliged to receive such a creature on equal terms.'

Smiling warmly, Teresa responded quickly. 'I so agree with you, but the Queen is always the soul of kindness and courtesy to everyone.' Remembering that the Queen always liked her to read aloud, Teresa wondered if this would not soothe and placate the irritated old lady. 'I usually read to the Queen in the afternoons—perhaps you would like me to read to you now?' she asked.

'Later, perhaps. For now you may tell me all the Court gossip. Start with those nearest the Queen, then you can tell me all about Montespan and her cronies, villainous crew.'

Determining that she would say nothing about the Marquise or her friends—for to talk of them was still too painful and, besides, she could not decide upon what

terms the Duc stood with her—Teresa entertained the
Duchesse with accounts of the doings of the Court since
she had been there. So able was she to recount the con-
versations, anecdotes, and little intrigues that she soon
had the Duchesse laughing and greatly entertained.

'You had better tell me your name, for I cannot keep
calling you *mademoiselle*.' She was wiping tears of
laughter from her eyes, for Teresa had been telling her
about an elderly courtier's attempted courtship of a
notable lady of the Court, and its disastrous outcome.

'I am Teresa Rochefoucourt. My mother——'

'Not Armand Rochefoucourt's child? Merciful
heavens! Why did you not say so? I cannot credit that
you have talked of inanities for the past twenty minutes
and never breathed an important word!'

Ignoring the rudeness and unfair assumptions made
in such a statement, for Teresa had formed a very accurate assessment of the Duchesse's character, she merely
smiled and replied, 'Yes, my father was Armand
Rochefoucourt, but I must tell you that he and my
mother and brother died when I was ten years
old——'

Once more the Duchesse cut across her conversation.
'The fever! Ah, how well I remember it. I suppose I
must have lost half my friends and acquaintance.' She
spent the next half-hour relating the various stages of
illness and affecting endings of, what seemed to Teresa,
at least the entire upper echelons of the French nobility.
'So you are Armand's little girl. Ah, how many years
ago that seems.' The Duchesse seemed lost in a reverie
of distant dreams. 'Then he married the great friend of
Maria Teresa, and then we heard no more of him.'

Accord seemed to have been established for the time
being, and Teresa breathed a sigh of relief, for she had
begun to find the company of the Duchesse rather ex-
hausting. She wondered if she might propose some other
scheme for her entertainment, for she feared that at any
moment they might stray into uncomfortable channels
of conversation. If the Duchesse were to ask her about
any of those people present at the satanic rite, she would

hardly know how to answer. Any conversation relating to the Duc must be painful and embarrassing, and she fervently hoped that it could be avoided.

As though reading her mind, the Duchesse demanded to know where she had met Guy d'Abbeville.

'His aunt was the Abbesse of the convent where I was placed after the death of my parents. I met him there——'

Eyes widening, and putting up a hand to cover her mouth, the Duchesse affected astonishment. 'Never say that Guy courted you in a convent! I have heard tales of his wild ways, but surely this is too much.'

Anxious for reasons beyond her comprehension to defend him, Teresa instantly leapt to his defence. 'I was about to make my appearance at Court,' she lied. 'And his aunt approved our marriage.'

'So it was all arranged before you even left the convent? It must indeed have been a love match.' Far from being censorious, the Duchesse seemed impressed, and began to look at Teresa as though there might be more to her than a pretty face.

A servant chose that moment to announce that they had a visitor, and Teresa turned with relief to see who had come to call upon the Duc, for it could hardly be a caller for the Duchesse or the Comtesse.

'I am so pleased to find you at home, Mademoiselle Rochefoucourt.' The Marquise de Montespan entered the room with all the aplomb of an old and valued friend. 'What a great pity that the Duc is from home, but I gather that he is to return quite soon. May I be introduced to your friend?' She seemed chagrined to see the Duchesse.

Teresa was amazed at the poise of the Marquise—how insolently she looked at the Duchesse and demanded an introduction! No enemy would enter the house of another with such assurance. Unless the Marquise had a very special relationship with the Duc, Teresa thought, with more cynicism than she would have thought possible a month earlier.

If Teresa had expected the Duchesse to be outraged after her strong words of an hour ago, she was mightily mistaken. That lady appeared all delight to have the introductions performed, and behaved with such interested civility towards the King's mistress that Teresa was astonished.

After some commonplaces had been exchanged, the Marquise explained that she had been in the town of Versailles on rather distressing business. 'I have heard that two very prominent members of the Court are dead.' Teresa's blood began to run cold—had something happened to the Duc?

Watching the Marquise's lovely face affect distress as she disposed her elegant person on a small chair, Teresa found it difficult to believe that this silk-clad creature, perfumed and delicately painted, was the same woman who had taken part in the satanic rite of yesterday. Cold hands held her emotions in their power. Of whom did she speak, when she talked of prominent members of the Court? Was the Duc not the most prominent member of the Court?

'You will be very sad to learn that your friends Charles Villiers and Richard Beauchamp are both dead.' Teresa gasped with horror—not at the Marquise's news, but at the expression of malevolence which accompanied it.

'Why have you come here?' Teresa whispered through dry lips, for the lovely creature who watched her with such hate-filled eyes personified evil. She found the Marquise's presence unbearable. If the Duchesse had not been present, she would have had the courage to order her to leave instantly.

'I was sure that you would wish to know,' the Marquise replied smoothly. 'It seems that they must have fought a duel with each other, for both were discovered in the forest, dead of sword wounds.' A silvery laugh rang out. 'It is rumoured that they fought over some young lady whose name escapes me.'

'Doubtless, my dear, the Court is full of nobodies these days, whose names escape everybody.' The Duchesse had been watching the Marquise, who flushed and bit her lip, then began to turn the great diamond bracelet on her slender wrist. At the height of her power, when Louis had been besotted with her, she would have known how to deal with this insolent old woman and this stupid girl. They would not have dared shown their faces at Court; she would have forbidden it. Now she had to tread carefully.

All day the Court had been rife with rumour. It was inevitable, she knew—half her friends and acquaintances seemed to have disappeared, and she could find no one to give her any information. When Teresa had run from the little house in the forest they had been angry, for they had felt cheated, but, with the exception of Père Dubois, they had been too drunk and drugged to pursue her. When they were less dazed, they had begun to see the frightful implications of her flight. Bound together in secret and diabolical complicity, they could remain secure in the knowledge that one would never dare betray the other. But Teresa had seen them all, and could identify them. They had all prepared to swear that she was one of their number, and threaten her with exposure to keep her quiet.

Sure that Teresa would be here, the Marquise had, in desperation, come to bargain for her silence. It had been an unpleasant shock to find that wretched old harridan San Rémy, a guest of the Duc, for with Teresa Rochefoucourt adequately chaperoned, some, at least, of her bargaining power was lost. She had hoped to add more threat of exposure to her list, thinking that Teresa had spent the night alone with the Duc.

When she had heard that Villiers and Beauchamp were dead, and the others missing, she knew that the Duc had killed them and became afraid for her own life. If only she could find someone who would give her information. Many times throughout the day she had tried to see Louis, but he was closeted with his advisers, she had been told. That vile, sly Madame de Maintenon had gone about her duties with her usual expression of secretive composure until the Marquise longed to box her ears. If the King should discover that she was one of the number of people in the satanic circle, then she was lost, for Louis would abandon her without delay. If she were lucky, she would escape with her life.

Her charmed, perfumed, glittering life was over and, unwilling to admit that she no longer had the power to attract the King, she had chosen to blame Teresa Rochefoucourt. Again and again, the words of Teresa's confession leapt to her mind's eye. Maintenon married to the King! It could not, must not, be true. Teresa had some power, and the Marquise had wished to use it for her own advantage and then watch the destruction of the girl who was now her greatest enemy.

All her hatred and fears were fused and directed at Teresa. The King had smiled at her, everyone liked her, the Duc wished to marry her. With her flaxen curls, large blue eyes and mischievous smile she had become the darling of the Court, loved by all, and without an enemy in any camp. I was the darling of the Court once, she thought sadly. I will become so again; I must.

'When you recollect the name of the young lady, you may tell us, for I am sure we shall be hugely entertained, Marquise. In the meantime, you must not allow us to detain you, for I am sure someone as well known as yourself must have many calls to make. Summon a servant, Teresa, to show the Marquise out.'

In the face of so masterly and comprehensive a dismissal, the Marquise had little option but to leave, vowing that when she had regained her position of power she would make sure that that old hag, San Rémy, became as unwelcome as the plague at the Court. Plague! She thought suddenly of an old servant who had applied to her for help—it seemed that she was stricken with smallpox and likely to die. There was some story of being in extreme poverty and starvation—she could hardly recall, really! If she were to help every poor person in France, she would not have an *écu* left for herself. And servants should make provision for such times as they were unable through laziness or ill-health to work. It was not her affair.

Trying to recall just when old Mathilde had applied to her—she rather thought it was a few weeks ago—she fervently hoped that the old woman was still alive, for her wicked mind had conceived a plot. It brought a smile to her face and lightened her step. She returned to the palace in better humour than when she had left it, although her instinct told her to be wary of the King.

Summoning a servant, she demanded to know the whereabouts of the letter sent by the priest of the parish in which Mathilde now lived. Spreading out the page, she examined the closely written sheet—St Germain! What luck! It was a mere stone's throw away; although if the King knew that smallpox was so close to Versailles he would be in a fearful rage. Directing her kitchen to pack a huge hamper of food, and the sewing woman to pack up some blankets and clothes, she sent them to the old servant.

'Leave the hampers on the doorstep, knock on the door, but do not wait for any reply. The old woman will then have a nice surprise.' If she told the servant that he was to go to a plagued house, he would not obey her orders. 'Take this letter and leave it on top of the food hamper.' Handing him Teresa's confession, she prayed the stupid old woman was not dead. She would return to the house in the Avenue du Vieux Versailles and tell Teresa Rochefoucourt where she could recover her confession. By the time she got it back it would, hopefully, be infected with smallpox; if Teresa did not die of the pox, at least her looks would be so altered that the Sun King would never again look on her with desire.

CHAPTER TWELVE

'GUY, I would much rather not go to the forest.' It was impossible to put her thoughts into words, but she wanted him to understand that the very thought of returning to that house, the scene of such a painful experience, was repugnant to her.

'My darling, I do not wish you ever to do anything that does not please you, but I think that this is important. I watched you last night at the King's music evening, and you looked so wretchedly unhappy and haunted by sadness that I could scarcely bear it. If there are any doubts or fears lingering in your mind, then I wish to lay them all at rest so that we can be happy together.'

Teresa's fears and doubts had little to do with her experiences, and very much to do with Adelaïde and the Duc. Not daring to ask him if any attachment still existed between them, she was prey to her own jealous thoughts and suspicions.

It was a cloudless day that promised heat and endless sunshine; wisps of mist still clung to the bushes and tree roots. The pathway along which they were riding was still damp, but with the lovely aroma of the forest in summer. How very different it was, with birds fluttering from tree to tree, singing; leaves strong and bright in many shades of green. It was so very different from the wild torment of the forest in the storm. It was difficult to keep reminding herself that it was the same place. As they rode deeper into the forest, she recalled that it was the Duc who had first shown her the house and warned her not to enter it. How had he known of its existence? How curious that she should still love him while having such suspicions of him.

Trembling slightly, for they had entered the clearing where she knew the house was situated, she looked about her with amazement. Of the house there was no sign at all—not a single brick or piece of timber. The only evidence that it had ever existed was a large, irregularly shaped patch of bare earth. Small birds pecked hopefully at the earth and flew off with little darting movements when the horses approached. A faint, pleasant breeze rippled across the clearing and fanned colour into Teresa's cheeks. A great weight seemed to lift from her shoulders, and she looked with tremulous relief at the Duc.

'What happened to the house?'

Tethering his horse, he helped her dismount, and hand in hand they walked into the clearing. 'I had it pulled down, and ordered that everything should be taken away. You see, there is nothing left to make you afraid. I wanted you to see for yourself.' Her hand began to tremble in his, for the disappearance of the house did not make the questions in her mind go away. 'I know that you are wondering what has happened to those vile people who brought you here. Do not think about them, for they can never again have the power to hurt you.'

'It is said that Charles Villiers and Richard Beauchamp died as a result of sword wounds. Did you kill them?' Her voice sounded strangely calm, as though they were discussing the reception that they had attended the evening before, and what the Duchesse and the Comtesse had worn, and what was said and not said.

'You may rest assured that all the men present that evening can no longer threaten you in any way at all. The women have been exiled.'

Such a brief statement, concealing so much grief for those they had loved and betrayed. Henri Deschamps had gone to the reception with them, his face a strained mask, his eyes empty and blank. With great tact and infinite kindness, Adelaïde had talked to him, shielding him from those who would pester him with the questions of the avidly curious. Such an understanding had been built up between them by the end of the evening

that both Teresa and the Duc had expressed the hope
that his grief over Marie's deceit and banishment would
not last long.

'We begin to think and talk like an established married
couple.' He had grinned and pinched her chin, so that
those watching whispered that surely they could not have
been involved in the mysterious events and remain so
light-hearted.

The Duc had no intention of telling her of the duels
he had fought in the dawn hours. His challenges had
been expected and accepted. Henri, as his second, of
necessity was the only one admitted to his confidence,
for he had been able to confide only part of the events
to the King. Contemptuously, he thought of those who
had snivelled and lied and tried to tell him that Teresa
was a willing party to the satanic rite that had almost
ended with her murder. Only Charles Villiers had fought
with a kind of desperate courage that had wrung from
the Duc his unwilling admiration.

Although out of love with his mistress, the King had
been shocked and disillusioned by the part played by
her. The Duc had not told him of Teresa's involvement
with the group who had plotted to take his power and
authority; her part had been that of victim, but he
doubted his ability to convince anyone of that. His own
father had died in a rebellion against the crown; in some
measure his own loyalties would always be suspect. That
he could deal with, but he found unbearable the thought
that Teresa should be suspected of any crime which she
had not committed.

Having initially deprecated her pretty, winsome frivolity, he now longed for it to replace the grave expression
and subdued manner. Taking her in his arms, and feeling
the instinctive yielding of her body, he became aware
again that she was a passionate, loving woman and began
to yearn for the consummation of their marriage.

Feeling the pressure of his lips on hers, desire flamed
through Teresa and she wanted the embrace never to end.
Doubts began to recede as the fire of their mutual passion
began to consume her, and she felt a delicious throbbing

rhythm urge her body closer to his. Nothing mattered
any longer, for at this moment she felt loved and desired. Guy d'Abbeville had known and made love to
many women who were generally his own age or older,
skilled in dalliance and experienced in love affairs.
Teresa's awakening love and ardour were a source of
delight to him, arousing him in a way that was new and
strangely more exciting than he could have dreamed
possible.

How little needed to be said when one was in love.
His touch was at one and the same time tender and urgent
with desire, his kiss giving and demanding. Little nu-
ances of feeling hitherto unknown to her brought into
sharp focus the endless and varied pathways of love that
stretched into a golden future. For the time being she
could forget that he loved Adelaïde also, that he might
have owned the house that had been pulled down, that
he might be plotting with the King's mistress. So many
questions, so many questions! She gave herself up to
ecstasy and decided that, just for this blissful moment,
they did not count.

'I wish we could have the house to ourselves, just for
today,' he murmured against her cheek. Taking her face
between his hands, he stared hungrily into her eyes, 'I
do not think I can wait until our wedding night, Teresa.'

She perfectly understood his meaning. Her lips
trembled and her eyes shone with luminous desire. She
felt that if she spoke she would spoil the magic of this
moment.

'I suppose we had better return to the house, for the
Duchesse thinks that my sister and her husband might
arrive, although I am tolerably certain that they will not,
as I sent a messenger with word that the château should
be prepared to receive a visit from the King and Queen.'

Her eyes widened in dismay, and she moved away from
his embrace. 'I had quite forgotten about that. Do you
think that they still plan to go to Provence? The Queen
said nothing to me when I attended her yesterday. Surely
at such a time...' Her voice trailed away.

'At a time when some of his most notable courtiers have been discovered in a plot to take his power, and have been involved in satanic rites. Louis is a law unto himself. Probably the biggest blow to his vanity has been the discovery that a mistress of whom he had grown tired also plotted against him.'

'What will happen to her?' Teresa admitted to herself that she did not much care, but feared that the Marquise's evil influence might once more be felt.

'The King is very fond of the children she has borne him; I imagine that he will make some suitable arrangements for her.' Having a fair idea that these arrangements would involve the Marquise removing herself to live on a very reduced income at some distant destination, he did not elaborate further.

'I am afraid of her, Guy.'

Putting an arm around her shoulders, and walking with her back to the horses, he sounded cheerfully unconcerned. 'There is no harm she can do you—I will see to that.'

In considerably lighter mood, she accompanied him back to the house in the Avenue du Vieux Versailles. The sun shone with new brilliance and the air was alive with the sounds of summer. The doubts and questions still niggled away at her mind, but seemed less and less important with each mile they covered. How lovely the house looked! It wore a festive, welcoming air; tubs of bougainvillaea were arranged in the courtyard, richly purple in the afternoon sun.

Adelaïde and her mother were sitting at the back of the house where a stone terrace overlooked a tiny lawn. As Teresa had now come to expect, Adelaïde looked stunningly beautiful. There was something about her creamy complexion and great velvety eyes that echoed the beauty of the garden awakening to the heat of the sun. Henri Deschamps, looking strained, but less unhappy, was listening courteously to a rambling and occasionally vindictive account of most of the older members of the Court. A particularly salacious and, Adelaïde was sure, entirely fictional piece of gossip was being related about an austere elderly Countess, which made Henri twinkle appreciatively at Adelaïde.

The Duchesse loved Adelaïde, and, while she had brought her to Versailles in order to further her own schemes for a marriage with Guy d'Abbeville, she could see that she was in a fair way to forming an attachment with Henri Deschamps. A man of the stamp of her late husband, Albert: pleasant, courteous, light-hearted. Ah, well! Mentally giving a philosophical shrug, she resigned herself to await the announcement that the two would marry. Disappointment was uppermost in her heart, for she felt sure that if Teresa had not been in Versailles, her little Adelaïde could have had the comfort and security of being the next Duchesse d'Abbeville. Having suspected that there was something mysterious about the coming marriage between the Duc and Teresa Rochefoucourt, she had now come to like the girl very much indeed. There were no faults that a little polish would not correct, and she looked forward to the time when d'Abbeville brought her to Provence, where she could guide, advise and bully her to her heart's content.

The gossip and speculation had apparently died down, although the more experienced realised that it was merely fermenting beneath the surface and would probably erupt later. The participants in the satanic rite had been dispatched, with the exception of the Marquise, to their various fates with such speed that there was time only for hasty farewells and not for explanation. Many waited without pity to see what was going to happen to Athénaïs de Montespan; that the King's love for her was quite dead was obvious to the least intelligent.

Later there were cards in the *salon* beyond the banqueting hall. A great crowd had assembled to watch the play, mainly because they wished to witness at least some of the events about which there was a great deal of speculation. The Marquise, dressed in gold, her flawless skin almost translucent, was in high spirits and laughed and talked gaily to Madame de Thiange. If her gaiety was a trifle brittle, and her eyes glittered as they rested on Teresa, who was playing at another table with the

Duc, the Duchesse Marie-Victoire, Adelaïde and Henri, few noticed. In fact, many assumed that the talk and speculation surrounding the King's mistress must be false rumour.

Every time Teresa lifted her head she found the Duc watching her, a depth of understanding in his dark brown eyes; occasionally his gaze would deepen into intensity, and she was obliged to look away, blushing, aware that she was responding to him in the most vulgar way.

Rapping her fingers, the Duchesse admonished her. 'Pay attention to your game, Teresa. You are throwing away points. I cannot bear inattention to cards, it shows a lack of serious purpose.'

Her remark made the occupants of their table smile. Teresa's lips quivered. 'Dear Duchesse, I have needed a serious purpose ever since I came to Court, you have solved my problem for me.'

Henri Deschamps was amazed at the change in the Duc, who smiled tenderly at his future wife. From being the angry man of a few weeks ago, he had changed into a man in love. Teresa had shown a depth of character in dealing with the shocking events of the past week, that he had not suspected; she seemed more mature and poised. Marie's defection had been a terrible blow that he still found hurt deeply; he was probably the only person, apart from the Duc, who knew the full horror of that evening. When Guy had told him what they had intended to do to Teresa he had been appalled, both for her sake, as he had grown very fond of her, and because Marie should have been involved. He tried to tell himself that it was possible that she did not know what was to happen to Teresa, but that still did not excuse her presence at the satanic rite. Every feeling was revolted when he thought of her; he began to think that he could not trust his own judgement about anything, and experienced self-derision as painful and humiliating as the realisation that the Marie Besneval he had loved had never really existed. The Comtesse Adelaide Souvré was kindness and beauty, but could he be sure that he was not once more mistaken?

A few weeks ago he had thought that he had cause to pity Guy d'Abbeville, for he had believed him to be deeply unhappy in the choice of marriage partner. Now he bore the appearance of a man content and in love, while he, Henri, was wretched. How fate made fools of them all, he reflected wryly. Would Marie think of him at all while she repented her misdeeds in a remote convent? Knowing Marie as he thought he did, he felt sure that she would soon find some way of amusing herself.

Athénaïs de Montespan was a different proposition. Every so often she would pause in the act of throwing down a card, and direct a baleful glance at Teresa. If she hoped to attract unwelcome attention to her in that way, she had missed the mark, for most present assumed that her actions sprang from jealousy. It had escaped no one's notice that the King seemed much enamoured of Mademoiselle Rochefoucourt. Many speculated that she would be the King's next mistress.

A ripple of excitement stirred the perfumed air as one of the King's men announced loudly that the King approached. He entered the room and waved everyone back to their seats, then, without looking at his mistress, who had looked eagerly in his direction, walked over to the table occupied by the Duc and his party.

Raising the hand of the Duchesse Marie-Victoire to his lips, he complimented her on her appearance. 'You always ornament Versailles, Marie-Victoire. We could wish for your presence more often.'

'For the pleasure of hearing such compliments, sir, I would gladly risk breaking every bone in my body on those dreadful roads to attend Court more often.'

'I cannot believe that Provence should be so lacking in people who cannot appreciate wit and charm when they meet it.' Louis was delighted with the Duchesse; she knew exactly what to say to please him. 'As to the roads, I believe that I will not be able to test them yet, for the Queen tells me that I really must be here to welcome the Austrian delegation, and so we must give up the idea of an expedition to Provence.' He sighed and looked with genuine regret at the Duc.

Guy d'Abbeville stiffened; he could not tell if the King was forbidding his return to his home. Vain, fickle and peevish, Louis acted frequently on whim. When he had first said that he would like to accompany the betrothed pair on a visit to Provence, it seemed as though he had tacitly agreed to end the Duc's enforced stay at Court.

'Mayhap we could welcome the King and Queen to Provence at some later stage?' he responded coolly.

'There is no hurry.' The King was peevish. 'Why must people always be in such a hurry to make changes? I detest changes; they are not good.'

All pretence at conversation had stopped in the assembled courtiers and their ladies, as all watched the exchange with avid curiosity. The Marquise had not been pleased when the King had so pointedly snubbed her by going directly to the table of the Duc. There had been a time when he had had eyes only for herself, and everyone else in a room had had to crane forward to get his attention. Now his glances were for that flaxen-haired girl who had caused her downfall. Her secret glee had sustained her through the ordeal of playing cards under the eyes of so many ill-wishers; when she thought of Teresa going to St Germain to recover her confession from the old servant, and of her fate, she almost laughed aloud. The King had an abnormal fear of illness, and particularly of infectious illness. Even if Teresa were to escape the worst consequences of the smallpox, she would certainly never be allowed to return to Court.

But the King had just said that he detested changes. Did that mean that she would continue to be his mistress? A tiny hope began to seed. Although he was now bowing over the hand of the Comtesse Souvré, his civilities appeared to be mechanical, for, beautiful though she was, the King was not interested in her. He seemed more interested in looking at Teresa Rochefoucourt, and listening to the outrageous sallies of the old Duchesse.

'There! I vow I have lost so many thousands of *livres* tonight that I shall have to pay you with my diamond necklace.' The Marquise spoke loudly and looked provocatively at Louis. 'But it was given to me by one whom I love dearly, and it would break my heart to part with it.'

Madame de Thiange looked sharply at her friend, and tried hard not to gasp aloud. In the days when the King only had eyes for his mistress, he would have paid her debts without a murmur. Any expressions of her devotion had been received with ecstatic smiles and shining eyes. Now he turned from speaking to the Comtesse and looked in their direction—not directly at the Marquise, but at some point just above her head. Standing straight-backed, magnificently attired in crimson brocade, the Bourbon King looked haughty and aloof. The effect was unnerving, and the Marquise blanched.

'The Marquise has gambled and lost. I believe that she has played above her income, and will have to accustom herself to living in much reduced circumstances.' Turning his back on the Marquise, the King was all smiles and fulsome charm to Teresa. 'We all look forward to your wedding day, my dear. There has been little enough to make us smile these past few days.' It was the only allusion that he was ever to make to the events of the preceding days; his thoughts and feelings were hidden behind a mask of awesome royalty.

Teresa saw the Marquise falter and glance uncertainly around her; once more she was conscious of the fickle loyalties pervading the Court, for none looked with sympathy or kindness on the woman so completely and publicly abandoned by her lover. The King was raising Teresa's hand to his lips, and she strove to appear flattered and pleased, for she had felt apprehensive when the King had returned an evasive answer to the Duc's invitation. Exerting a slight pressure on her fingers, the King held her hand and looked into her eyes. Like the Duc, he had dark brown eyes, but where one glance from the Duc had the power to raise or deflate her feelings, the King merely made her feel uncomfortable.

Attempting to resume her interrupted game of cards, the Marquise was unable to resist glancing at Teresa from time to time, giving her looks of mingled loathing and fear. Until now she had felt secure in the knowledge that Teresa would never speak of the house in the forest or the events which had occurred there. Now, she was not so sure; there was a new confidence about her, a maturity that she had previously lacked. In love with the Duc she might be, but to be the King's mistress, as she well knew, was to have virtually supreme power at Court. Recalling those heady days when she had basked in the warmth of the Sun King's love, they had exchanged the deepest confidences.

If Teresa Rochefoucourt became his mistress then she would surely reveal that she had been the victim of the satanic rite. Believing that his mistress had been a participant in that rite had meant he no longer wished to see her, she was forced to accept now that she would never win him back. But if he discovered that anyone had wished harm or death on the object of his affections, that person would perish in the Bastille.

Gathering up her cards and trying to appear unconcerned in the face of the dreadful threat which now hung over her, she attempted to smile into the thin, cruel face of Madame de Thiange.

'I cannot continue with this game, I am out of humour. Would you care to find another partner?' Forcing herself to look as calm as possible she rose from the table.

'Of course, dear Marquise,' Madame de Thiange was all sweetness. 'We all understand that you have had a terrible shock. Doubtless you will wish to retire. But,' she paused delicately and looked towards the King, still laughing and talking to the Duc d'Abbeville and his party, 'is it wise to flee?'

'Flee?' the Marquise gave a brittle laugh. 'I am merely retiring to my quarters. Gambling bores me to death.' Ignoring the king and sweeping regally from the room without a backward glance, she returned to her apartments.

Once there, she went into her private room and began to think furiously. It had been a foolish move to have sent that confession to St Germain, for with it in her possession she had the means to defend herself against accusations. She could show him the confession and explain that Teresa had been a willing participant in the satanic rite and not for the first time. Those ridiculous predictions for Madame de Maintenon! Quite untrue, of course.

The knowledge that she had been rejected for a young girl was somehow easier to bear than the thought that she had been overthrown in favour of a plump, middle-aged woman with nothing at all to recommend her. Madame de Maintenon had been strangely friendly and communicative of late, praising the children, remarking on their progress in their studies. It was still impossible to believe that she had used Teresa as a medium for gaining information. Probably, the girl had told her what she had wanted to hear.

Banishment seemed a sweeter fate than the Bastille; she must either recover the confession quickly, or ensure that Teresa Rochefoucourt go to St Germain and contract smallpox. That little page, Paul—she would see him and demand that he gave Teresa the message. Perhaps, she smiled maliciously, they could go together. That would ensure that they were both removed. That would teach him to leave her employ without so much as a word!

'Well, Teresa, you have certainly made an impression on the King.' The Duchesse gave her a very meaningful glance and, observing the blush staining her cheeks, laughed suddenly. 'Lord! What a simpering generation you all are. In my day, to have won the admiration of his father, Louis the Thirteenth, was every girl's dream. Now, the King makes himself agreeable, acts with gallantry, and all you can do is to blush like a nun. These are not good seats, Adelaïde. We shall see nothing of the play from here. Not that I like Molière—he is only barely tolerable—but I suppose one must be in the fashion.' The Duchesse, who had chosen the seats, was now attempting to move the entire party to another part of the park in which the play was to be staged. When the King had invited them to accompany him from the card *salon*, they had not been able to refuse. It was a fine, warm evening, and all around them the air hummed with the frequently repeated story of the King's public repudiation of his mistress. In concert, they implored the Duchesse to remain where she was, for to be moving as the play was about to begin would be very annoying for the actors.

'Actors! Mistresses! Tcha! I care nothing for them. Did you see that creature storm from the room as though she were indeed the Queen she has frequently thought herself? And all because the King indulged in a little flirtation with a pretty girl.'

Henri and Adelaïde, as though in unspoken accord, immediately began to talk of other things, for the Duchesse had a penetrating voice that carried over the park with disastrous clarity. If the King should return and overhear her, he would surely be annoyed. Promising Teresa that he would play the lute for her at the conclusion of the play, he had gone to confer with his musicians to see if they had an instrument worthy of his talent.

Only Teresa and Guy d'Abbeville were hugely amused by the Duchesse, and exchanged many glances of merriment. Each time the glances became of longer duration, until finally their eyes met and were held fast. It was as though they alone existed in the park on this warm evening in summer, motionless. She saw that a small pulse throbbed at the corner of his mouth, and his eyes had darkened with desire.

The actors had begun to declaim their lines, but Teresa heard nothing, for the Duc had moved to stand behind her chair, and, sharply aware of his physical presence, she yearned to be alone with him. To be so close and yet not to be able to touch or be touched by the man she loved above all others was ecstasy in suspense.

The characters in the play had begun to shout loudly and laugh. Under cover of this noise and the generally excited reaction of the elegant audience, the Duchesse leaned across to address Teresa. 'Do you know, Teresa, that if you were to capture the King's fancy, your place at Versailles would be assured—but he would never permit you and Guy to return to Provence. I do not think I would like that at all.'

'Mama! That is a shocking thing to say. Now you will really put poor Teresa to the blush, and she has been so enjoying herself.'

Teresa, looking up into the Duc's face in a swift, agonised glance, had been afraid to voice the fear which had been gnawing at her all evening. A little smile played about his mouth, and his eyes held an expression that made her heart leap tumultuously.

'I do not care where I live,' he spoke softly. 'As long as it is with Teresa.' Touching her cheek in the lightest of caresses, that was both careless and deeply intimate at the same time, he smiled into her radiant face.

He does love me, she thought with breathless wonder. He must, or else he could not have made such an admission. At such a moment her love for him overflowed, bathing her in an almost tangible aura of loveliness. Adelaïde was a beautiful woman, but whatever he had once shared with her now belonged entirely to Teresa.

'Very prettily said, Duc.' The Duchesse spoke tartly. 'But if you two are to stage a scene more affecting than Molière's nonsense, you had better carry her off to that little house of yours in the forest, for I am sure that half the Court are more interested in you than in the actor.'

It had been his house! That was what the Duchesse had said. The vile little house, used for such dreadful purposes, had been his property. It was the Duc who had shown her the house, and who had forbidden her to enter it. Who else but the owner would have the authority to have it pulled down? Teresa felt her bright world crumble into grey, jagged disarray; it was as though a beautiful picture had been torn up and rearranged so that the pieces did not fit properly. Guy d'Abbeville, Athénaïs de Montespan. Were they lovers? Had they some deadly association for diabolical purposes? The Marquise's page had appeared in his service on the morning following the satanic rite—why?

Seeing that Teresa's face had stiffened into a white, horrified mask, the Duchesse became alarmed, and then irritated. 'For the sake of all the saints, child! Do not tell me that you are so surprised or shocked by what I have said. You cannot look at Guy d'Abbeville with your heart in your eyes, nor allow him to devour you with indecent looks, and not expect anyone to comment. Believe me, I have only put into words what anyone watching you must be thinking. It is not so very dreadful.' Giving a short bark of laughter, her *maquillage* cracked slightly. 'Just wait until Saturday! If you are still as maidenly and easily shocked after your wedding night, then I shall have misjudged young d'Abbeville. What are you making those faces at me for, Adelaïde? What is it you are trying to say?'

With hidden smiles, those who had been unable to help overhearing the Duchesse's remarks turned their attention back to the play, assuming that Teresa's frozen shock was a consequence of her virtuous shrinking from the old lady's bold and forthright speech.

Unable to bring herself to look at the Duc, Teresa kept her attention rigidly on the play, and even forced herself to laugh when everyone else did. It was some silly piece poking fun at the style of dress affected by the King and his chosen courtiers: it seemed that Paris thought the sight of a man wearing a plain military-style jerkin was hilariously funny. Quite unable to see the humour in this, for she had always thought the Duc excessively handsome in such garb that showed his tall, well-made body to such advantage, Teresa's laughter became more and more mechanical.

When he placed a hand gently on her shoulder, she flinched away, unable to bear his touch, terrified that her treacherous body should betray her mind. Looking away from the actors, whose antics no longer accorded with her own tormented sentiments for she felt listless and heavy-hearted, she caught sight of the Comtesse's lovely profile. The picture in her room, of Adelaïde, kept by the Duc—was that kept for reasons of sentiment, or because he still loved her? In the convent at Villepreux, he had told his aunt that he would rather go to the Bastille than marry her; had he changed?

Admitting to herself that this marriage had been forced on him, she also admitted that she had no right to expect his love. But he *had* told her that he loved her—he had held her in his arms and kissed her so long and so deeply that they had seemed as one loving being. Utterly confused, and too hurt and disappointed to think clearly, she simply longed to leave the park. Where could she go? It was impossible to return to the apartment she had shared with Marie Besneval; that had already been allocated to someone else. Dared she ask the Queen to shelter her? Impossible! Return to the convent at Villepreux was also impossible, for the Abbesse would never receive her again. A lifetime spent with a man whom one loved but could not trust would be a nightmare; it would involve a compromise of principles that she had not realised that she had until they had been tested.

Bending down so that his lips almost brushed her ear, the Duc spoke in a quiet voice. 'Would you like me to take you back to the house? I could say that you are indisposed.' Such an affectation of concern!

'No, thank you, it is not necessary.' If the Duc really had been involved with the satanists, she might be in danger, and it was vital that she did not let him know that she suspected him. 'It would be most unseemly, for the King has promised to play the lute for us. He would think it very odd and rude if I went away now.' Marvelling at her own composure, she began to regain control of her disordered senses. The Wicked Duc, that is what they called him, she recalled; I wonder what he did to earn that name? Did it have a more sinister significance?

Marie Besneval had said that she and the Duc had loved each other and hoped to marry. Had he talked to Marie as he had talked to her? Perhaps it was he who had introduced Marie to that house, and had betrayed her when she had most needed him. At one point Teresa had been prepared to accept Marie as a guest in the Château d'Abbeville in order to watch her with the Duc. Until recently she had suspected that he might be in love with Marie; then the Comtesse had come to Versailles with her mother. Through the sheeting rain of that dreadful night, she had seen the Comtesse in the arms of the Duc—had seen them kiss. The little dressmaker, Celeste, had told her that she had overhead the remark that no wedding would take place between herself and the Duc. Marie Besneval had been, she was quite sure, one of the women in the apartment of Madame de Maintenon. Round and round these thoughts tracked in her head, until she felt as if she would scream with frustrated anger. Were they all involved in some plot of which she had no knowledge? Everything she had thought she knew about the Duc was contradicted by the facts that she was now obliged to face.

'Well, that nonsense is over, I am pleased to say,' declared the Duchesse, who had watched the comedy with every appearance of enjoyment. Looking about for some acquaintance or friend, she spotted an elderly admirer and, patting her ringlets like a young girl, trotted briskly across the lawn to waylay him.

Immediately Adelaïde turned to her. 'I am afraid that Mama made you unhappy with her foolish talk . . .'

Feigning astonishment, and summoning up a merry smile, Teresa addressed her. 'Unhappy? How silly! The Duchesse amuses me vastly with her talk. I can promise you that I find your mother more amusing and stimulating than any other lady in Court. Fond as I am of the Queen, there is too much propriety and not enough joking when I am with her.'

If her remarks sounded inane, none appeared to notice. Henri, intercepting a doubtful look from Adelaïde, broke in eagerly.

'That is exactly what I feel about her, Teresa. She is such fun that I am rarely in her company for longer than five minutes when I find myself laughing at her drolleries.'

Taking the seat vacated by the Duchesse, and pulling it close to Teresa, the Duc took her hand in his, looking at her seriously, as though he would read her troubled thoughts with the intensity of his look. 'You and I must talk, Teresa.'

Pulling her hand away from his, for she experienced a delicious thrill of anticipation, she laughed lightly. 'Indeed we must, but not, I think, at this moment. For, look! The King approaches with his lute. You would incur the royal displeasure if you did not sit up and look fascinated.' Valiantly achieving a sunny smile, she determined that none should know of the turmoil in her mind. The Duchesse and her daughter had provided her with enough to think about, but she could not do it in public. She needed to be alone to sort out her own thoughts and troubled feelings.

The Duchesse returned from her little *sortie* much invigorated, and prepared to be pleased by the King's music. Louis, positioning himself directly before Teresa, was a noted and accomplished musician. It was probably the only point at which his vanity and talent coincided, and the result was an exquisite and tender rendering of the music of a love song, so hauntingly sweet that many produced scraps of lace with which to dab away tears.

As the music blended with the warm, summer evening air, Teresa again became conscious of the Duc's presence. Although she could not see him, for he stood, once more, behind her chair, she knew that she would sense him wherever he was. When Madame de Maintenon had used her as a medium in order to discover what was in the future, Teresa had been both puzzled and disgusted. Later, thinking over the events, she had wondered why she had been chosen, and had assumed it was because she was very young, a newcomer to Court, and could not, therefore, have been prejudiced by any preconceived ideas.

Now, deeply and painfully in love, she discovered that all her senses were heightened and sharpened, and she had an intuitive knowledge of where the Duc was and that his eyes were on her. But his thoughts remained his own, and she felt unable to determine if he spoke truthfully when he said that he loved her.

Setting aside the lute, Louis accepted the rapturous applause which greeted his performance, and looked with pleased expectancy at Teresa. Involuntarily, she put out both hands in a gesture of appreciation, for she had been moved by the beauty of the music and the skill of its executioner. Beaming with delight, his lips twitching slightly, Louis came towards her and, lifting both her hands in a graceful movement, kissed her fingertips.

'If my poor performance has given you joy, *mademoiselle*, then that is all the reward I seek.' His eyes, greedily taking in the soft beauty of her face, gave lie to his words. Louis thought himself the supremely confident centre of a web of pomp and splendour, where the players moved amorously to the background of ornament and music. That the web could be dark and murky, that players played for stakes beyond their social and financial means, never troubled him. He was the Sun King—where he commanded, all obeyed without question.

Teresa Rochefoucourt was young and very beautiful. When she smiled at him her blue eyes sparkled and, he imagined, invited him to intimacy. There was a candour and directness in her manner which refreshed his jaded palate; the thought of making her his mistress whetted his appetite. Duc Guy d'Abbeville would have to accept the fact that the King desired his bride. Although he liked the Duc, he had been alarmed and impressed with the speed with which he had dealt with that unsavoury episode in the forest. That had demonstrated to the King that the Duc had the ability and strength of purpose to achieve any end he sought. What if he should seek to overthrow the monarchy? If one man in France could bring about such a terrifying state of affairs, it was the Duc. The Duc d'Abbeville must never be allowed to return to Provence; he must be kept here, under the regal eye. If he disliked that, he could change his quarters to the Bastille.

'I have a capital notion! It is such a lovely evening, why do we not take a gondola along the canal? We could sup in one of those little arbours that I have had constructed.' The King addressed the party generally, but his eyes sought Teresa's approval of the scheme.

Clapping her hands, she exclaimed, 'How lovely! I have not yet been on the canal. What fun! Do say we may accept,' she pleaded prettily with the Duc. The King had unexpectedly provided an excellent reason for separating her from the Duc, the Duchesse, the Comtesse and Henri Deschamps. Their unspoken sympathy and attempts to alleviate any distress she might be feeling was irksome. Any discussion following the disclosure that the house in the forest had been owned by the Duc must be postponed, for she was quite unable to deal with the subject at the moment. If his ownership of the house had been above board, then why had he not told her about it?

'What an ogre you must think me to beg my permission. As though I would seek to deny you any pleasure!' The Duc smiled at her, his harsh face softening in a way that few had ever seen. Fully conscious of the shock she must have had when she had heard that the house in the forest was his, he longed to comfort her. It had never been his intention to tell her that he owned the house; the circumstances surrounding his ownership had been disagreeable, and he had preferred to forget that it had ever existed. It belonged to a part of his past that he could not take pride in; he did not wish to think about it, let alone talk about it.

'Seek the Duc's permission where the King has commanded?' Louis tried to appear flippant, but only succeeded in sounding peevish. 'Does it please you to disobey me, d'Abbeville?' The tone was petulant.

'Whether it pleased me or not, Your Majesty must know that I would always obey him.'

The Duchesse, alive to the great honour bestowed upon them by being invited to join the King in this expedition on the canal, was anxious to avail of it before the King became fractious and changed his mind. The Grand Canal had been finished in 1672, and the King had brought Venetian gondolas to Versailles, complete with colourfully dressed gondoliers who were housed in the place on the canal known as Little Venice. When the King went out in his little flotilla, it was always a ceremonious occasion, for he insisted that musicians followed his progress. If they found playing music in a moving gondola difficult, they never complained, and those privileged to hear them all agreed that to glide down the canal in the cool evening air to the strains of Lully's music was bliss.

'What a lot of bother about nothing,' she declared sharply. 'We shall never be so honoured or entertained again in our entire lives! Permission? We are all gratitude and excitement. You may command *me* to your heart's content, for I am all eagerness to obey such a delightful command.'

The slight tension which had settled over the party during the exchange between the Duc and his King lifted, for Louis had heard what he wanted to hear. All smiles and condescension, he waved a hand in the direction of the Grand Canal, and, offering his arm to Teresa, escorted her to the gondolas.

The Duchesse, her daughter and Teresa were to travel in the King's gondola, and they looked suitably flattered and attentive as the King described some of the lovely features that he had had installed along the canal and in the park. They were all described as his own inventions, products of his genius, creations designed to accentuate the glories of the monarchy. Every so often he paused as though expecting Teresa to reply, but as she was wholly unskilled in the art of flattering a King, she did not know how to reply. It was left to Adelaïde to murmur the right responses at regular intervals; this she did in a calm, quiet manner, and Teresa could not help but admire her poise and dignity. In fact, Teresa was afraid that Adelaïde's forthright mother might utter some remark to which the King might take offence. Sensing that the King had somehow been antagonistic towards the Duc, she did not wish any unwise words of the Duchesse San Rémy's to add to the uneasiness which pervaded the atmosphere. Only the Duc, sure of his love's heart, seemed unaffected.

Stealing a glance at the Duc as the King assisted her into the red-cushioned gondola, Teresa saw that he was laughing and talking with Henri Deschamps as though he had not a care in the world. Irrationally, she began to feel incensed. The King had made his desires very plain—surely, if the Duc loved her as he said he did, then he should be jealous or, in the very least, concerned. Sitting beside the King, with Adelaïde and the Duchesse seated opposite them, she experienced a little thrill of pleasure as the gondola began to move along the water. It was a novel experience, and Louis was charmed by her ingenuous enjoyment of the simple pastime. When he began to flirt with her, she wished that the gondola bearing the Duc and Henri was not so far behind them, so that he could have heard her enraptured acceptance of the King's gallantries. But the lesson she wished to teach him was quite wasted, for every time she looked back at him he was deep in conversation with Henri. Becoming more animated, she allowed the King to pinch her cheek and call her his new jewel of Versailles. The Duchesse watched them with maliciously twinkling eyes, while Adelaïde became more and more uncomfortable as they floated past verdant banks of trees, bushes and flowers.

With an expert flick of his wrist, the gondolier poled the gondola towards a small landing-stage, and, thrusting the pole deep into the water, simultaneously it seemed to Teresa, flung a rope around the piece of wood jutting from the small pier, and secured the gondola. Leaping with agility on to the pier, the gondolier began to assist first the King and then the ladies on to firm ground.

'Where are my servants?' Louis looked around him, pouting slightly. 'I particularly wished that a cold collation should be laid out in the little arbour close to this spot. It is a charming place—I thought of the entire design myself, you know, with only a little help from the Marquis de Lengeron. You recall him, Marie-Victoire? He is a most able and agreeable man. Ah, here is a groom! Now you shall see how cosily and informally a King may entertain his friends. I particularly in-structed that there should be no ceremony this evening, just a little collation for my friends. Tourville! Tourville! Is all prepared?'

The groom, immensely tall and sad-looking, stepped forward and bowed to the King. 'Everything is just as Your Majesty has ordered.' Teresa wanted to laugh, for he looked as though he had come to tell the King that someone had died. The gondola bearing the musicians was just drawing level with the pier; of the Duc and Henri, there was, as yet, no sign.

'Good! Good! Now, *mademoiselle*, take my arm, for I cannot risk you falling on that little step you see ahead of you, and breaking your pretty ankle. At least,' he bent his head and whispered confidentially in her ear, 'I *assume* it is a pretty ankle, but I dare say I shall have to see it for myself.' Smiling fulsomely, he walked ahead of the Duchesse and Adeläde.

After a short walk along a very pretty pathway, bordered with big pink flowers that gave off a faint fragrance, they arrived at the King's cosy little arbour. It was as large as a small *salon* in the palace. An enormous table had been laid with every kind of food: partridges, chicken, dishes of green peas, jugs of cream, pastries made in the shape of birds and flowers, and, in addition to this, there were eggs stuffed with spiced mushrooms on beds of crisp green lettuce, beside a great silver dish bearing capon stuffed with oysters. How on earth were five people to eat this gargantuan feast? Teresa wondered, sure that she could only manage a strawberry from the basket at the edge of the table. The great quantity of champagne must surely be intended for a very much larger party than theirs!

The King urged the Duchesse and the Comtesse to sit on the elegant little chairs, more suited to a drawing-room than an arbour, and help themselves to as much food as they cared to eat. 'For, you see, it is all to be quite informal—we help ourselves, we dispense with servants.' He pinched Teresa's arm and his moistened lips curved sensually. 'We can then be very private,' he whispered into her ear.

At first amused by the scene and the King's manner, she became alarmed when he led her not to the table, but back on to the path that led away from the canal, towards which the chairs faced.

'I am going to show *mademoiselle* some very beautiful statues in the little clearing close by.' Without giving the other women a chance to reply, he walked away with an unwilling Teresa on his arm.

A group of exquisite white marble statues graced the centre of a little glade. Stopping in wonder, Teresa looked at the group of wood-nymphs, their hands flung out, robes flowing, and a look of abandoned pleasure on their marble faces. They were at once delicate and sturdy, their fluid lines a testament to the sculptor's art. Once again, Louis took credit for this lovely creation.

'It was a great piece of work to get this done, you know. I had to send to Italy for the men to execute this for me. Naturally, they worked under my instruction the whole time. Afterwards they told me that they did not know how they would have managed without me. Never in their entire careers had they had such instruction and guidance from any living being. For a while I was tempted to have them remain at Versailles, but they were unfortunately obliged to leave at very short notice.'

While Louis was marvelling at the contemplation of his own genius, Teresa wondered if they had earned a large fee for their diplomacy as well as their skill.

'Of course, this paltry sight cannot compare with one so lovely as you, my pretty girl.' Sliding an arm around her waist, he breathed heavily into her face, his lips thickening with desire.

Into her mind flashed a memory of another glade in the forest, of another man, kissing her until she had yearned for a completion of their physical union with a ferocity and intensity to match his own. As the King pressed his lips on to hers, she could feel her gorge rising. Spontaneously pushing him away, her nose wrinkled in distaste, she averted her face.

'What is this?' Louis was dismayed and surprised. 'You gave me every encouragement. This is no time for maidenly shrinking. Come, my pretty girl, you shall know what it is to be loved by a King.'

His further attempts to kiss her were frustrated by her face becoming very white and convulsing. Watching these actions with some alarm, he saw her put her hand to her mouth.

'I . . . I think I am going to be sick, if it pleases Your Majesty,' she gasped.

'It does *not* please me!' he responded, incensed. 'Kindly try to control yourself. Never before have my attentions been received less worthily; it pains me to see that I have so misjudged you.'

Desperately trying to control her unwelcome physical reaction to his lovemaking, she spoke jerkily. 'It is just that I love the Duc, my husband-to-be. I meant no offence to Your Majesty. Please, believe that.' Involuntarily, she put out a hand as though to ward him off. It was so reminiscent of her earlier gesture of welcome that he froze angrily.

'Doubtless you love your future husband. But it is not in my experience that a woman who loves a man seeks to entice and encourage me into this unseemly and ridiculous position. I fear that, between you, you and your Duc have sought to make me an object of ridicule. No one ridicules the King of France and escapes!' He was haughty and majestic; how had she ever thought of him as a figure of fun? 'You will remind your Duc that the Bastille awaits those who offend the King of France. Come, *mademoiselle*, I trust that you are sufficiently recovered to return to the rest of your party.'

With blinding clarity, Teresa saw that she had placed the Duc in a position of the greatest danger. If Louis had only issued veiled threats earlier in the afternoon, he had now shown his hand very clearly. Given a chance, he would send Guy d'Abbeville to the Bastille. It was at that moment, as the King escorted her back to the arbour, that she once more recollected the existence of her confession.

CHAPTER THIRTEEN

'But, Marquise, you do not understand! I must have that confession, today! I beg that you will give it to me.'

Athénaïs de Montespan could hardly believe her eyes when Teresa was admitted to her apartments. All day she had racked her brains, trying to find a suitable means of contacting her and then inveigling her to go to St Germain. When she had summoned the page, Paul, the impudent brat had refused to answer her summons. Even her own servants, aware of the fate that hung over her, were becoming slovenly and impudent. Despite the gravity of her situation, she had not given up hope that the King would relent and that their mutual passion would be rekindled. It had been an agony of jealousy and torment for her when Louis had fawned over this girl; looking now at her shadowed eyes and pale cheeks, it was difficult to discern the charms that had fascinated Louis.

'Mademoiselle Rochefoucourt! How very kind of you to visit me. Your confession? I cannot give it to you, much as I would like, for I no longer have it.' The Marquise smiled maddeningly.

Teresa stopped, and her mouth formed into a round of amazement. 'Do you mean that Père Dubois still has it? But,' Teresa faltered, on the verge of tears, 'I thought that he had left the Court.'

Left the court! The Marquise could not decide if Teresa was an imbecile or a clever woman feigning innocence. 'Oh, yes, he has most certainly left the Court,' she responded bitterly. 'But he has not got your confession. I know where it is, but first you must tell me some things that I wish to know. Then I will tell you where your confession is, for it is a dangerous piece of paper.'

Covering her pale cheeks with slim hands, Teresa's eyes widened. 'I know that, and I could not bear anything to happen to him.'

Pausing, as she had been about to speak, the Marquise looked at her, puzzled. 'The King?'

'No! The Duc d'Abbeville.' Teresa sounded agonised.

Swiftly the Marquise tried to recall what the contents of the confession had been. There had been something about the Duc having taken this girl, the Queen's god-child, from the convent at Villepreux. Surely she could not, in the light of succeeding events, think that there was anything in the confession to bring shame upon the Duc? If anyone could be found wanting as a result of making that interesting little document public, it would be the little fool herself. But there were possibilities here—possibilities that she would like to explore. If Teresa was so enamoured of the arrogant Duc d'Abbeville, then she could be made to suffer even more.

Moving gracefully across the luxuriously carpeted room, she could not—would not—believe that she must give all this up! The Marquise rang a small silver handbell that rested on a gilt table near the door. After what seemed an age, a servant responded to the summons and stood impatiently at the door. She was looking over her shoulder.

'What do you want?' she demanded rudely. 'I have other duties to attend to beside pandering to your needs. Madame de Maintenon said I was to stay close by her; she will be annoyed if she learns that I have performed any service for you.'

Teresa gasped with astonishment. The Marquise had taken part in a ceremony that was to culminate in Teresa's death—she might not have realised that, but she had not been present for any good purpose. But this servant could not know that, and the Marquise had held complete sway over Louis's Court for many years. A few weeks ago her word had been law, her smallest whim had been obeyed, and now the servant spoke of 'pandering' to her. Once more she reflected on the fickle nature of the Court, where favourites were appointed and dismissed with in-decent haste. Should she have been unwise enough to have become the King's mistress, this could now have been the fate that awaited her. Sympathy stirred within her, unwillingly, for this tormented, unhappy woman. Whatever her own personal feelings were, she must not forget that the Duc's life might depend on her recovering that confession. She must discipline herself into concealing her hostile feelings for the Marquise.

An unbecoming flush of anger stained the Marquise's cheeks, but she did not retort or reprimand the insolent servant. 'A few days ago I sent a man into the village of St Germain with some hampers of food and clothes for an old servant of mine. Please find the man and send him to me.'

'Find the man? Certainly not! I've got better things to do than hunt the length and breadth of Versailles for some lazy servant. If you want him, my lady, you go and find him yourself!' With that she flounced away, leaving a scarlet-faced Marquise open-mouthed.

'You cannot know how I suffer,' she told Teresa, tears of anger running down her reddened cheeks.

But *you* must know how you intended *me* to suffer, thought Teresa, appalled at the woman's hypocrisy.

'I shall be separated from my children, that is the part I cannot bear. My darling little baby, I shall never...' Her voice was suspended by tears, and, despite her resolve, Teresa was moved. 'If you are to become the King's next mistress, I beg that you will be kind to them.'

Teresa was unable to answer, for Madame de Thiange burst into the apartment, her crimson skirts billowing, thin mouth working excitedly.

'Marquise! I came directly I heard the news! It is too exciting, and the whole Court is in uproar. But you know me, I am not one to take pleasure in the downfall of a friend. You will never guess who has been created a Marquise!'

Eyes flashing, fingers curled dangerously, the Marquise whirled around and looked with suspicion at Teresa. Instinctively she flinched, for she had seen the King's mistress look at her that way before.

'Not her!' Madame de Thiange was contemptuous. 'It is your children's governess, Madame de...or, I *should* say, the Marquise de Maintenon. There!' she gave a high titter of laughter. 'I knew that you would be as surprised as I.' Her narrow eyes sparkling with malice, she assisted the Marquise de Montespan to a sofa. 'Very shocking news, is it not? I vow and declare that I almost fainted myself when I heard. What can it mean, do you think? Do you suppose that the King and de Maintenon actually...but, no! The idea is too preposterous. At least, that is what they are all saying—behind her back, of course, for to her face they are all bowing and scraping. I came away, for I could not bear such hypocrisy.' Flushed and animated, the woman looked almost pretty, and Teresa felt sick.

'Thank you, *madame*. It was most kind of you to bring me the news, but I should not like to detain you, for it will be politic for you to return to the Marquise.' The Marquise pulled some shreds of dignity around her and nodded to the woman already hurrying gleefully from the room.

As soon as she had gone, the Marquise slumped forward, her arms across her chest, elbows on her knees, eyes blazing in a whitened face. 'You knew about this, did you not? You predicted it. Did you play some part in my downfall, and the raising up of that old hag to such a position?' What terrified Teresa more than the woman's demented appearance was the low, hissing voice she used—quite unlike the musical tones she usually employed.

'You mistake, Marquise. I care only about the Duc d'Abbeville.'

Teresa's quiet, rational tone enraged the woman still further, and she found that the sight of the beautiful young girl trying to protect the man she loved an unbearable sight.

'Well, he does not care about you! Did you think he did?'

'He loves me.' Teresa spoke faintly, feeling waves of hatred emanate from the other woman.

'He never loved you, you little fool! Did you know that it was his house we used in the forest, the night we planned to kill you?'

The venomous expression, the hissing voice, combined to make Teresa sick. 'The Duc did not know about that; I overheard the men talking.'

'Oh, yes, he did. Did you think that they dreamt up the whole plot? *I* fed them ideas—ideas that the Duc told me to feed them. There! I see that I have surprised you. You did not know that, did you? It was the Duc who wished to seize power. You had served your purpose, and he wished to be rid of you.'

As her world turned grey and chills of fear began to run up and down her spine, Teresa heard her voice come from afar. 'And why does he still wish to marry me? For he does, you know.'

'To protect himself. He thinks that you know too much. If you are married to him, then you cannot speak against him. Very clever! All men are clever—they use women to serve their ends, and then abandon them. Believe me, my dear, you have all my sympathy.' She laughed shrilly.

'I do not want your sympathy!' Teresa cried. 'I want my confession. Let me have it and be gone, for I cannot stand any more of your lies. You even set your page in the Duc's house to spy on me!' Fear and disillusionment had made her rash.

The Marquise quivered with excitement—was it possible that she did not know about the page going into the Duc's service?

'If you have any affection for the Duc—and I assume you must or you would not have sent him your page—then, for the love of God, please give me that confession.' As fast as the Marquise was regaining her composure, Teresa was becoming distraught.

Conceiving a plan that would ensure that the page suffered as much as Teresa, she spoke glibly. 'Foolish child! I did not send Paul to spy on you, I sent him for a much better reason. Paul is our son.'

Staring at her blankly, Teresa said, 'Your son? The son of Louis?'

Wagging a finger, and smiling archly, for the Marquise was beginning to enjoy her game, she replied, 'The son I bore the Duc. Oh, it was all so long ago, and naturally it was kept very quiet. These little episodes usually are, you know.'

Feeling as though she had stepped into the maze on a dark night, Teresa tried to fight off the nightmare feeling that threatened to rob her of her sanity. 'I thought that he had loved the Comtesse Souvré,' she said weakly.

Desperately, the Marquise tried to recall where she had heard that name before. The face of a very beautiful dark-eyed woman swam into her mind's eye. Adelaïde San Rémy. Had there not been some scandal? Something about d'Abbeville wanting to marry her—or did he elope with her? It was all so long ago that she could not recollect. No! Wait! She had it. D'Abbeville had loved her, declared his love to the world, and his Adelaïde had chosen another! Was not his rival also his friend? Yes, she was sure that was the case, and, moreover, d'Abbeville was supposed to have forced a duel on to Albert Souvré.

'He does love the Comtesse, but her late husband, Albert Souvré, stipulated that if she married the Duc d'Abbeville after his death, then she would lose her fortune. In marrying you, he can have your fortune— he is an excessively greedy man—*and* have his lover. One can hardly blame him!' She shrugged her shoulders. 'Men are all the same, *chérie*, you will soon discover that.'

How hateful that term of endearment was on her lips! 'I do not envy you your life in Provence—the Duc is the son of a traitor and a whore. Do not look so shocked, it is no secret.'

'I must leave you. The Queen has requested that I attend her.' Teresa rose stiffly from her seat, feeling that if she did not leave this hateful place immediately she would become hysterical. The Marquise had told her so much that might be the lies of a wounded, defeated woman; on the other hand, she might be speaking the truth. The Duc had told her nothing, explained nothing.

'Stay! Do you not wish to find your confession?' Biting her lip, afraid that she had said too much, the Marquise tried to appear sympathetic, for she very much wished Teresa to go to St Germain and contract the smallpox. 'All this has been a terrible shock for you, I can well imagine, for when I was young I, too, permitted myself the luxury of falling in love. It does not last, my dear. Your confession is with an old servant of mine, a Mathilde Quesnay, in St Germain. I am not sure where she lives; it somewhere near the church, I believe. Go to her now, today, and recover your property. I lodged it with her where it would be perfectly safe, for Mathilde cannot read.'

Teresa had no idea what she said, nor how she left the apartments of the Marquise, only that minutes later she was curtsying deeply before the Queen.

'What a long time it seems since you looked at all your jewels.' Maria Teresa's face was lit by a sweet, grave smile, as pure and untroubled as the woman she had just left had been wicked and demented. 'Today I give them all into the keeping of the Duc. He will be here in a moment.' Colour flooded Teresa's pale cheeks, and the Queen attributed this to her pleasurable anticipation. 'My lawyers have prepared all the deeds of settlement. You need not be concerned with the details, for they relate mainly to the disposal of your income among your children. Your husband will attend to all those matters for you.'

Looking about the room in which she had spent so many happy, untroubled hours, Teresa could not help reflecting how much she had changed since she had come to Court. A few weeks ago she could not possibly have listened to the words that the Marquise had spoken and remained outwardly calm and poised—that she had learned from the Queen and Adelaïde.

'Take this piece of sewing, Teresa. My eyes are troubling me today, and I cannot continue for some minutes. It is an altar cloth, for the royal chapel. I particularly wish it to be finished for this afternoon, where a very special wedding takes place.'

Teresa's eyes flew from her stitchery to the Queen's softly smiling face. 'Wedding, Your Majesty?' Her heart skipped a beat; surely the Queen could not mean her own wedding? That was not to take place until Saturday. She must recover her confession first!

'The King has agreed that you and the Duc can be married this afternoon. As you know, he had some notion that you would be married on the day that the Austrian delegation arrives. We were all to depart immediately for Provence; a charming idea, but one, I believe, we must put off until another time. Men can be very difficult at times, as you will discover, but with love and patience they can all be managed. Louis does not wish to see the Austrians, but I have persuaded him that it would not be the act of a great King to absent himself from Court at such a time. It would be better for your marriage to take place immediately; we can then give the occasion the accord and respect that we would wish. Already the King is busy planning the most extravagant festivities.' A smile of genuine amusement gleamed for a moment. 'It is remarkable how easy it is to manage the most difficult man. At least I have not lost that power.' This was said without irony, and Teresa felt humbled. The Queen, in demanding so little of life, made her feel selfish.

In the background she heard the Princesse d'Elbeuf murmuring, and knew without turning around that the Duc was in the room. As he bowed gracefully over the Queen's hand, she saw how broad was his back, how assured his bearing; her heart ached with love and betrayal at the one time. As he turned to her, his eyes burned with ardent desire and a smile quivered at the corner of his mouth. Was he acting? Had Athénaïs de Montespan been speaking the truth? Like Adelaïde, she was a woman of great beauty and poise—did he prefer that type of woman? Youth and inexperience made Teresa vulnerable, and afraid to trust her own feelings. If half the monstrous accusations made by the Marquise were true, then the Duc did not, and never would love her.

'We marry this afternoon, Teresa.' He was holding out his hand, his manner strong and confident, a teasing smile in his dark eyes when he saw her blush and hesitate. 'Come, let us take the Queen's blessing.' Holding her hand, he raised her up and they knelt before the Queen, side by side. Their hands joined in prayer, she was quite unable to summon any sober thoughts, for his close physical proximity made her pulses race, and her breath became curiously short.

At the conclusion of her blessing, the Queen smiled down on them. 'Now, Duc, you and I must attend to some business matters. Teresa will prepare for her wedding here, in my own apartments, and my women will attend her. Do not look so anxious, Teresa, for I have sent to your dressmaker for your gown, and I am very pleased with it. It is charming.'

Teresa felt as though she had been suspended in time. It was as though she had been robbed of the power of all her senses—she should hate that proud, arrogant face so close to hers. Resentment should be uppermost in her mind, for he had made the most delicious love to her, and yet his deeds in the past had earned him the name of Wicked Duc.

It would be unfair and childish to expect that a man of thirty should have no past, for he must. But the thought that his child by the Marquise de Montespan had been casually introduced into his household shocked her as much as the accusation that the man she was to marry was the son of a traitor and a whore. Inexperienced she might be, and unformed her views certainly were, but she was just enough to admit that no child could be responsible for its parents. Was it possible that this man whose very presence in a room made her every fibre quiver responsively, was the man who had plotted against his King?

'Would Your Majesty permit me a moment alone with my bride?' How assured he sounded. When the Queen nodded assent, his fingers curled around hers as they rose from their kneeling position.

'May I suggest that you both spend a few minutes in prayer in the royal chapel?' With her usual tact, the Queen had provided an ideal and opportune time for them to talk before their marriage.

Already the chapel was full of lovely blooms, their fragrance mingling with the faint aroma of incense. The King's choir, under the able instruction of the choirmaster, was practising the music for the wedding. There was an air of bustle and gaiety; everyone loved a wedding. Lighting candles before a statue of the Blessed Virgin, Teresa and the Duc stood for a moment in a silence full of unspoken thoughts and unanswered questions. The gravity of the contract that she was about to enter into was made apparent to her in that moment, and, with a revulsion of feeling, she felt unable to contemplate a life with this man until she had answers to

her questions, and until she had recovered the confession
that might put his life in danger. If he had not told her
the truth, neither had she been fair to him. She had to
recover that confession, and with all possible speed.

Taking her hand, he raised it to his lips. 'We shall
soon be man and wife, my darling. You cannot know
how that fills me with pleasure.' Confused and miserable, she snatched her hand away, for her body was at
war with her head. Had he spoken such words to
Adelaïde? Did they laugh at her behind her back? The
face of the page, Paul, rose to her mind; was he—could
he be—the son of the Duc and the Marquise?

'I do not wish to marry you, Duc! Please, do not press
me for reasons, for you will not tell me the truth, I know
that. Once, you told me that you would prefer the Bastille
to marriage with me. Now, I tell you that I am so confused and unhappy that I would prefer death to marriage with you.' Tears of unhappiness ran down her
cheeks, unrestrained. 'You do not…cannot…have ever
loved me.'

It was the moment for the Duc, regardless of the fact
that they were the object of furtive scrutiny of the chor-
isters and servants busy in the chapel, to take Teresa in
his arms and kiss away her fears. For a man so experienced in love, he behaved with a clumsiness that he later
regretted bitterly.

'It is true that I have not always loved you,' he began,
stepping back from her, his voice and manner stiff with
embarrassment and the hurt of rejection. 'That is hardly
surprising, since this marriage was forced upon
me——'

Humiliation and anger now sent away the unhappiness and confusion. So! This marriage was forced upon
him—he still harped on that outworn melody. There was
no trace of the former tender affection and ardent desire
in his eyes or voice. Had that been assumed? It must
have been, or could not be so readily abandoned.

'This marriage was also forced on me!' she reminded
him vehemently. 'If you think I take pleasure in the
thought of a union with the son of a traitor and whore,
you are vastly mistaken, sir!'

Appalled at her own words, she stopped suddenly, for there was an expression of such murderous hatred in his eyes that she recoiled. Turning on his heel, he strode from the chapel, and did not see the tears, now of contrition and remorse, stream down her pale cheeks.

The preparations for the wedding were all carried out by other people; Teresa moved like a sleep-walker through the next few hours. From time to time, she was aware that the Queen came to see her, that there were exclamations of awed surprise about her ethereal beauty, the diamonds she wore, the translucence of her skin. It was only when Adelaïde Souvré came to present her with a little white mantilla of finest Provençal lace that colour flooded her pale cheeks—the delicate colour of a wild rose.

'Ah! That is so much better, now you have some colour,' the Princesse d'Elbeuf approved. 'It is good that your friend is here. You must stay, Comtesse, for *mademoiselle* should have a friend of her own to accompany her.' A murmur of assent rose from the ladies who continued to fuss around her like bees moving over clover.

'I shall be happy and honoured to accompany you to the chapel, Teresa.' Adelaïde spoke quietly, much concerned, for she saw that Teresa was unhappy.

When the Duc had returned a short while ago to the house in the Avenue du Vieux Versailles, he had been in a thunderous rage, barking orders to servants with such unaccustomed severity that they flew to obey his commands. Beneath his rage, she who knew him well had detected the same ravaged grief that she had witnessed in him all those years ago when she had told him that she would not—could not—love him, and that she was to marry Albert Souvré.

It had been impossible to avoid the knowledge that the Duc was deeply in love with Teresa Rochefoucourt, and that she returned his love, for their every glance revealed their feelings. Something dreadful had occurred, and she was at a loss to think what it could be. Was it possible that Teresa had heard the story of the house in the forest—not her own unhappy experience there, but

an older and more dreadful one? It was for the Duc to
divulge that, not his friend.

Affection for the man who had once loved her made
her come to the palace to see if there was some help she
could give to put matters right. Seeing Teresa standing
motionless, listless, and with a haunted look shadowing
her eyes, she knew that something had occurred which
had created a rift between the lovers—something that
boded ill for their forthcoming marriage.

'Comtesse, how charming you look in that shade of
yellow. Only people of your colouring should wear that
shade.' The Queen had entered the dressing-room and
nodded kindly dismissal to the ladies present. Adelaïde
had dipped into a low curtsy and was preparing to
withdraw.

'Do not go, Comtesse. I wish you to wait here with
Teresa. In a few minutes my chaplain will come and take
you both to the chapel; we shall follow in your train.
You see, Teresa,' she twinkled, 'today, it is you who must
take precedence over everyone.'

Alone with Adelaïde, Teresa took her courage in both
hands. She had to know if it was true that she and the
Duc were lovers.

'There is something I must ask you, Adelaïde,' she
blurted out. Thank heavens, thought Adelaïde, for she
had begun to fear Teresa's silence, and wondered if she
would even utter her wedding vows. 'Is it true that you
and the Duc are lovers and plan to continue in that state
after we are married?'

'I will not ask who told you such an infamous lie!'
Adelaïde's eyebrows rose in pained surprise. Whatever
she had been expecting, it was not this. 'It is untrue and,
besides, I think that Henri, who has asked me to marry
him, would have something to say on that subject.'

Eyes rounded in surprise, Teresa gaped at her. 'You
are to marry Henri? But, I thought that you and the
Duc...'

'If we loved each other he would be marrying me, not
you, and Henri would not have proposed to me. What
a strange idea, Teresa.' Adelaïde was perplexed.

'I heard that the Duc would not marry you because
that would mean that you would have to give up the

inheritance from your husband, and that your husband
had stipulated that you were not to marry the Duc.'
Teresa spoke so quickly that she was breathless.

'Whoever told you such nonsense was out to make
mischief. My late husband's property reverted auto-
matically to his next male heir—we did not have any
children. In any case, the Duc is an immensely wealthy
man; such considerations need not weigh with him. As
to Albert stipulating that Guy and I should not marry,
you must know that he requested the very opposite.
When he was dying he gave Guy a portrait, his own
favourite portrait of me, to hold in his safe-keeping, and
asked him to care of me.'

Teresa felt her world turn topsy-turvy; Adelaïde was
so clearly telling the truth that she felt ashamed of herself
for voicing the vile accusations that had been made
against her.

'And his son?' she whispered through stiff, dry lips.
'His son, the page, Paul, his son by the Marquise de
Montespan?'

Adelaïde's kindly compassion began to fade visibly;
she looked haughty and distant. 'Do I understand you
to mean that these monstrous allegations were made by
the Marquise de Montespan?' Teresa nodded dumbly.
'And you took her word? I see that you did, or you
would not be questioning me. Do not be a fool! Paul is
the nephew of Gaston who owns the inn, Gaston's, in
the town! Everyone knows that. The Duc gave him a
position in his household because he was one of those
instrumental in securing your salvation from the house
in the forest. But surely the Duc must have told you all
this?'

'No, we did not discuss any of it.'

'Then, why on earth have you quarrelled? I take it
you *have* quarrelled, for I have never seen Guy in such
a murderous rage.'

Miserably Teresa looked at her. 'I told him that I did
not wish to marry the son of a traitor and a whore.'

Her face rigid with disdain, Adelaïde stepped back
from her. 'I see. That explains a good deal. I will accompany you, *mademoiselle*, because the Queen commands it and the chaplain is already at the door.

Otherwise I would wish myself a hundred miles from your presence.'

For the gentle Adelaïde to speak thus was as much a blow as the Duc's anger. The words—clear, honest, truthful words—of an honourable woman had made her more wretched than the Marquise's vile lies.

After the wedding ceremony, of which Teresa recalled very little, the King had planned that they were to travel on gondolas up the canal and feast in an arbour. Later in the evening, there was to be a firework display followed by a grand ball. She had cast only one scared look at the Duc's face throughout the wedding ceremony, and that was when he had put the mantilla aside from her face and bent to kiss her. Sunshine had dappled across the altar, which had been laden with the silver and gold vessels of the rite of the mass, over the massed blooms, now giving off a heady scent, and over the dazzling jewels worn by the sumptuously clad courtiers and their ladies. The Duc's face had been a grim mask; his eyes, dark and blank, had held her own expression for a long moment. The kiss, when she had received it, had been as cold as the icicles that clung to her heart.

Stepping into the gondola, she recalled her vision in the apartments of Madame de Maintenon with sickening clarity. The person, just married, who experienced overwhelming sadness, was herself. All might look at them and comment with looks and words on the beauty of the bride and handsomeness of the groom; but she felt that she was the unhappiest girl in France.

The arbour in which they had eaten—although Teresa had only picked at the delicious food—was the size of a small ballroom. Louis was in high glee, and it seemed as though all animosity must be forgotten—certainly he beamed with good humour all afternoon. This was exactly the sort of occasion best suited to his theatrical and extravagant tastes. Teresa was glad to sit down, for they had spent what seemed to her an interminable time standing while the official registers had been signed after the marriage, and the formal homage received from the most prominent members of the Court.

Teresa and the Duc were sitting on high, plush, gilded chairs, and could see clearly the musicians playing from gondolas on the canal, and the Court moving about the feast tables—talking, laughing, and indulging their favourite pastimes of gossiping and flirting. If Henri Deschamps and the lovely Adelaïde were not yet deeply in love, there was sufficient esteem and mutual respect to ensure that their union would be a happy one.

'Duc, Duchesse, may I pay my compliments to you both and offer my heartfelt wishes for your future happiness?' The Duchesse Marie-Victoire had approached without Teresa being aware of her presence until she spoke. How strange that sounded. Duchesse. She supposed that she would have to get used to it. The old lady was talking to the Duc, and Teresa was lost in a haze of thoughts. Marriage! Tonight she would be expected to share his bed. At one time that idea would have thrilled her; she would have been as eager for the consummation of their marriage as he. Now, faced with his implacable mood, she knew that it would be impossible for her to give herself to him. Watching the Duchesse move away, her wrinkled face alive with excited speculation, Teresa felt revolted.

As though guessing her unspoken thoughts, the Duc turned to look levelly at her. 'You need not look so terrified, Teresa. Until you choose, you shall never be more than my wife in name. You and I are bound together in this unholy union, but I shall not make you suffer in any way.' What pierced her heart more than the words he used was the tone of sadness, of weary resignation to an unpleasant fate.

The Marquise de Maintenon looked as though she were a large black cat who had awoken from a long sleep in the sun to find a bowl of cream beside her. Extending a plump hand to the King, she walked with him to where the newly married couple observed their wedding festivities.

Bowing her head and curtsying, she rose slowly, and when her eyes were level with Teresa's she gave a look so pregnant with conspiracy that Louis looked from one to the other sharply. The sun vanished quite suddenly from the sky and, as the light faded ominously, Louis looked up, his face shadowed, eyes narrowed.

'I fear that we are to have another storm. What an ill-omen for you both. It is as well that you are to remain at Versailles, for, if the sun is to shine, it is sure to do so here.'

'It is said that the climate of Provence is pleasant at this time of year, Majesty. I regret, deeply, that you cannot pay us the visit that I so much anticipated with pleasure.' The Duc's calm, unemotional voice was at variance with the watchful tenseness in his eyes.

'Provence at this time of year? Tcha! What can you want with gallivanting off to Provence in the middle of summer? The climate of Versailles is infinitely superior to that of Provence, as you must know. I cannot allow you to take your fair bride to Provence until she has witnessed the glories of a Versailles summer.' Waving a lace handkerchief in the air, he patted the plump hand of the new Marquise and smiled foolishly into her full face. 'Do you not agree, my dear Marquise, *hein*?'

The atmosphere, charged with the tension of the approaching storm and the tangible disappointment emanating from the Duc, made Teresa shiver with fear. The King had signified more markedly than before that the Duc could not return to his Provençal domain. Huge drops of rain began to fall, and everyone started a frantic scurrying about for shelter. The King summoned the gondolas, and, in the general confusion inevitably accompanying a hasty exit, the Duc took Teresa's hand and hurried her to a pathway through massive flower-bushes. How romantic it would have been under other circumstances. At the end of the pathway, a light coach drawn by two black horses waited. Holding open the door of the coach was Paul, his face a blend of respect and pleasure at the sight of his new mistress.

As she climbed into the coach, she thought that she must tell the Duc—tell him everything. If they were to have any chance of happiness, there must be truth between them. He would help her recover the confession, and put aside her absurd and increasingly silly fears about the Marquise de Montespan; she would abjectly beg his pardon for the pain she had inflicted when she

had called his father a traitor and his mother a whore.
It mattered not to her who or what his parents had been.
Moving to one side of the seat, she made room for him
to sit beside her, but he remained standing outside, giving
an order to the driver to take her back to the house in
the Avenue du Vieux Versailles.

'Do you not accompany me?' She was sharply
disappointed.

'No,' he replied heavily. 'It is better not. I will say that
you are overcome by the events of the day, and will return
for the ball, later. It is inconceivable that the King will
now wish to hold a firework display.' His instinct was
to take her hand in his, for he saw his own disillusioned
unhappiness mirrored in her eyes, but he was afraid that
if he spent any longer in her company he would throw
caution and pride to the four winds, take her in his arms
and beg that all misunderstanding between them be put
at an end. To force himself on an unwilling bride played
no part in his plans for his future happiness.

'Shall I see you again this day?' Fearful that he would
withdraw from her completely, she longed for an opportunity to explain matters to him.

Misinterpreting her question, he thought that she
feared his presence, and was further wounded. 'You shall
not be alone with me again, I shall ensure that. Have
some rest, Teresa. Try to recover your spirits, you have
no need to fear me.'

Slamming the door of the coach, he signalled to the
coachman to drive on, and the last view she had of his
face was one so tortured with unhappiness that she wept
all the way back to the Avenue du Vieux Versailles.

By the time the coach drew to a halt outside the house
she had formed a plan, and could hardly wait to put it
into execution. She would change, command the driver
to take her to St Germain, recover her confession, and
be back in the Avenue du Vieux Versailles by the time
the Duc returned to collect her.

'Stay!' she commanded the driver, who was preparing
to dismount. 'I wish to go on a short journey and must
change my clothes.'

'Don't know about that,' he grumbled. 'Didn't get no
orders as to no other journey.'

Too determined to pursue her plan, Teresa could brook no delay or disappointment. 'You have just received an order.' She spoke imperiously, no longer the seventeen-year-old Teresa Rochefoucourt from the convent at Villepreux, but the Duchesse d'Abbeville.

'Yes, Duchesse. Certainly, Duchesse.' He climbed back on to the driving seat, his face a mask of stoic servitude.

Within minutes Teresa re-emerged from the house, the servants agog in the doorway, for she had explained her errand to none, and was climbing back into the comfortable interior of her husband's coach.

As the vehicle bowled along she estimated that, if her business could be completed promptly, she should be back in the house within an hour and a half. How long ago it seemed that she had travelled this long, straight road! It should have changed, she thought irrationally, for she had changed so much.

The village of St Germain was situated a short distance from the convent, and luckily she spoke to a young man in the dress of a shepherd who immediately directed her to the home of Mathilde Quesnay. Mouth agape, pushing aside thick, shaggy locks of hair with a large, dirty hand, he had been about to say something else to her, but she was in too much of a hurry to stop and exchange gossip with a peasant. As the coach stopped outside a small neat abode, she reflected that he had probably wished to enquire her business with Mathilde—she could imagine little happening in this sleepy village. The arrival of a stranger would be an event that would be discussed endlessly.

Barely waiting for the horses to settle into stillness, she wrenched open the door of the coach and jumped down. Pushing open a wooden gate, she went to the front door of the small house and knocked for a minute. When she received no reply she pushed the door and, finding it open, entered an exceedingly dirty room. There were remains of half-consumed food everywhere, a fire smouldered in the hearth, and above it, suspended from a hook, was a kettle. Every sort of litter and confusion reigned in that tiny room.

'*Madame? Madame?* Is anyone here?' Teresa called out, for, despite the appearance of an empty room, she

was certain that someone was here. The filth and muddle
revolted her, for she had expected that a former em-
ployee of the palace to be of good and respectable family.

Glancing around, she saw that a piece of paper had
been lodged behind a wooden box that held the remains
of bread. Jumping, she recognised the paper—it was her
confession, she was certain of that. Stepping forward to
retrieve it, she put her foot on something soft that moved
and emitted a moan.

Almost jumping into the air, so startled was she, Teresa
looked down to find that what she had thought was a
bundle of old rags proved to be a human being. Stooping,
she pulled aside the tattered rags covering the person
and stared into the face of the dreaded smallpox. Cold
sweat broke out all over her body; fear crawled over her
skin like a plague of parasites. So heavily marked with
recently healed wounds that were turning into a mass of
deep, ugly scars was a face, and it was impossible to tell
if it was male or female. It must be Mathilde Quesnay.

Teresa knew what she had to do, and her mind clari-
fied and began to work quickly. Going to the door, she
opened it and called to the coachman. 'Do not come in,
there is smallpox here. Go and find me some clean water,
bed-linen, food and kindling for the fire. Leave everything at the gate, but do not enter the house, for you
may become infected.'

The coachman's eyes nearly started from his head
when he heard what she said, and so quickly did he drive
away that she doubted if he would obey her commands.

Clearing a space on what appeared to be the bed, she
lifted Mathilde on to it, and, gently pulling aside the
rags, saw that most of her pox marks had turned to scars.
Guessing that this must mean that the fever had passed
and was no longer infectious, she attempted to make the
woman more comfortable. Her debilitated state appeared to be a consequence of the neglect she had suffered, and Teresa fumed angrily at those who had left
her in such a pitiable condition.

She had misjudged the coachman, for he returned and
dumped many things, including buckets of water, at the
gate of the cottage. Without allowing her to explain that
the dreaded fever had passed beyond its infectious stage,

he leapt back on to the coach and drove away at such speed that he was out of sight by the time she reached the gate. The effort of carrying everything into the dingy room almost exhausted her, but it was soon accomplished. As she was quite unused to domestic work of any sort, it took her a long time to light the fire, boil water and clean the room. But when Mathilde was washed and dressed in the clean shift that had been thrown into the bed-linen, she did not look nearly so bad as when Teresa had first found her.

'Bless your kind heart, dearie. You are the first person I have seen in weeks. Apart from that food and blankets left by the Marquise de Montespan, I have had nothing for a couple of weeks. I had to burn the clothes to keep warm. I had no energy to do anything. Now, here I am, in a nice clean bed, with a lovely fire and this delicious broth to eat! I almost feel my old self again. Thank you.'

Now that she had completed her self-imposed task, Teresa had leisure to reflect that her own future looked very bleak indeed. There was now no possibility of her returning to Versailles, for she had not said why she was going. The Duc would think that she had left him, and he would certainly never risk coming to a plagued house.

In that she had wronged him, for she was sitting by the fire, watching the woman who now slept peacefully and naturally, when she was startled by the sound of hoofs in the distance. Closer and closer they drew, until, with the sound of a great commotion, they stopped outside the cottage. About to get up and open the door, she was prevented by its being rudely thrust open.

The Duc stood on the threshold, his face haggard, all pride and arrogance stripped away. With an inarticulate sound in his throat he crossed the small room in a stride, gathered her into his arms and crushed her in an urgent embrace.

'My darling, what in the name of God are you doing here? Did you fear me so much that you had to flee— and to the house of a smallpox victim? Can you not imagine how I should feel on receiving such news?'

'Fear you?' Her eyes were like stars. 'I never feared you, Guy.' Haltingly, she told him of the events that had led up to her presence in this cottage. 'And, until this moment, I had forgotten all about my confession. It did not seem so important as caring for this old woman.'

'It was never important, you foolish idiot,' he said lovingly. And, taking the paper, he thrust it into the heart of the fire. 'You say that you believe that the woman will be all right. Well, then, I shall go to Villepreux, to the Abbesse, and request that the good nuns take care of her. I shall pay them. Then I am taking you home.'

Home! How pleasant that word sounded; but she could not go yet. He had come to her, regardless of the fact that she might have been exposed to the smallpox—that above all things demonstrated to her that he loved her. He had not even referred to the fact that he had thought of the possible danger to himself. In the warmth of his embrace her fears had all disappeared, her love rekindled to heights of passion that had been dormant until now.

'Guy, I must apologise for saying that your father was a traitor...' Too ashamed to continue, she could only look at him contritely.

'I shall explain it all to you.' His voice was vibrant.

'No, do not. I do not deserve an explanation. It was the greatest piece of folly to listen to that evil woman.' Putting up a hand to cover his mouth, she smiled mistly at him. 'I do not care what your parents did or were, I love you, and wish to be your true and proper wife forever.'

'Let us go outside, Teresa, for the air in here is oppressing me. Also,' he kissed her hands and wrists, 'I wish to be alone with you.'

The threatened storm had blown over, and the air smelt fresh and clear; stars, pale and winking, were already piercing the milky, violet sky. Stopping short, Teresa looked at the coach which had brought the Duc to St Germain—it was piled high with luggage! He had meant to travel elsewhere! Was he leaving her? Was that the reason that he had come here? Was it to say goodbye? Dumbly, she stared at him, her heart leaden, as he began to speak.

'When I was a child, a very young child, my father, along with others, rose up against those who ruled in the place of Louis. He was only a child himself then. They were called the Frondeurs. Their cause failed, and many were killed or executed. Generally it is believed that my father was killed. He was not. After he was captured and imprisoned, my mother came to Versailles to plead for his life. She loved him.' That simple statement spoke volumes to Teresa, and a lump came to her throat as he continued. 'A man of very high position promised that he would secure a pardon for my father, or at least ensure that his life was spared—but there was a price to pay. Loving my father as she did, she paid that price. My father was executed, and the man who forced my mother to break her marriage vows abandoned her. Finding that she was expecting a child, my mother remained in Versailles, alone, and went to live in a house, the one in the forest, that had been given to my father by the King. It was there that she died, giving birth to a stillborn daughter. That is why I loathe and detest the palace, with its insincerity and insubstantial loyalties.'

It had not been necessary for him to tell her that; she could fully enter into all his feelings, for she shared them, although she had come to hers by a different route. For several minutes she remained silent in deep and real sympathy for a woman, long dead, who had so suffered for her love.

'Believe me, Teresa, that house always had vile associations for me. When I was obliged to be in Versailles, I had another built, and loaned or leased the house in the forest.'

'Do we return to Versailles now?' she ventured timidly. She had to know if he intended leaving her.

Throwing back his head, he laughed, and the sound rang out on the clear evening air—a merry sound, deep and attractive. 'Louis has commanded me to leave Versailles, and not to return for a very long time. A command I am very happy to obey.'

So he had not come to seek her out, he was on his way to Provence! 'I thought that he wished you to stay at Court.'

'So he did, but when he heard that you were in a house with smallpox he became distraught and terrified lest you should bring the disease back to Versailles. I was with Adelaïde at the time. No! Take away that wan look, I was *not* making love to her. The only woman I want to make love to is my own darling wife. She had been telling me what had passed between you, and then I understood all the hurts and torments you had suffered. My darling,' he pulled her to him and began to kiss her again. Pushing him back gently, she looked into his face.

'And then?' she asked softly.

'Why, I told him that I would carry that order to you myself. If you were in danger, I wished to share it with you—and that is the truth, my own heart. In a dreadful rage, he commanded that under no circumstances were either of us to return; we were to go to Provence or the ends of the earth—whichever suited us best.'

He had never looked so handsome as he did then. There was a buoyancy, an eagerness about him that was infinitely more attractive than the bored, cynical indifference she had so often seen on his face.

'So! We go home to Provence,' she breathed softly. 'Guy, when we get home, I want you to promise me that we can take care of women like that.' She nodded at the cottage. 'They must never be abandoned. And if any unfortunate woman should find herself in the position of your dear mother, then you must promise me that they will never be abandoned on your land.'

Looking deeply into her eyes, his own alight with love and passion, he spoke. 'Is it a domineering little Duchesse I have married, to be giving me orders and commands?' he teased her lovingly.

Smiling up at him provocatively, she said, 'In Provence, you can be yourself, and I can be myself. There will never be any pretence.'

Cupping her chin in his hands, he said softly, 'When I first set eyes on you, I asked you if you had come to rob me. I was right, you did rob me.' Seeing her faint puzzled look, he explained before he bent to kiss her. 'Of my heart.'

Unwrap romance this Christmas

A Love Affair
LINDSAY ARMSTRONG

Valentine's Night
PENNY JORDAN

Man on the Make
ROBERTA LEIGH

Rendezvous in Rio
ELIZABETH OLDFIELD

Put some more romance into your Christmas, with four brand new titles from Mills & Boon in this stylish gift pack.

They make great holiday reading, and for only £5.40, it makes an ideal gift.

The special gift pack is available from 6th October. Look out for it at Boots, Martins, John Menzies, W.H. Smith, Woolworths and other paperback stockists.

ROMANCING THE PHONE

Win the romantic holiday of a lifetime for two at the exclusive Couples Hotel in Ocho Rios on Jamaica's north coast with the Mills & Boon and British Telecom's novel competition, 'Romancing the Phone'.

This exciting competition looks at the importance the telephone call plays in romance. All you have to do is write a story or extract about a romance involving the phone which lasts approximately two minutes when read aloud.

The winner will not only receive the holiday in Jamaica, but the entry will also be heard by millions of people when it is included in a selection of extracts from a short list of entries on British Telecom's 'Romance Line'. Regional winners and runners up will receive British Telecom telephones, answer machines and Mills & Boon books.

For an entry leaflet and further details all you have to do is call 01 400 5359, or write to 'Romancing the Phone', 22 Endell Street, London WC2H 9AD.
You may be mailed with other offers as a result of this application.

British
TELECOM